WHEN THE FAT MAN SINGS

For Leonard Gross, a friend for all seasons

♦

A man's got to make at least one bet every day, else he could be walking around lucky and never know it.

—Jimmy Jones, Hall of Fame horse trainer

ONE

♦

Passing

The fat man had drawn a large crowd around the table, but not because he was winning. In fact, he didn't seem to know what to do with the dice. Whenever they reached his end of the table, he would pick them up gingerly, as if they might be too hot to touch, then put them down again directly in front of him. He would scatter fifty- and one-hundred-dollar chips all over the layout, then reach for the dice a second time, shake them awkwardly with both hands, and fling them out onto the hard, green felt of the tabletop like an old woman tossing bread chunks to a distant family of ducks paddling in a pond. The technique did not work. The dice invariably came up with the wrong numbers, either craps on the first roll or a seven on the second or third. By the time I became really aware of him, he must have lost thousands.

I had squeezed myself into the mob and gradually worked my way to the front row, about halfway down the table from him. Despite his inability to make even a single pass and the coldness of the table as a whole, the crowd did not seem inclined to scatter. Few of them, however, had come to play; most of them were just there to catch the fat man's action. I realized at once that he was a celebrity, but I hadn't figured out who yet and I didn't much care. I had an hour or so to kill before I had to get back to work over at the Hilton and I was feeling lucky. I watched the fat man lose another few hundred on somebody else's roll and waited for the dice to come my way.

1

"*Porco Giuda,*" the fat man said, "someone has put the Evil Eye on me!"

An old cowboy standing next to me hitched up his jeans and cocked his Stetson forward over his eyes. "Damnedest thing I ever did see," he said. "He can't shoot dice for shit and he don't even know how to bet."

"The table's cold, I guess," I hazarded.

"Cold? We were doin' okay until this dago fella showed up," the cowboy said. "Minute he got here the fuckin' layout froze up so hard cattle could die on it. Damn fool don't know what he's doin'."

I watched the fat man place fifty-dollar chips on all the hardways bets and on Any Craps. "I gather he doesn't do this for a living," I said.

The old cowboy looked at me in amazement. "God no," he answered. "Hell, he'd have been a skeleton by now."

The stickman pushed the dice toward me. "You want to shoot, sir?"

"I came to play," I said, putting a ten-dollar chip on the Pass line.

"Hey, mister," the fat man called out to me, "how you feel?"

"Fine," I said.

"You are feeling lucky?"

"I didn't come here to lose."

"Okay, you wait," the fat man said and snapped two fingers at the croupier.

The man glanced behind him and caught the pit boss's eye, then turned smilingly back and shoved another huge stack of chips toward the fat man's end of the table. "Yes, sir, of course."

The fat man picked up bunches of them in both hands and looked anxiously at me. "So you think you lucky, huh?"

I nodded. "Everyone's lucky sooner or later."

"Okay, I go with you," the fat man said. "What you do?"

"I'm planning on making at least seven passes," I said.

"That's good, I like that." He placed two hundred dollars in chips all over the numbers. "How about hardways?"

"It's a dumb bet," I said. "And why don't you wait until I come out?"

"Come out? What is that?"

I looked at the croupier. "I'm planning to shoot a natural," I said. "Why don't you take him off on the come-out?"

"You do what he say, okay?" the fat man told the croupier.

"Yes, sir, you're off," the croupier confirmed.

I asked for fresh dice and picked out another pair of ivories from the bunch the stickman offered me. "Here we go," I said, pretending to a calm I did not feel.

"By God, I think you're gonna do it," the old cowboy said and slapped twenty dollars himself on the front line.

I shook the dice twice and sent them bouncing off against the far corner of the layout.

"Seven, you win," the croupier intoned. "All right, we've got a hot new shooter. Make your bets."

"I tell you he is lucky," the fat man informed the table. "Now, *mio caro*, you shoot some numbers, yes?"

I shot some numbers, yes. I held the dice for thirty-five minutes, during which I made six passes and threw dozens of numbers in between. The cowboy and I, playing judiciously and professionally, picked up over two grand apiece, but it was peanuts compared to what was happening at the fat man's end of the table. He had doubled, tripled, and quadrupled his action on the numbers during my hand, so that by the time I finally threw a seven and wiped out the towers of chips he had going all over the layout he must have enriched himself by at least thirty or forty thousand dollars. And he had himself a wonderful time doing it. Every winning bet brought a great beaming smile of pleasure over his large, bearded face, and he would snap the fingers of both of his curiously small, delicate-looking hands around his head, as if they were castanets. *"Santo cielo, che meraviglia!"* he exclaimed as he raked in his winnings. "You are a saint, you are *il Padre Eterno* Himself!"

I didn't know exactly what he was saying, as my knowledge of Italian was limited, to say the least, but I knew it was complimentary. I didn't argue with him. When I started to leave the table, he motioned me over to him. "Listen, you come to hear me tonight, all right? I leave a pass for you to my table. Then you come to see me backstage, okay?"

"I'm sorry, I can't," I said. "I'm working myself."

"You working? What you do?" He had a dark but high-pitched voice that rang some sort of bell in my head. "What is your name?" He stared at me with great concern, his little black eyes intently searching my features for a clue to my identity.

"Shifty Anderson, I'm a magician," I explained. "I work at the Three Kings; it's a hotel downtown. Tonight I've got a convention at the Hilton."

"A magician? You make people disappear?"

"I haven't tried that yet. No, mostly little things—coins, cards, stuff like that."

"A magician! Is incredible! *Sì, incredibile!* You work every night?"

"I'm off tomorrow."

"Ah, then you come to hear me. I only sing once a night, this week only. You come. You ask for my table and then you come to see me, okay?"

I knew who he was now. How could I not have known? "Sure," I said. "Thank you."

"You not thank me," he said. "Here." He thrust five one-hundred-dollar chips into my hand.

"No, that's all right," I said. "I won quite a bit myself."

"My friend, you take them," he said, folding my fingers around them with both of his hands. "You save my life tonight. I am now almost even."

"Almost even? Maybe you ought to try some other game."

He laughed and the sound of it threatened to shatter the glasses on a passing cocktail waitress's tray. "It does not matter," he explained. "I always lose, my friend. Except tonight. *Grazie.*"

"That's okay. I'll see you tomorrow evening."

I left him and headed across the lobby toward the bar. The old cowboy fell into step beside me. "You're a good shooter, kid," he said. "You even got that dago out."

"That dago," I said, "is not your everyday kind of Italian."

"No? Who is he?"

"That's Fulvio Gasparini."

"Sounds like some kinda vegetable, don't it? What's he do? Own a spaghetti factory?"

"Nope. He's a singer, maybe the best in the world."

"A singer? Not country music, I guess."

"Opera."

"Opera. That's where them people stand around in them funny hats and shout a whole lot of stuff at each other?"

"You got it."

The old cowboy shook his head in dismay. "It don't seem like a respectable way to make a livin'," he said, "but I guess some folks'll pay good money to see just about any kinda foolishness."

Happy Hal Mancuso, my agent, was waiting for me in the Xanadu coffee shop and he did not seem overly pleased to see me. I guessed that he had put on at least another five pounds in the two months since I had last talked to him and he seemed to squat in his booth like an angry frog on a lily pad. Even so, he looked frail compared to Fulvio Gasparini, whose bulk would have awed even a professional football player. Hal was just fat; Fulvio Gasparini was a walking monument to the power of song.

"Where the hell have you been?" Hal asked as I slid swiftly into the seat across from him. "I've been sitting here for forty minutes."

"Sorry. I got hot." And I told him about my six passes. "I couldn't turn my back on the money."

Hal looked grim. "I ought to worry about you, Shifty," he said, "but then why should I? You don't worry about yourself. It's bad enough you're a diseased horseplayer, but now I get you a job working the best downtown dining room in Vegas and you'll probably piss all your money away in the casinos. You're sick, you know that?"

"Hal, forget it," I reassured him. "I'm a horseplayer, yes, but a gambler, no. I had twenty minutes to kill, so I thought I'd shoot one hand. I got lucky and I can use the money."

"You won two grand?"

"A little more."

"Give it to me. I'll bank it for you and that way you won't blow it, at least right away."

"Hal, I'm a big kid now. I can manage my own affairs."

"I wish I could believe that." He looked more than ever sunk in gloom, but then that was his operating style. He hadn't acquired his nickname in the business by accident. In fact, I had been the one to hang it on him and it had stuck. "So how's it going?"

"Fine." I told him that I was doing very well, which was the truth. The Three Kings, one of the newer spots downtown, had given me a nice place to work, a spacious, quiet dining room furnished in neo-Victorian splendor, with the tables and booths all far enough away from one another that I could circulate and impress individual groups of diners without disturbing their neighbors. My basic salary was five hundred a week and I was clearing another couple of hundred a night in tips, sometimes more on the weekends. "I don't even miss the horses all that much."

"That's because you can bet on them at the race book, right?"

"I haven't been over there more than three times in the month and a half I've been here, Hal," I said. "I only really enjoy the racing if I'm on the scene, you know that."

He shook his head, as if he had just been told by a confirmed alcoholic that he was still boozing but had it all well under control. I had long ago given up trying to convince him that I was not a degenerate gambler, but I couldn't simply accept his negative view of my life. I was first of all a magician and second a horseplayer, and it was a point of honor with me that I defend that view of myself. Even to Happy Hal Mancuso, whose outlook on life inevitably assumed that all was for the worst in this worst of all possible worlds.

"How much longer you got here?"

"Two weeks," I said. "But I think they'll want me back."

"That's good. I'll follow up on it."

"Do you have anything else cooking for me?"

"I got two cruises booked, but not till March."

"I guess I'll see if there's anything for me at the Magic Castle, when I get back to L.A."

"I'm working on some stuff. I might have a TV spot for you, a couple of days' work."

"That's good."

He sighed, exhaling as if from under the entire weight of the world's ongoing injustices. "Some profession you picked, Shifty," he confided. "You want to be a magician, you could at least have worked up the big illusions. I could get you real money for that kind of act, but no, you gotta mess around with bits of string and paper balls. Jesus Christ, you'd be better off bartending or working in a bank or something. You ever thought about changing your act so we could make some money? You're a reasonable-looking young guy—"

"I'm turning forty, Hal."

"Well, you look younger. You get yourself a good costume, lots of pizzazz and stuff, maybe get some good-looking broad to work with you, with a nice set of gams and all, work up one of those acts like where they make elephants disappear or you change the broad into a hyena or something, and we make some money. You got to think about it, don't you?"

"Why?" I shot back. "You're talking show biz, Hal. I'm a magician. What I do is a skill and I work very hard at it."

"There's no payoff, kid."

"I'm doing all right and I'm not married and I have no kids and I live alone."

"Like a goddamn monk, that's how you live."

"I have nothing against women."

"Shit, you know what I mean."

I did. We had had this discussion about my future, or lack of it, so many times that I no longer paid much attention to it. I defended my position because I thought I owed it to myself and to my profession, the only one I had, which I loved and believed in. Anyway, both Hal and I knew that neither of us would convince the other, so we went through the routine without damaging our relationship in the slightest. Basically, I was certain that Hal liked me and even admired me, in a grudging, backhanded way. I was perhaps the only client of his for whom he had no hope of advancement or real money, but he kept me on because I probably represented a challenge to him. And especially because he liked me.

"Listen, I have to go," I said, glancing at my watch. "I picked up a two-day convention of dentists at the Hilton. Don't worry, I'll send you your commission."

"I don't need the fifty bucks," Hal said. "Keep it. Blow it on the horses."

"By the way, I never did ask you what you're doing here."

"I got a comic working over at the Sands, a guy named Hugo Mandelbaum. He wanted me to come over and catch his new act. He says he's killing the people and that I should make him a star."

"Is he and will you?"

Hal shrugged, with the resignation of Atlas shifting the burden from one shoulder to another. "Probably not and no. You never heard of this guy?"

"No. Is he any good?"

"I'm not sure good is the word," Hal said. "He's dirty. That's what makes people laugh these days."

"When are you going back to L.A.?"

"Just as soon as I can. It ain't paradise, but if I stay here I'll contract a social disease."

"I finish in a couple of hours," I said. "Want to have a nightcap?"

"You can sit through Hugo's act with me," he answered. "Meet me in the lobby of the Sands at ten o'clock."

I left him there to his habitual misery. Voltaire would have loved him.

I finished up with my party of dentists by dinnertime and pocketed a nice check for the two hours. I had worked up some routines involving a set of false teeth and the use of borrowed dental instruments, instead of my usual props, and it all went over very well. My Ring on a Stick, for which I used a metal pick and a platinum band, was especially effective, and I closed out my act with cards, always my forte. My friend Vince Michaels, the finest close-up artist I know, and my mentor in magic, always said I was the best with cards and who was I to contradict him?

I caught up to Hal again at the Sands and we went into one of the lounges to catch Hugo Mandelbaum in action. "This is gonna make me sick, I know it," Hal said as we sat down at the ringside table Hugo had reserved for us. "This guy thinks cancer is funny."

Hal's comedian turned out to be a middle-aged man pretending to be in his thirties and with an approach to his audience that bordered on open hostility. He wore black slacks and a pink shirt slashed open to his waist, revealing thick tufts of curly hair entwined around a tangle of gold chains. He had thick black eyebrows, dyed black hair sculpted into flowing waves that dashed against his forehead, and a set of perfectly capped white teeth that he flashed on the audience whenever he expected it to laugh, which happened not as often as he could have wished. The men in the room liked him, partly because so much of his patter was clearly contemptuous of women, but the latter were intimidated by him and shrank from his insults as if from something contaminated or diseased. I found myself wondering why Hal represented him. His was not the sort of act that could be booked on *The Tonight Show*. In fact, I thought to myself, he'd have been most at home in a sewer.

"A guy goes to a whorehouse and he says to the madam, 'I got five hundred bucks here and I want the worst piece of ass in the joint,' " Hugo said for openers. "So the madam looks at him and she says, 'Honey, for five hundred bucks you can have the best girl in the place. Not only is she stacked, with terrific bazongas, but she's a great lay.' 'I don't want a great lay,' this joker says, 'I want the worst. I'm homesick.' "

The act went downhill from there. From time to time I glanced over at Hal, who sat immobile on his chair, his pudgy hand around a wineglass, and never so much as cracked a smile. "My agent is here tonight," Hugo told the audience about halfway through his monologue. "My agent. You know what an agent is? I'll tell you what an agent is. An agent is a guy who stands out there on the beach and he watches you battle these huge fuckin' waves trying to get to shore. If you make it, and while you're lying there, half-dead and bleeding from the mouth from the tough time you've been having, he comes over and he leans down and he taps you on the shoulder and he says, 'Can I be of any assistance?' "

Hal did not laugh at that one either, but then I had never seen him laugh at anything, good or bad. After Hugo had finished his act with a horrendous story about drugs, homosexuals, and routine defecation, Hal leaned toward me. "What do you think?" he asked.

"I think he's sick," I said.

"Yeah?" Hal slumped back in his chair. "I got him a grand a week and they want to renew him. I think I can get him fifteen hundred."

"There's no accounting for tastes," I said. "The women hated him."

"Why wouldn't they?" Hal answered. "Hugo's a threat to every decent instinct in the human race."

The comedian came strutting through the audience and joined us. His offstage manner, I soon noted, was as tasteless and abrasive as his act. "You're a magician," he said to me after Hal had introduced us. "Can you make my herpes disappear?"

"I'm a magician, not a miracle worker," I said.

Hugo turned to Hal. "Great, wasn't it?"

"I'm not sure *great* is the word, Hugo," Hal said. "You are not going to win a good-taste award."

Hugo laughed. "The last good taste I had was a chorus girl's pussy. So when are you going to know?"

"I think the deal is set. You have another four-week guarantee with a renewable option and the money's right."

"The money's never right. I should be making millions."

I was suddenly very tired and I stood up to go. "So long, Hal, I'll be talking to you," I said. "Nice to meet you, Hugo."

"So you're a magician," he said. "Listen, I got a ten-inch wand here I could sell you. Did you ever hear the one about the guy who went to have his prostate operated on and the surgeon cut off his balls?"

I fled from him into the lobby and stopped in the restroom before heading home. After an evening with Hugo Mandelbaum, even a Vegas men's room seemed like a breath of fresh air.

TWO

◆

High Notes

I had never in my life heard any-thing like Fulvio Gasparini. At first, as I sat there in my ringside seat at the Xanadu, I couldn't believe my ears. The man had simply walked out on that immense stage, acknowledged the applause with a slight bow and a charming, toothy smile, and promptly embarked on the big, tearful aria from *I Pagliacci* that Caruso had made famous. At first I thought he was using a hidden mike instead of the ones mounted unobtrusively at the edge of the stage, but then I realized that that sound was almost unamplified. He stood well back from the footlights, his feet planted solidly on the boards, his head tilted slightly back and his arms flung out as if to embrace his listeners, and let fly. The notes poured from him in a great torrent of dark, velvety tones that rolled out over the orchestra. When he soared up to the climaxes, I was forced to gasp. His high notes were like trumpet blasts, clear and clean and thrillingly beautiful. Best of all, however, was the consummate, polished style with which he molded his phrases. There was no sobbing or scoop-ing or shouting, just a long, modulated, delicately shaded line intended to convey the true emotion of the song; everything seemed designed to honor the composer's intention with economy and clarity. I was stunned.

The entire program lasted forty minutes and not once did he let down. Admittedly, the evening had been tailored to keep a Las Vegas audience entertained, but within that limitation the tenor never compromised. He sang every schmaltzy aria and song, from

Mascagni and Puccini to Tosti and such Neapolitan favorites as "O Sole Mio," as if they really mattered. In between renditions, speaking with a thicker Italian accent than I had recalled him using during our session at the craps table, he charmed the audience with chatter about his family life in Italy, his warm and comic relationship to his wife, Carmela, his two young sons, the farm animals they cared for on their property in southern Italy, and his early adventures in opera. He had a fund of good anecdotes about himself and his colleagues, past and present, and he told them well, with a good feeling for detail and excellent timing. Unlike Hugo Mandelbaum, he knew how to manipulate an audience and get it to root for him. When he walked off after a thrilling rendition of the aria from *La Bohème,* the applause was thunderous and a woman at the next table stood up on her chair to shriek bravos at him.

Fulvio sang two encores, both with a young American soprano named Anna Willows, whom he introduced as his pupil and protégée. One was something called the "Cherry Duet," from a Mascagni opera, the other a medley of operetta favorites. In these numbers I noticed that he held himself back, rarely rising to full voice, so as to allow Miss Willows to shine. She was a tall, slender redhead dressed in a low-cut, velvety black gown that clung to her figure and revealed beautiful arms and shoulders, as well as an ample bosom. She had a sweet, true soprano, but nothing out of the ordinary. Had Fulvio wanted to, he could easily have obliterated her.

When they had walked off hand in hand, with Fulvio smiling and blowing kisses to his public, I sank back in my chair, as if I had been lightly rapped on the head with a club. "What is the matter?" my table companion asked. "Are you not feeling well?"

"I'm fine," I said. "I've never really heard him before, that's all."

"This? This is nothing. This is a *porcheria.*"

"A what?"

"A dirtiness. A waste."

"Not to me. I've never heard singing like that. I like Pavarotti and Domingo and I remember Caruso and Gigli on records, when I was a kid, but this was at least as good. What a voice!"

"*Sì,* you are right. But this is not Fulvio. This is *mondizia.*"

"Mon—what?"

"Garbage, you understand? *Merda.* Shit."

For the first time I paid some attention to him. I had arrived just before the show began and I had barely had time to introduce myself, shake his hand, and sit down. He was a small, stoop-shouldered, cadaverous-looking Italian with surprisingly strong hands, a long, slightly hooked nose, and bright brown eyes. His gray hair stood up in unruly patches over a high forehead and he was dressed in a baggy brown suit that flapped on his thin frame like laundry hung from a tree. He had sat through the show unmoved, his arms folded against his chest and his face impassive. He had been the only one in the room not to applaud Fulvio's performance.

"I guess the money must be good," I ventured.

"The money is everything," the little man said sarcastically.

"Well, a man has to make a living."

"I do not see the necessity."

"What did you say your name was? I'm sorry, but I didn't catch it."

"Pipistrello, Achille," he said, holding out his hand again, even though I had shaken it on arrival. *"Piacere."*

"My pleasure."

"You are a friend of Fulvio's from where?"

"From last night," I explained. "We were shooting craps together."

Achille Pipistrello grimaced with distaste. "This place is a calamity," he grumbled. "If we do not leave here . . ." He allowed the sentence to remain uncompleted, but impending doom was the implication left hanging in the ozone.

"Are you Signor Gasparini's manager?"

He snorted derisively. "I am his accompanist and coach," he explained. "Fulvio has learned all of his roles with me."

"Ah, I see. You travel with him."

"It is not easy," Achille Pipistrello said. "It is a life for a dog."

"Look, I don't know much about opera or singing in general, but I think what I just heard was terrific."

"But of course," Pipistrello answered, blinking his eyes in dismay. "That is why this is disgusting. It is like Michelangelo sculpting the *Davide* in *marzapane*, you understand? It is like da Vinci painting a beard on the *Mona Lisa*. It is a calamity."

"Have you told Fulvio what you think?"

"But of course, but he does not listen. He listens now to the Lagrange woman, a most dangerous *femmina.*"

"Who's she?"

"The manager."

"And the Willows girl?"

"Ah," Achille Pipistrello exclaimed, as if to clear his throat of an unpleasant catarrh, "she is a worm. One day Fulvio will roll over on her in his sleep and crush her to death. That will be a blessing."

We got up together and walked backstage to Fulvio's dressing room. He was sitting in front of a wall mirror and removing his makeup. People came and went on various errands, but the minute Fulvio saw me his broad, bearded face lit up like a klieg light. "Ah, my savior," he said. *"Come va?"*

"Fine, fine," I assured him. "You were terrific, really."

The tenor laughed with pleasure, then glanced beyond me in the mirror to where Achille Pipistrello was leaning gloomily against the wall by the door. "You met Achille?"

I nodded. "Yes."

"And of course he tell you this is a crime I am doing."

"Something like that."

"Stronzo," the singer barked at his accompanist, then looked back at me. "You know what is this word?"

"No."

"It is 'turd.' Achille is a *stronzo.*"

The accompanist scowled, turned, and walked out the door, slamming it behind him.

"I guess he feels you're selling out here," I said. "He wants you back in the opera house."

"All my life I am in the opera house," the tenor said. "It makes me tired. Here I sing a few songs and I earn in one week what I am earning in two months in the theater. It is a change. Life is a change."

"Anyway, you're through in another few days, aren't you?"

"Sì. Then we go to Los Angeles for the Johnny Carson show and after that the Met."

"New York?"

"Sì. Otello, of Verdi. You know *Otello?"*

"I've heard it on records."

"I sing four times the *Otello* at the Met. And then to Napoli."

The door popped open and Anna Willows walked in. "Fulvio, you promised," she said, pouting slightly.

"Ah, *sì, due minuti,"* Fulvio called to her. "Oh, Anna, this is my gambling friend, Signor Anderson. *È un mago.*"

Her eyes opened wide with surprise. "A wizard? You tell the future?"

"Not exactly," I answered. "I'm a magician. I'm working at the Three Kings downtown."

"How nice," she said, immediately losing interest. Her attention refocused itself on Fulvio. "We're late and I'm hungry," she said.

"Two minutes is all," Fulvio said. *"Cristo, le donne!"*

Still pouting, Anna Willows let herself out of the room again. I found myself wondering about the current status of the tenor's marriage, that wonderful, warm family picture he had painted for his audience during the course of the show, but then, I reasoned, here he was, thousands of miles from home, away for months at a time in strange cities, surely he had a right to an occasional dalliance and why not with a knockout of a lyric soprano?

"*Un altra stronza,*" the tenor informed me cheerfully. "*Mio caro,* I am *contornato*—how you say?"

"Surrounded?"

"*Sì,* surrounded by *stronzi.* Ah, but that is life. Tell me, you wish to gamble again?"

"Tonight? I'm afraid not. I'm pretty tired and I don't want to lose it back."

"No, not tonight. Tomorrow, in the afternoon. There is a private place upstairs here. You come tomorrow, at three. *Va bene?*"

"Well . . ."

"We play roulette. You know roulette?"

"I won't play the American wheel."

"Why you not play?"

"Two zeros," I explained. "The house has too much of an edge."

"Ah, but upstairs we have the European roulette," he assured me. "One zero. You come, we play. *Va bene?*"

"*Va bene.* But I have to warn you, Signor Gasparini, I'm not a big player."

"I play, you bet for me, we win much money. You are lucky, I can tell. Okay?"

"Okay. Three o'clock?"

"*Sì.* You ask for the Penthouse Garden and give my name. And, *mio caro,* my name is Fulvio. You are Lou?"

"My close friends call me Shifty."

"Sheefty? Oh, I like."

The door opened again and Anna Willows, looking annoyed this time, stuck her lovely head into the room. "Fulvio! Please!"

"*Oofah,*" the tenor exclaimed. "*Va via!* I am coming!"

I said goodbye to him and let myself out past the irritated Miss Willows, who let me go without so much as an acknowledging glance or even a small nod. I walked past her down the hallway toward the exit, turned the corner by the stage door, and came upon Achille Pipistrello again. He was hunched against the wall and smoking a long, thin, black Tuscan cigar. In the pale neon light he looked yellow and frail, with great dark hollows under his eyes. "Good night," I said, starting past him.

He reached out a hand and took my arm. "You see Fulvio tomorrow?"

"Yes, we have a gambling date at three o'clock upstairs. He wants to play roulette."

Pipistrello nodded gloomily. "He is losing much money."

"Well, he's a bad gambler," I said. "Maybe I can help him to lose less money."

"*Si?*" The accompanist looked at me in genuine despair. "You are also a gambler?"

"No, I'm not. Basically, I only bet on horses, because I know something about them. But I know *how* to gamble, let's put it that way."

"Horses? *Dio mio,* but Fulvio is mad about horses," the little man said. "He is buying horses now."

"Really? Where?"

"Everywhere. I do not know where this will end."

"Maybe I can help," I said. "Listen, I know you can't win at casino gambling, but you *can* win at the horses. At least I can help Fulvio to lose less."

"He is crazy," Achille Pipistrello said, "and they are ruining him."

"Who? Miss Willows?"

"No, she is nothing. The Lagrange woman. Anna is a creature, that is all. But the Lagrange woman is dangerous."

"Dangerous? In what way?"

Before he could answer, we heard a door slam and the noise of Fulvio's departure from his dressing room. He was laughing loudly and joking, as he and Anna Willows and two or three other people, apparently other members of their late-supper party, headed in our direction.

Achille Pipistrello blinked in alarm and squeezed my arm. "You help Fulvio, all right? You help him not to lose so much money," he said, his little brown eyes glittering fiercely in his sallow face. "These people, they destroy him." And he hurried past me up the corridor toward the stage area like a small crab scuttling to safety under a rock ledge.

THREE

◆

Oases

The next morning, my friend Jay Fox, the prince of handicappers, arrived in Las Vegas. He called me at about eleven o'clock at the Three Kings, where I had a free room for the duration of my engagement, and caught me with lather all over my face. "Shifty, what's going on?" he asked. "You killing the people here?"

"The old Fox," I answered, glad to hear his voice. "What are you doing in town?"

"I'm here for the Million-Dollar Challenge at Caesar's," he said. "I've been checking in for the past hour, but there's a screw-up. I'll tell you all about it at lunch. Can you make it?"

"Sure. How's it going at Santa Anita?"

"I'm about even, but it's early in the meet. I thought I'd drop in here for a few days and try my luck."

He told me all about it over sandwiches and coffee in a small restaurant I had found two blocks off the Strip. It was quiet, the food was good and reasonably priced, and there wasn't even a slot machine in sight. "How'd you find this place?" Jay asked me.

I grinned at him. "When you're in the desert, you do what the smart Arabs do—you look for an oasis. It's all right, isn't it?"

"Very nice," he said, "especially after what I went through this morning."

Jay's betting syndicate had put up ten thousand dollars to back their champion in the Million-Dollar Challenge, a handicapping contest sponsored by Caesar's Palace. One hundred contestants

16

were each to put up an entry fee of ten thousand dollars, with a first prize of half a million and nine other awards of lesser sums going to the ten top finishers. The contestants were to handicap nine races a day from any of four different tracks all over the country and had to bet a minimum of two hundred dollars per race, with the maximum payoff on any win bet limited to twenty to one. "That's so one huge long shot doesn't vault you over people who are picking a lot more winners than you are, but at lower odds," Jay explained. "It's theoretical money, of course. The ten thousand bucks buys you an equivalent number of points. The winner is the guy who has the most points at the end of the four days. But it's a no-go."

"How come?"

Jay smiled. "Thirty-two of the first fifty-six checks the casino received bounced, so they've canceled the contest."

"So horseplayers die broke. Are they picking up your expenses?"

"Oh, sure. And they're now putting on a much less ambitious contest, for a fifty-thousand-dollar first prize and a buy-in of only a grand, so I'm going to stick around for four days and try my luck."

"With the syndicate money?"

"Nah," Jay said. "At this level I can risk my own loot and keep any profit I make all for myself. Want to come in with me? I'll let you buy in."

I promptly took out my wallet and peeled off five one-hundred-dollar bills and handed them to him. "I'm in for half," I said.

His eyes opened wide with astonishment. "Wow, you must be hot at the tables," he said.

"Not bad." I told him about my adventures shooting dice with Fulvio Gasparini and my forthcoming date with the tenor to try our luck at European roulette. "And I'm told he loves the horses," I concluded. "His accompanist said so."

"Bring him around," Jay suggested. "Win or lose, I'd love to meet him. Sounds to me like you latched on to a gold mine, Shifty."

"We'll see what happens when we lose," I said. "Sooner or later in this town you have to lose."

"But in the meantime you've got a nice free ride going. Play the string out."

"I intend to. Now fill me in on what's been happening."

We talked for an hour or so, while Jay brought me up to date. He was in good form, comfortably in charge of his destiny and coming off good fall meets at the L.A. tracks. Things had been a bit slow since the opening of Santa Anita the day after Christmas, but

Jay seemed unperturbed. He never killed them early in any meet, he pointed out; it always took several weeks for him to get in the groove. It was a question of watching and waiting, betting cautiously and passing a lot of races, until he could discern a pattern to the action, establish a track bias favoring speed or come-from-behind horses, catch animals coming back a second or third time in situations that promised rewards. "I'm on the edge of a breakthrough right now," the Fox said. "That's why I thought I'd try this contest. I can bet for real at the race book and chase the prize money at the same time."

I was fond of Jay Fox and few things in life gave me more pleasure than talking horses with him. We had met at the track a long time ago and become friends, even though our life-styles were quite different. I thought of myself primarily as a professional close-up artist. Horse racing was my secondary occupation, something I did for love as well, but not to hang my whole life on. Jay, on the other hand, lived only for his handicapping skills and his action at the track. He had once been a professional tennis player, good enough to be competitive in the years before the big bucks became available on the tournament circuit, and he could have had a successful teaching career in Los Angeles, where we both lived. His black, curly hair was thinning on top and he had put on some weight since his playing days, but he still moved like an athlete, with a bouncy, cocky air set off by a pair of bright-blue eyes. He was also personable and he knew a lot of Hollywood people, most of whom he'd met at the track. But he had turned his back on all that to become a professional horseplayer. He bet for himself and for a syndicate of six or seven people, who each put up one or two thousand dollars a meet and paid Jay a cut of any winnings he made for them. And he worked very hard at his risky craft, spending a minimum of eight to ten hours a day poring over his charts and notes in order to handicap each card. "You know, Fox," I had once said to him in the middle of a bad losing streak, "the same hard work and dedication applied to a business career and you could be Lee Iacocca."

"That's work," he had replied.

"And this isn't?"

"To me it's fun," he answered. "Fun is what turns you on. Work is just a way of wasting your life."

"Aesop would have loved you," I said. "He got the fable of the lazy grasshopper and the virtuous ant all wrong."

Jay had pushed himself back from his *Form,* now all covered with multicolored notations and mysterious cabalistic signs indicating who knows what subtleties of interpretation, and placed his hands behind his head, as he beamed condescendingly in my direction. "Shifty," he said, "there are two things you'll never hear any man say on his deathbed."

"And what are they?"

"I should have worked more and I should have married earlier."

How could I argue with him? Wasn't the pursuit of happiness one of the guarantees in the U.S. Constitution? And what could make either of us happier than a ten-to-one shot hitting the finish line first with our money on his soft nose? What Jay Fox did for a living was not recognized as an honorable occupation by the consensus of American public opinion, but it was more in tune with the music of the spheres than what most people did for a living. At least Jay wasn't cheating or killing anyone. At old Saint Peter's Gate he would not be turned away simply because he had delivered his life over to something as aesthetically rewarding as a horse race. I couldn't imagine a god unwilling to risk a couple of bucks on an overlay, especially if Jay Fox liked its chances.

After lunch, Jay went back to Caesar's Palace to complete his arrangements for the handicapping contest, which was scheduled to begin the next day, and I went back to my room at the Three Kings to rest up for my assault on the roulette wheel. I found a message to call the Lagrange office in New York collect. No sooner had I done so and explained who I was to the cheerful gay male voice at the other end of the line than a woman cut in to our conversation. She had a crisp, no-nonsense sound to her.

"Hello? Mr. Anderson?"

"Yes."

"I'm Jeanine Lagrange, Mr. Gasparini's personal manager."

"How do you do."

"May I ask who you are and what your connection to my client is?"

I told her. "So there's no real connection at all that I can see."

"I'd like to keep it that way, Mr. Anderson."

"Did Mr. Gasparini ask you to call me?"

"Of course not."

"Then how did you get my name? Who told you about me?"

"It's my business to protect my clients' interests," she said. "That includes keeping track of who they see and what they do in their spare time."

"I can tell you're very good at it."

"I'm very well paid to be."

"Miss Lagrange, I don't think of myself as a threat to your client's welfare," I explained. "He's a very bad gambler."

"I know that."

"I saved him a lot of money the other night at craps and he thinks I'm lucky for him. He asked me to play roulette with him this afternoon. That's about the extent of it."

"I'd prefer that you break the engagement," she said. "It's hard enough keeping Fulvio healthy without involving him with gamblers."

"You'll forgive me for saying so, but I don't think you have a very good idea of who I am or what I do."

"You're a close-up magician and you work at the Three Kings."

"Right so far. I also know how to gamble and your client doesn't. He's going to gamble with or without me, isn't he?"

She exhaled audibly into my ear. "I'm afraid so."

"I can cut his losses. What harm can I do him?"

"Fulvio needs to concentrate absolutely on his art."

"Then he shouldn't be in Las Vegas," I said. "Art is not the game here. You booked him into the Xanadu, I presume."

"He's being paid fifty thousand dollars a night."

"He's probably losing it all back at the tables. You ought to fix it so he sings only in cities where gambling is illegal."

"That wouldn't stop him."

"I suppose not. Well, it's been nice talking to you—"

"Wait a minute. I hope I made myself perfectly clear."

"I guess you did."

"Good, I appreciate it." And she hung up on me without even saying goodbye. Some people have no manners.

The penthouse suite at the Xanadu sprawled over two stories, with a cool, darkly lit bar on the lower level and the gambling rooms upstairs. The decor was mildly reminiscent of a rain forest and there were even several live, brightly colored parrots in cages suspended from the ceiling. The cocktail waitresses, who seemed interchangeably delicious to me, were dressed in a style I can only describe as whorehouse tropical, with flowered skirts slit up to the hip bone and garlands draped casually over their otherwise naked bosoms. The gamblers admitted to these sacred precincts paid no attention to such distractions; they were mostly middle-aged white men dressed either in expensive business suits or flashy sports coats, and they had come to play. To a real gambler a woman represents a dangerous distraction, a hazard to be avoided or overcome, like a water jump or an excess of weight in the saddle-bags. These ladies were as safe from harassment, I figured, as if they had been employed to hustle cookies at a church fair.

I found Fulvio Gasparini in the bar, where, attired in a blue-striped suit, he loomed magnificently over a cup of what turned out to be tepid tea laced with honey, and his eyes lit up when he saw me. "Ah," he exclaimed, *"il mago!* Now we win money!"

"That's what you always say, Fulvio," Miss Willows observed, "but all you do is lose." She was sitting across from him, looking sulkily beautiful in a long white-silk dress with an ermine cape draped elegantly around her shoulders.

"Today is different," Fulvio said. "We have *il mago.*"

"I'm not a real wizard," I assured him. I took Miss Willows's hand, squeezed it, then feigned surprise when a little rubber rabbit popped out of her palm as I released it. "Oh, it got away again," I said, snatching it back. I clapped my hands together and made it vanish. "Now where did that little devil go?" I asked. "Ah." And I pointed to Miss Willows's cape. "Would you mind?"

"What? Mind what?" Her eyes were now focused on me in wary surprise.

"Your cape," I said. "I think Herman's in there."

She reached up and found the tiny rubber beast nestling under her chin. "Oh," she said, amazed. "How did you do that?"

"Magic," I answered, "that's all."

"You'll need more than magic to make a winner out of Fulvio," she informed me, handing the bunny back to me.

"Oof, Anna," the tenor said, "you are always saying no to everything. Life is to enjoy. Right, *mago?*"

"Sì, sì," I agreed. "Let's at least have some fun."

The tenor stood up and looked down at his soprano. *"Vieni anche tu?"*

"I'll stay here," she said. "I hate to watch you lose, Fulvio."

"Women," the tenor said, taking my arm as we moved toward the stairs, "they do not understand about life. They are always complaining and shutting the doors to pleasure. *Che noia!"*

I wondered briefly whether I should tell him about my phone call from Jeanine Lagrange, but I decided against it. I think it would have made him angry, and it would have distracted him from our main purpose, which, that afternoon at least, was to detach the casino from a portion of its capital.

At that hour the gambling rooms of the private suite at the Xanadu were not crowded. One baccarat table was active and there were players at two blackjack layouts, but the craps table was empty. We walked past it to an end room where a bored croupier and two assistants were presiding over a standard European roulette wheel, then being tested by a party of Arabs. They all seemed to belong to the same family or tribe and played together, holding whispered consultations with one another before putting their chips, all in denominations of a thousand dollars and looking like small breakfast trays, into action. I made Fulvio pause to survey the scene for at least several spins of the wheel before we joined them, even though I could tell that he was seething to get into action himself. "It's important to see if we can sense any pattern to the play," I explained. "You have to have a feel for what's going on, Fulvio, before you risk your money."

"*Bene, bene,*" he said, bouncing impatiently on the balls of his feet, his eyes glued to the wheel as it endlessly revolved and the tiny, white-ivory ball bounced from one numbered slot to another.

I pulled him aside, which wasn't easy, something like trying to tug an oil tanker away from its moorings. "Listen, Fulvio," I said, "we're going to play a cynic's system."

"Eh? *Cosa?*"

"Ordinarily, I'd suggest that we play the house numbers, the zero and the two adjacent slots, the twenty-six and the thirty-two," I explained. "One of those should hit every eleven spins. One streak of eleven losses and we wrap up. Do you understand?"

"No, but is okay," the tenor said, his eyes still hungrily fixed on the gambling layout. "You play, I bet, okay?"

"Yes, but today we're going to vary the action," I continued, not because I expected him to grasp what I was up to, but because I felt I owed it to him to clarify what I intended to do; it was his money that was at risk. "These Arabs are playing as a family unit. They're all betting the same even-money propositions. I think we ought to bet against them."

"Why you do that?"

"They're risking a lot of money," I explained. "It's hard for me to imagine that the Xanadu is going to allow these wogs to take their casino away from them."

"You mean they cheat?" Fulvio asked, his eyes opening wide in astonishment.

"Probably not," I said, "but if they are, why not benefit from it?"

"*Mago,* you do it," Fulvio said. "Now we begin."

We walked up to the wheel and watched the Arabs stack their

trays up on even numbers. I waited until the wheel was in motion, then nodded to Fulvio, who promptly bet two thousand dollars on odds. The little ivory ball spun out of the twenty-six and jumped into the seventeen slot. The croupier pushed two thousand dollars our way. "Ah, *bene!*" Fulvio exclaimed. "*Bravo, mago! Che meraviglia!*"

Roulette is a boring game, devoid of any real skill and with long stretches between spins of the wheel. It becomes less tedious when you are winning, and in our case I managed to keep the tedium factor to a minimum. Over the course of an hour, by playing with the house against the embattled Bedouins, we managed to win well over half the time, until we had assembled a small mountain of chips. The Arabs must have dropped half a million at the table, but seemed unperturbed at their failure. After they departed cheerfully from the scene, I took Fulvio's arm. "How much are you ahead?" I asked.

He made a quick count. "Twenty-four thousand, *mio caro,*" he chirped. "You are a genius!"

"Let's stop," I said.

"But why?" he asked, looking dismayed. "Is good beginning, no?"

"Our friends have left," I pointed out. "We're on our own now."

"And so?"

I could tell the fever was still on him, so I resigned myself to possible disaster. "I would quit for tonight," I said, "but if you must, Fulvio, then let's play the house numbers."

He began betting one-hundred-dollar chips on the zero, the twenty-six, and the thirty-two. We hit the zero on the seventh spin and proceeded to have another good run, with one of our three numbers popping up every half-dozen plays or so. By the end of another hour, Fulvio's winnings had doubled. I excused myself for a minute and went downstairs to the men's room, hoping that Fulvio would manage not to go crazy during my absence.

Anna Willows was sitting at the bar, where she seemed to have achieved a disturbing degree of intimacy with the bartender, a dashing type of about thirty with a handlebar mustache and the quick, greedy eyes of a speculator. "Well," she said, as I emerged from the restroom and passed her again, "how much are you losing?"

"We're winning about forty thousand," I said, "unless Fulvio's blown it all back during the last five minutes. Sorry to disappoint you."

Her cool green eyes opened wide in surprise. "Fulvio's winning?"
"I don't usually gamble to lose," I said. "We're having a good streak. As soon as it runs out, we'll stop. I hope."
"He's wild," the bartender said. "He'll play all afternoon."
"Not if I can help it."
"This is Lorenzo," Anna said, indicating the bartender. "He keeps me entertained while Fulvio is losing."
"Hi," Lorenzo said, nodding coolly my way. "A drink?"
"Make it a light beer," I told him. "I never drink when I'm risking money."
"That's smart." He went about his task, while I glanced at Miss Willows. She seemed to be temporarily lost in thought. I found myself wondering if she and Lorenzo had gone beyond the casual intimacy of the bar scene.
"I guess I was wrong about you," she said.
"In what way?"
"Fulvio's a celebrity. He attracts a lot of scroungers and hangers-on," she explained. "I figured you were no different."
I now knew who had called Jeanine Lagrange, but I saw no need to make an issue of it. "You could help."
"How's that?"
"How about coming upstairs in about thirty minutes with a terrific headache?"
"I'll do it."
"Good." I pushed myself away from the bar. "Now I better get up there and see what's going on."
My fears, I discovered, were realized. During my absence the tenor had begun spraying bets all over the layout and had been losing. It hadn't taken him twenty minutes to blow nearly a third of his winnings back. I managed to get him under control again by insisting that we stick to our system, but the wheel had turned cold. We hit a zero on the tenth spin and a twenty-six after another eight revolutions, but then lost eleven consecutive plays. I took Fulvio's arm. "Let's go," I said. "We've played our string out."
The fat man shook me off like a bothersome insect. "No, no, *mago*," he said, "the luck turns, I know it." And he slapped three more chips on our numbers.
"Fulvio, if you're not going to listen to me, I'm going." I even took a couple of steps toward the exit.
"No, wait! Ten more minutes and I come!"
"Sorry."
I felt that my chances of prying him away from the table were

poor, but luckily the situation changed abruptly with the sudden appearance of Miss Willows. "Fulvio," she snapped, her hands angrily on her hips. "I'm going. I have a terrible headache!"

"*Santo cielo,*" he moaned, "these women!"

"*Stupido,*" she snapped and turned to go.

Gasparini hesitated, then flung one last chip toward the zero as he left. Just as he reached the door, the ball slid into the slot and the croupier sang out, "Zero, you win, sir!"

Fulvio looked stunned. "You see?" he said to Anna. "You see what you do?"

"I don't care, I'm going," she answered, starting out.

Fulvio gazed at me, then broke into a huge grin. "What you think, *mago,* eh? *Bravo,* you win!" He waved toward the layout. "Is for my friend, the wizard," he called out. "You pay him, okay?" He looked my way again. "*Ma che fenomeno!*" he said, clapping me so heartily on the shoulders that my knees buckled. "I have won twenty-five thousand dollars. You come to see me tomorrow morning, all right? Eleven o'clock, *va bene?*"

I smiled at him. "*Va mucho bene,*" I said, improvising. I watched him lumber happily off after Anna, then turned toward the roulette layout to retrieve my winnings, a total of thirty-seven hundred dollars. Nice work, if you can get it.

After my stint at the Three Kings that night, I dropped in at Circus Circus, where my favorite blackjack dealer worked. Her name was Dawn Caputo. We had once been something to each other, but the affair had evaporated a couple of years earlier, mainly because she had discovered that I had psychologically shut her out of the most important part of my life. She was now in her late thirties, a small, trim-looking, dark-haired woman with a kind smile and long legs, but with a few too many lines around her eyes. She had been married to an itinerant jazz musician and divorced and supported an only son named Ronnie, a nice kid of eleven to whom I'd become very close during the months we had been together. But she had realized eventually how little I had to offer any woman, apart from some good times and a lot of sprightly conversation. I was a close-up artist and a horseplayer, two occupations that do not yield immense and secure rewards, and I lived like a hermit in a one-room Hollywood apartment festooned with old posters, programs, and *Racing Forms.* I could be a lover, but never a husband or a father. And when she had realized that, she had walked away from me, regretfully and with some tears, but permanently and definitively. As an old horse degenerate had once explained it for us, "Broads are okay, but you can't put a saddle on their backs and work 'em out of the gate. Worse, you can't bet on 'em. And they ain't gonna bet on you, that's for sure."

Dawn got off at midnight and we walked out of the casino, with its trapeze artists and balancing acts doing their stuff over our heads as usual, and went into the coffeeshop. We chatted for about half an hour, while Dawn unwound. Dealing is a tedious, repetitive job, but it produces real tension, most of it from the players, not all of whom are gifted with grace and the milk of human kindness. Over the years Dawn had learned to cope with it, but there is a price to pay. It showed up in the lines around her eyes.

"So how are you doing, Shifty?" she asked. "It's been a few days."

"I know," I said. "I've been busy." I told her about my dentists and Hal and my gambling forays with Fulvio Gasparini.

She laughed. "Boy, he sounds like a real character."

"He is. Now he thinks he can't lose, as long as I'm around, which, of course, is crazy." I took a sip of coffee and leaned back against the seat of our booth. "And I hear he just loves the horses. Wait until he finds out about Jay and me and climbs in on that action."

She looked at me and smiled wanly. "You want to jump my bones," she said softly. "Is that what you're doing here?"

"Well, something like that," I admitted. "But we can just talk, if the prospect appalls you."

She giggled. "Oh, Shifty, you're nothing if not transparent. You know I can't take you home."

"I know. How is Ronnie?"

"In terrific shape," she said. "He's doing real well in school and all. Nice kid. Asks about you occasionally."

"I'll take him to the movies or something. Would he like that?"

She nodded. "You bet. You know, you're one of his heroes."

"That's a big responsibility, all right. I guess I let him down once, when you and I split up. I'll try not to do that again."

"He's over it now. He really likes you."

I took her hand. "My place?"

She hesitated a moment, then squeezed my fingers. "Why not?" she said. "You always were a good lay."

Before I could pay the check, I was horrified to see Hugo Mandelbaum heading in our direction. He reached our booth before I could prepare Dawn for the encounter. "Hey, babe," he said, grinning and sitting down without waiting for an invitation. "How's it going?"

"Fine, Hugo. What are you doing here?"

"I got a chick that works here, pal. She's a cock and tail waitress."

"Hugo's a comedian," I explained to Dawn. "He's one of Happy's clients."

"A comedian? I wouldn't have guessed in a million years."

"Yeah, I'm the best," Hugo said. "Listen, did you hear the one about the guy who goes to his doctor for an examination and the doctor tells him he's only got six months to live, so he should move to Cleveland and marry a nice Jewish girl?"

"I've heard it," I said.

"Yeah, but she hasn't," Hugo said, focusing on Dawn, who was looking at him as if she had suddenly been confronted by an unclean sink. "So the guy says, 'Why should I move to Cleveland and marry a nice Jewish girl, if I only got six months?' "

No one answered him.

" 'It'll seem like a lifetime,' " Hugo concluded, laughing loudly and nasally at his own joke.

Dawn laughed, too. "Okay," she said, "not bad."

"Stop right there, Hugo," I instructed him. "That's the cleanest joke you ever told, I'll bet."

"It's the only clean joke I tell," the comedian answered. "Did you hear about Mrs. Nussbaum, when she went to the gynecologist?"

"No, and we're not going to," I said, standing up and tugging Dawn after me.

"We have to go now," she said. "It was nice meeting you, Hugo. I think."

Later, as we lay quietly in each other's arms in my room on the tenth floor of the Three Kings, Dawn said, "Why do you know such goofy people?"

"Just lucky, I guess." I sat up and looked at her. A pink glow from the neon lights in the street below cast her body in soft shadows and her eyes were hidden. I kissed her gently on the lips. "Want to try again?"

"Not tonight, lover. I'm tired."

"I didn't mean tonight. I meant—you know . . ."

She smiled. "Not on your life, Shifty. You can't go home again. Don't you know that?"

FOUR

♦

Action

Jay Fox was in his element. I found him sitting in the race book at Caesar's at a broad counter facing a bank of color television screens on which odds were flashing and horses were running. Surrounded by his charts and big black notebooks, he was calmly scrutinizing the *Form*, while all around him incipient panic reigned. Most of the contestants were scurrying to and from the betting windows, moving through the permanent neon haze of the large room like insects in pursuit of domestic debris, while waitresses on various errands of mercy threaded through them like warrior ants. Overhead, the PA system rattled off useful information on the action at tracks all over the country. The mood of these festivities made my skin itch. Jay, however, remained untouched, a placid island in an agitated ebb and flow of acquisitiveness.

I sat down beside him. "Well?"

"Just hold on a moment, Shifty," he said, glancing up now at a screen to check the odds on a horse he had isolated on one of his statistical sheets. "I think I got one here." He snapped the notebook shut, checked his *Form* one last time, then rose like the phoenix to move toward a betting window.

"So?" I asked, when he came back.

"I put two bills on this speedball in New York," he answered, "just to get things going here."

A few seconds later, the race, a six-furlong sprint for three-year-old allowance horses, went off and we watched it on the monitors.

Jay's selection, the favorite, ran exactly as he figured to. He burst out of the starting gate, opened up two lengths in the first quarter-mile, stretched his lead to four around the turn, and, though tiring some at the end, won handily by a length and a half. The animal paid $5.60 to win, not a munificent sum, but Jay seemed satisfied at the outcome. "That was stealing," he said. He sank back in his seat and sighed, like a contestant relieved to have come up with a crucial right answer on some morning game show. "That was my maiden foray," he observed. "It's probably the only bet I'm going to make this morning. Most of our action, Shifty, is going to be at the California tracks this afternoon, where I know what I'm doing. It's going to be a long day in here."

"Can you take a break?"

"Sure. I got about an hour now. The next race is a cheap sprint for New York–bred fillies, which is like handicapping frogs, so I don't even have to watch it. Come on."

He got up and we walked out of the room into the lobby of the hotel, where a long line of raucous male guests, a convention of some sort, was checking in at the registration desk amid the comforting mechanical clatter of the slot machines inhaling metal. We sat down at a table in the bar area, ordered Cokes, and stared out over the swarm of gamblers. "A heartwarming sight," Jay said. "I like the idea of a whole nation of people dedicated to that greatest of American principles—getting something for nothing."

"In these joints, if you hang around long enough," I said, "what you get is nothing for something."

"So how'd it go yesterday?" Jay asked me, after a long sip of his Coke.

I told him. "The guy thinks I'm a lucky charm."

"Maybe you are, Shifty."

"All I do is keep him from throwing his money away," I said. "Percentage plays, that's all. But he calls me his wizard."

"You got something going there."

"I guess."

"Nearly six grand in two days? Shifty, that's good action. Best of all, it doesn't cost you anything."

"It's not my style, Jay."

"What isn't? Winning money?"

I let that one pass; he knew what I meant. At the track, as in everything I do, I'm basically a loner. I don't tout people and I don't try to climb in on their action. To Jay a free ride is the ultimate edge any gambler can achieve, but it just makes me uneasy, as if I'm violating some basic trust or code of honor on which I've tried to build my life. "He wants me to travel with him," I said.

"Where to?"

"All over, I guess. New York, Rome, Naples, back to New York, everywhere."

"Terrific. What's he going to pay you?"

"It's a guaranteed six months."

"How much?"

"Four hundred a week, against fifteen percent of the take on any and all of his gambling action."

"Expenses?"

"All paid."

"Shifty, you've landed on a gold mine."

"Not the way he gambles. And anyway, in the casinos you've got to lose, sooner or later. All I can do is cut his losses. With the horses . . . I don't know. . . ."

"What don't you know?"

"It's . . . it's not what I do, Jay," I tried to explain. "I'm not a professional gambler, I'm a close-up artist."

The Fox looked at me in amazement, as if I had just told him I had found a satchel full of thousand-dollar bills on the street and was rushing off to the nearest police station to turn it in. "What is it with you?" he began. "I mean, are you on some nutty kind of religious kick? A guy makes you an offer like that, you play the string out."

"I guess." I must have looked unhappy.

"You guess? Is he willing to put it in writing?"

"He said so, but I don't think I'd need to. Anyway, I'd want to be able to get out in case it all turns sour. I mean, if we start losing, he could become disenchanted pretty quickly."

"The First Commandment is, Shifty, you don't walk away from a winning streak."

I shut my eyes and sank back in my chair. Fulvio Gasparini's beaming, bearded countenance loomed up before me. He was sitting up in bed, just as I had seen him earlier that morning, with a breakfast tray on his lap. It supported a gallon of tea, a loaf of toast, seven or eight boiled eggs, and a haunch of bacon. "Ah, *mago*," Fulvio had said, waving one huge arm at me as I entered the room, "we are going to be rich, very rich, and very happy! First I sing and then we play! *Che bella vita!*"

"Are you listening to me, Shifty?" Jay's voice cut into this expansive reverie. "Can you hear me?"

"I can hear you."

"What's waiting for you in L.A.?"

"Not much, at the moment."

"So?"

"So I don't know."

Jay looked pained, as if battling the onset of a mild attack of colitis. "Shifty, are you enlisting with the worker bees? What's happened to you?"

I decided to ignore this question. "Who's Gerald Monkton?" I asked instead.

"I know the name. Why?"

"He's a horse trainer."

"Oh, yeah. Originally from San Francisco, I think."

"He's Fulvio Gasparini's horse trainer."

"I'll look him up," Jay said. "I think he started on the county fair circuit, then was around the Frisco tracks for a while."

"He's in New York now, at least most of the time."

"What horses does Fulvio have?"

"He's just getting into it now," I explained, relaying to Jay what the tenor had told me earlier, during our breakfast meeting in his suite at the Xanadu. "He's going to put his money into good racing stock. Not broodmares or yearlings or stallion shares, but horses that are ready to run."

"That can be risky."

"Yes, I know."

"And he wants you to advise him."

"Not exactly. Gerald Monkton is doing all the advising, as well as all the buying and training. But when I told Fulvio I knew something about betting on horses, he lit up like an old print I once saw showing Mount Vesuvius in eruption. 'So I run my horses, we bet on them,' he said, 'and we make fortune.' "

"Sounds like a terrific way to go through life."

"Jay, I'm really not sure I want to be involved in all this," I tried to explain. "I mean, I have my own life to live. My magic—"

"Tell you what, Shifty," he interrupted, setting his empty glass down on the table like a punctuation mark, "if you don't want the job, you can pass it on to your old friend, the Fox. It would be a nice change in the routine and I'd finally get to see a little something of the world. I've never been to Europe. Of course, there's the opera part of it. I could put up with it, though. I'd buy some earplugs."

"Well, I'm probably going to say yes," I admitted. "I told him I'd let him know tomorrow. He leaves Vegas Sunday night and I'm going to catch up to him in New York. He wants me to come with him, but I can't. I have another week here and then I've got to stop off in L.A. for a couple of days at least."

"What for?"

"Clothes, and a couple of loose ends to tie up." I smiled. "And maybe Happy Hal will have a TV offer I can't refuse."

Jay sighed, paid for our drinks, and we got up to go. "Shifty, let me tell you something about life."

"It's a fountain."

"Ha ha." He took my arm and steered me back toward the handicapping contest. "You're on the carousel one time and you have only so many tries at the golden ring."

"Do I need a wisdom scene this early in the day?"

Jay laughed. "Go for it, Shifty."

By three o'clock that afternoon, when I stopped at Caesar's again, Jay had settled on a long shot named Freddie Sing Sing in the ninth at Santa Anita. "Not exactly a dead crab," he told me, "but he's got a real shot here. He's parked outside, but he has the speed to grab the lead and get over to the rail by the time the field hits the turn. Then, if the rider can give him a breather down the backside, he should be clear by the head of the lane and have enough left for the drive. He's a stretch-out going long for the first time and this trainer's pattern is to put two sprints into his animals before popping at a distance. And he'll be at least eight or nine to one in here against a couple of Dummy-God plodders. I'm going to go over the top on this one."

I laughed. "You know, Jay, I could listen to you talk like that all day."

"Yeah? They don't figure like that all day long, Shifty."

"No, I mean the argot," I explained. "This secret language we all talk."

"Secret? What's so secret? Didn't I make myself clear?"

"Perfectly—to me." I stood up. "I'm going to alert my opera star."

"Don't do that," Jay objected. "The way that guy bets, he could tip the play off and lower the price."

"I won't tell him what horse."

"How can you get away with that?"

"Trust me," I said, heading for the phones.

Signor Gasparini was unavailable, I was informed by a not very courteous operator, but I decided to track him down personally. I certainly wasn't going to leave my message for him with the hotel switchboard. I hopped into my car, the famous Datsun 310 once test-driven by Chuck Yeager in his first attempt to break the sound barrier, and rattled up the Strip to the Xanadu.

On the fairly safe supposition that he might be in but not taking calls, I went directly up to his suite, an apartment that occupied a corner of the top floor of the Tower to the Stars, a luxurious enclave for celebrities and high rollers at the very center of the sprawling Xanadu complex. As I stepped out of the elevator and started down the corridor, a door opened and Lorenzo, the bartender from the Penthouse Garden, retreated into the hallway, followed by a long, naked white arm. He said something I couldn't hear and then Anna Willows leaned out of the open doorway. She put her hand behind his head and quickly kissed him savagely on the mustache, then withdrew, shutting the door behind her. I was reasonably sure they hadn't seen me, but I turned in the opposite direction and lingered around the corner of the landing until I was certain Lorenzo had gone, after which I again headed for Fulvio's suite.

I could hear him in full voice from fifty yards away. He was singing some sort of a do-re-mi vocal exercise to a piano accompaniment and I decided to wait outside his door until he had finished. After three or four minutes, however, the piano suddenly stopped playing and I heard Achille Pipistrello mutter angrily in Italian. *"Cretino!"* Fulvio shouted at him, following that word up with a stream of others I couldn't understand. Achille muttered back and thumped angrily on a chord, as if to emphasize some sort of musical point. *"Merda!"* I heard Fulvio say. *"Da capo, allora!"* They began from the beginning again and this time finished, even though I could tell neither man seemed happy with the other after they had concluded. Achille was still muttering and I could hear Fulvio moving noisily around the room, like a restless animal in a cage and waiting to be fed. I rang the bell.

"Chi è?" Fulvio shouted, then angrily opened the door. He was dressed only in slippers and a bright-blue terrycloth robe that enveloped him like a Crisco wrapping. "Ah, *il mago!*" he said, his face dissolving at once into a surprised but welcoming smile.

"I'm sorry to disturb you," I said, "but I knew you weren't taking calls. I have something to tell you."

"You come in," he answered, stepping aside to sweep me past him. "You know Pipistrello."

"Yes. How are you?"

"Bad," the little man said, gazing up at me from his seat at the baby grand. "Very bad."

"He is my Evil Eye," Fulvio said. "He is making me to break my balls."

"I am making him to work," Achille snapped. "If you do not work at the voice every day, it fails. Fulvio does not wish to work. Pavarotti works, Domingo works. Fulvio Gasparini does not work. Fulvio Gasparini will disappear."

"My Evil Eye with the evil mouth," Fulvio said. "Go away."

"Sure, I go," Achille said, standing up and snapping down the piano lid. "I go and you will see what will happen."

"*Stupido*, sit down!" Fulvio commanded him. "I am not finished. I will talk to the *mago* and then we will finish, if it kills me."

"It will not kill you," the little man said. "You will sing. No, it will not kill you." And he sat down again, reopened the piano lid, folded his arms, and waited, like a bored seagull riding out a swell.

"So, Sheefty? What is it cooking?"

I told him exactly what was it cooking, pretty much in Jay's own words. A mistake, I soon discovered.

"*Cazzo*, what is this you are saying?" he asked. "*Non capisco.*"

"It is the litany of ruin," Achille said. "*La rovina, capisci?*"

"It's about a horse running in the ninth race today at Santa Anita," I explained. "My friend Jay Fox, the handicapper I told you about, thinks the horse will win."

"But where does this crab come in?"

"*Già.* What business has it?" Achille echoed him.

"A dead crab is what we call a horse that can't lose," I continued. "Actually, there's no such thing, of course—all horses can lose and do—but Jay thinks this one has a very good chance today. He'll pay a good price. I'm going to bet on him and I thought you might want to get in on our action."

"Get in—ah, *sì*," Fulvio exclaimed, smiling broadly. "You will bet a thousand dollars for me." He started out of the room.

"That's too much, Fulvio," I said. "I'll bet two hundred for you, no more."

The tenor hesitated, seeming to bounce on the balls of his feet as if about to leap into the air like an amorous bullfrog. "Only?" he pleaded.

"It's plenty," I warned him.

"No, I bet more," he said, again starting out of the room.

"I'm sorry, that's my limit," I said.

"*Your* limit?" He stared at me in genuine puzzlement. "Is not my limit."

"Look, I know I'm not officially on the scene yet," I declared, "but if you're not going to take my advice, then I can't work for you. You want me to help you get your gambling life in order? Well, I'm going to insist you let me do just that. I know how you bet, Fulvio. Two hundred dollars is plenty of action on this particular horse."

Fulvio shrugged and allowed his gaze to roam helplessly about the room. He made a point, however, of not looking either at me or at his accompanist, who was now perched on his piano stool like a cast-iron garden gnome. "*Va bene,*" the tenor said at last. "I get the money."

"It's okay," I said. "I'll bet it for you. You'll get a full accounting, but we'll straighten out all the details later. I'd better get back to Caesar's now and I guess you have to work some more here." I started for the door.

"How is this horse called?"

"Freddie Sing Sing."

"Oh, I like," Fulvio said. "I like very much."

"He won't win because he's got a cute name," I said. "If he wins, it'll be because he's ready to run."

"Go, *mago*, go," the tenor ordered, waving me on my way. "Next time I bet more."

"Fulvio, you don't need a ton of money at the races," I said. "You need winners."

On my way out the door, I caught a glimpse of Achille Pipistrello's face. The little man was staring hard at me out of those piercing brown eyes with an expression I interpreted as one of approval; I guessed I had made a permanent ally. "*Allora,*" he said, as I shut the door behind me, "we work now. *Finalmente.*"

By the time I passed Anna Willows's closed door, the tenor's rich, dark tones had begun to echo off the walls again. I found myself wondering idly, as the elevator whisked me down to the lobby, if Miss Willows only made love to her bartender while she could hear Fulvio in full cry down the hall from her. And what else did she do with her days?

♦   ♦   ♦

I got back to Caesar's in plenty of time to make our bets, a total of three hundred dollars to win on Freddie Sing Sing, and spent the forty minutes or so I still had to kill watching Jay maneuver his money through the competition. He had picked up a couple of other winners to keep him in mid-pack in the contest, but his day was clearly going to revolve pretty much on what would happen in the ninth at Santa Anita. I knew him well enough to know that he was excited, but to the outside world he appeared as serene as a hirsute Buddha. When the race finally went off, he jumped slightly in his seat, but before it was half over he had relaxed completely, his arms folded benignly across his chest and his eyes focused fondly on the television screen. Freddie Sing Sing had behaved exactly as expected and came coasting home, a winner by two lengths, at odds of nine to one. The win swept Jay up the standings and left him tied for third place at the end of the day, strongly in contention for the fifty-thousand-dollar jackpot.

"I wish they were all this easy," I said, getting up to inform my opera star of our coup.

Jay smiled. "They're running like little trained pigs," he said. "Where's your meal ticket? Why isn't he here?"

"He's practicing," I explained. "He's airing his lungs. You should hear him."

"I'll pass."

"I'll go call him."

"Then come back and you can buy me a celebratory drink."

Fulvio himself answered the phone this time. When I told him he was eighteen hundred dollars richer, he laughed. *"Formidabile!"* he exclaimed. "I come right down."

"No need to," I said. "I'm going to have a drink in the bar here with a friend of mine, then I'll bring the money to you."

"Good. Achille will not permit me to go in there," he declared. "It is the smoke. There is much smoke, no?"

"Yes, there is."

"Ah. It is most bad for the voice. Around horses there is always much smoke. Why is that, *mago?*"

"There's too much time between races," I explained. "Tension builds up. People smoke to relieve the tension."

"Peccato. It is too bad," he said. "At the races, in the open, it is not impossible. But here . . ." His voice trailed away like that of a disappointed child agreeing with an adult but hoping to be contradicted.

"You sounded in terrific voice," I said, ducking the opportunity.

"Ah, yes, my wizard," he intoned cheerfully into my ear. "Tonight I will sing like a god. You must come. You can bring the money then."

"I'll make the last part of the program," I promised. "I'm still working myself, you know."

"Of course. But soon you will be working only for me."

"If you call this work."

"You will see," he promised. "There will be much money. But listen," he continued, as I was about to hang up. "Have you seen Anna?"

"No," I lied, "I haven't. She's not in her room?"

"Women, *mago,* are much trouble," he said. "They are not like us. They are from a different universe, you understand?"

"I think so, Fulvio."

"Well, *ciao.* Until later. And *grazie."* He hung up.

Jay and I had a couple of margaritas, after which I decided to head back to my hotel; I had about an hour and a half to change and get ready for my nightly stint. I walked out through the lobby toward the main parking lot, liking the feel of all that money in my pockets and wondering idly now where Fulvio's soprano had disappeared to and whether her behavior earlier in the afternoon had been typical or merely a passing fancy.

It was dark outside and I was unaware of anyone else around me. As I stepped off the curb on my way to retrieve the Datsun, which was parked at the far end of the lot, I heard a familiar grating voice. "Shifty," it said, "how're they hanging, pal?"

Hugo Mandelbaum had evidently followed me out of the casino. He was dressed in a dark brown leisure suit, two-toned wingtips, and his usual complement of jangling jewelry; he looked like a pimp. "Hugo, we have to stop meeting like this," I said. "What are you doing here?"

"I came to see a frail about a fuck," he said. "Listen, what do you get if you catch AIDS from a cocktail waitress?"

"I know you're going to tell me."

"Barmaids."

"Hugo—"

"And if you get it from a virgin, it's first aids."

"Oh, my God . . ." I began to move briskly out of range.

"If you're infected by Ronald Reagan, you have presidential aids!" He called after me.

I broke into a swift jog across the parking lot, threading my way through that sea of cars like a scatback ducking tacklers. The man was becoming a menace, I reflected, as I reached the Datsun and leaned over to unlock the door. I don't remember now whether I ever got it open, because I was hit very hard from behind. The blow caught me on the side of the head and knocked me sideways against the next car. I recollect falling to my knees and wondering what was happening to me. I'd been hit by one of Hugo's heavier jokes, I figured. Then the asphalt rose up to meet me and the rest was silence, deep and slightly pink.

FIVE

♦

Small Moves

Hugo Mandelbaum came to visit me at the hospital, late the following morning. I was lying in bed, propped halfway up, with my skull swathed in bandages. I was alone, though I still retain a dim memory of hurried comings and goings around the screened-off bed next to me. Perhaps someone had died in it during the night and been whisked away, but I never asked and I didn't want to know. My head ached fiercely and I couldn't focus very well in the darkened room. I did, however, recognize my visitor. "Oh, Christ," I murmured, with a groan.

"The wrong prophet, sweetheart," Hugo said, vibrating with misdirected energy. "How're you doing?"

"One joke, Hugo, and I'm going to get up and kill you."

"Look, I just wanted to know how you were getting along, that's all. I got to you first."

"You did?"

"Yeah." He moved to the foot of the bed and leaned over it, his coarse features blurred in the dim light. "I mean, you kind of disappeared and then I spotted this guy moving real fast and I figured something had happened. I was the one who found you and called the cops."

"Thanks. I appreciate it."

"It's okay. I told them all about it. I guess they didn't get the guy."

"I don't know."

"They never get anybody. All cops can do is arrest hookers and

39

bookies. Shit, the fuckin' FBI couldn't find Patty Hearst for two years."

"Did you actually see him?"

"The bozo who hit you? Nah. Must have been a little guy, though, because you couldn't hardly spot him between the cars."

"I never saw him at all. I have no idea who hit me."

"Did he clean you out?"

"Yes. He got away with my cash, about three thousand dollars. Funny thing, though . . ."

"What?"

"He didn't take my wallet."

"Maybe he didn't have time."

"Maybe not, but I had it in my inside coat pocket. It wouldn't have taken him more than two seconds to reach in there."

"By then he had the money. What did he care?"

"You're right." I tried to sit up a bit so I could see him a little more clearly, but my head was throbbing and I couldn't make it.

"So what did he hit you with?"

"A piece of lead pipe, I was told. I was lucky."

"Yeah? Some luck, kiddo. With your luck, remind me not to get on an airplane with you. How long you in here for?"

"I don't know. Two or three days, maybe. There's no fracture. They did a CAT scan."

"Cats? What kind of cats?"

"It's called a computerized tomography or something like that, Hugo. It's an X ray."

"Oh. Say, I could work up a routine on that." He snapped his fingers and began to hum with incipient creativity. "Cats . . . cats . . . the pussy scan. Hey—"

"Hugo, I'm not strong enough for this."

He grinned, his teeth flashing white in the gloom. I could hear him tinkle his chains as he moved, looming up beside me now. "You got no sense of humor, fella. A couple of laughs and you'll be out of here."

"Or dead. Listen, Hugo, I have this really outrageous headache."

"Bad, huh?"

"Yeah. I have a concussion and I've got to take it easy. They worry in here about things like blood clots."

"Doctors. You better get your ass out of here before you really get sick. I mean, these guys don't get rich from *not* doing stuff to you, you know what I mean?"

"Yes, I think I do. Listen, Hugo, it was nice of you to come."

"No problem, no problem. I thought maybe you'd bought it. I mean, that son of a bitch really coldcocked you. You didn't move a fuckin' inch and you weren't breathing too good."

"Listen, maybe you could do me a favor."

"Sure, babe, shoot."

I asked him to phone my boss at the Three Kings and suggest he get in touch right away with Vince Michaels, who might be able to fill in for me these next few days, or he would know of some other good magician who could use the work. Then I gave him Jay's room number at Caesar's and told him to leave a message for him to call me. "He'll probably be at the race book," I explained, "but he'll be wondering what happened to me."

"Anything else? Want me to warm up a nurse for you?"

"You haven't seen the nurses in this hospital or you wouldn't say that."

"I saw them. It looks like the Bay of Pigs out there."

"Hugo, one other thing . . ."

"Shoot, kiddo."

"Fulvio Gasparini, at the Xanadu—"

"Sounds like a mouthwash."

"He'll want to know why I didn't show up last night."

"You fags gettin' it on?"

"Hugo, two-thirds of the money I lost was his. We had a wager on a horse."

"You mean you actually gamble on horses?" Hugo asked, in mock horror. "That's shocking. You deserved to get mugged. You're a fuckin' degenerate."

"Tell him what happened and where I am. He may think I stole his money."

"He trusts you, huh?"

"He hasn't known me very long."

"I haven't either and I don't trust you."

"Don't waste any jokes on him, Hugo. He won't understand them."

"How come? He ain't Polish."

"Tell him I'll try to call him tomorrow, before he goes. Or leave him a message. I'm not sure I can take too many calls today."

"So is that it?"

"I guess so. Thanks for coming, Hugo."

"Okay. So how about one joke?" He grinned at me, looking like a bejeweled gargoyle in the gloom of my room. "A good clean laugh wouldn't hurt."

"A good clean laugh is what you can't give me, Hugo," I said.

"And anyway, it will hurt. It's hurting already, but go ahead." By this time I figured I owed him at least one, so I braced myself against my pillow.

"Give me four good reasons for not being an egg."

"I can't think of any."

"You only get laid once," he said, "you only get hard once, you only get eaten once, and the only person who'll sit on your face is your mother."

"Goodbye, Hugo. Thanks for everything."

He moved toward the door, but turned, of course, for one final salvo. "You know how you get hearing AIDS? From listening to assholes."

"Hugo, be sure and take your jokes with you," I said, shutting my eyes to ease the pain. He laughed, one of civilization's spoilers, and bounced out into the corridor, shutting the door behind him.

I slept on and off most of that day. Every time I woke up, it seemed to me, it was because someone on the hospital staff had walked into the room on some dubious errand of mercy. It began to make me angry, until it was explained to me by the young resident medico in charge of my case, an apple-cheeked blond Hippocrates fresh out of a medical factory, that I was under constant observation. "You took a hard blow, Mr. Anderson," he said, as he took my pulse in the late afternoon. "We don't want you to go into a deep sleep right now. You were out for a long time, you know, and it might be a little difficult to wake you up."

He made this ominous pronouncement as casually as if commenting on the possibility of a slight drop in barometric pressure, so after he had gone I made a serious effort to stay awake. I couldn't quite manage it, but I stopped complaining about being roused by the series of jolly white-uniformed butterballs who swept in and out in relays from the nurses' station down the hall. What the hell, I figured, I might as well live.

My only other visitor that first day was a bored detective from the Las Vegas Police Department named Larry Sturm. He was in his early forties, much too young, I thought, to be as disenchanted with the world as he seemed to be. He was short and squarely built, with an open flat face, blank blue eyes, and a Whitey Herzog haircut, right from under a tight soup bowl. Without any preliminaries, he sat down beside the bed, took out a large pad and some forms, and began to quiz me on the events of the previous evening. He displayed no emotion of any kind and a complete disinterest in my admittedly minor misfortune.

"I gather we have no idea as to who might have done this," I observed, after he had finished and was evidently preparing to depart my bed of pain.

"Nope," he said. "No one saw anything."

"I thought my friend Hugo Mandelbaum might have seen something."

"The comedian?"

"Yes, some people would call him that."

"He thinks maybe the guy who hit you was short and dark, but he isn't sure."

"And that's not evidence."

"I don't think we could build a terrific case around it, even if we rounded up all the short crapshooters in town."

"You get a lot of these kinds of happenings, do you?"

"You putting me on, Anderson?"

"No, I'm curious."

"Well, maybe ten or twelve or thirty a night."

"You ever catch any of these people?"

"Sometimes we get lucky."

"Not a high-priority item, huh?"

"No. We had a couple of murders last night, eleven armed holdups, and two rapes. You're strictly small stuff."

"It's the story of my life," I said, "except that losing three thousand dollars is not small stuff to me."

"You're lucky. It's only money."

"I should feel comforted, but I don't. I wonder how the guy happened to pick me out. I was one of hundreds in there yesterday afternoon."

"You probably flashed your roll," Sturm said, standing up and preparing to leave. "Winners like to show off."

"I don't think I did," I objected. "I'm fairly cautious about doing that. I learned not to from hanging around racetracks."

"Yeah? Well, I guess he figured you were holding, and you were alone, right?"

"Yes. I was moving pretty fast, because I was trying to get away from Hugo."

"Who?"

"The comedian. So this man must have been waiting for me."

"Maybe."

"Well, that's the odd part, isn't it?"

Sturm nibbled on that bit of information, as if he had just picked it out from between his teeth. "It was quite a ways from the casino entrance," he said. "He was probably just waiting for anybody to show up."

"Probably."

"The casino people were pretty unhappy about it," he said. "Usually, we don't get too many muggings along the Strip. The hit-and-runs happen downtown, where the security isn't so tight."

"And the losers are a little more desperate."

"You got it. Well, that's it, then. You may hear from us."

"I won't walk on coals until I do."

"No, I wouldn't," he said, easing himself out. "Just watch yourself next time. And anyway you'd have lost it back eventually."

"Some consolation."

But I don't think he heard me. Poor Sturm, he obviously had a cop's eye view of the world, as a place of permanent loss and despair, utterly devoid of magic. It clearly wasn't up to me to cheer him up.

I suppose I should have stayed in the hospital the full seventy-two hours the resident recommended, but by the end of the second day I had had it. Not only was I feeling much better, with only an occasional dull ache to remind me of the blow I had taken, but I had indeed become uncomfortable about what else might happen to me if I were to linger too long in this palace of tears. The empty bed in my room had been filled on the second morning by a wizened ancient who had obviously been stiffed too many times out of the gate. He lay slowly but audibly expiring behind his screen of what I took to be an excess of Marlboro country, while teams of expensive specialists and technicians scuttled noisily in and out to ease him on his way. I wasn't getting any sleep at all by this time and reasoned that, in my weakened condition, I could easily succumb to the nearest passing virus, so I telephoned Jay to rescue me, which he did after his third day's stint with the ponies at Caesar's.

Apart from the sheer pleasure of escape, Jay was unable to provide much compensating cheer. His luck in the contest had turned sour and he had tumbled into the bottom rungs of the standings. "I haven't had a winner in two days," he said gloomily, as he eased us away from the hospital entrance and headed for the freeway. "I've lost six photos, been fanned on the turns, shut off in the stretch, and disqualified twice."

"Our luck she is running not so good," I observed. "Do we have any chance at all?"

"None," he answered. "We'd have to hit a couple of big long

shots, but even then, the way these contest rules are set up, it would take a miracle."

"So there goes another five hundred," I said, "to add to the three grand I lost in the parking lot and the twelve hundred it cost me to check out of the hospital."

"You can have a terrific opinion at the track," Jay commented, "but there are going to be days when you're in for a lot of aggravation."

"You tighten up and ride it out, Fox."

"Yeah, but not here. I'm heading back to L.A. tonight. This place is a meat grinder."

"And at Santa Anita you can see the animals in the flesh," I said. "There are aesthetic compensations."

"The track is not an art gallery, Shifty. It's a small war."

I dropped the subject, because I was reasonably certain by this time that his losing streak with the horses had probably been compounded by an equally disastrous run at the tables. When your luck turns bad, it usually affects all areas of your life. Nobody knew this better than the Fox, who had long since paid his dues to the Dummy God and needed no moralizing or advice from anyone on the subject. So I commented briefly on the weather, cold and sunny, and passed on the less offensive of Hugo's jokes, which at least distracted him to some extent from his misery. By the time we pulled up in front of the Three Kings, he had remembered to ask me about my plans. "I don't know," I told him. "I couldn't get hold of Fulvio and I haven't heard from him. He closed last night and he may have already left town. I'll probably see you back in L.A."

"He can't hold you responsible for losing his winnings, Shifty."

"It depends on whether he believes what Hugo told him or not."

"He's still showing a huge profit, isn't he?"

"Unless he's blown it back in my absence." I let myself carefully out of his car and stood up, feeling a bit dizzy and disoriented. "So long, Jay, and thanks."

"You going to be okay?"

"Sure. I'll see you back in L.A."

Feeling about as substantial as a bag of popcorn, I made my way carefully back up to my room, where I found a couple of phone messages. One was from Vince Michaels, informing me that he had just missed me at the hospital but that I was not to worry; he had arranged to fill in for me and would be in touch later. The second was from Anna Willows, asking me to call her and leaving me her room number at the Xanadu.

I went into the bathroom and splashed some water on my face. I didn't care much for what I saw in the mirror, the haunted-looking countenance of a Holocaust survivor, but I attributed it in part to the neon lighting, which in Vegas hotels tends to age you a month a day. Or perhaps it was just the air of the place. I remember Dawn once telling me that living in Las Vegas was equivalent to being mummified. "After you're here for a while," she said, "if you try to leave, you just crumble into dust. We're like those people in that old movie about Shangri-La, frozen in time." She was right; it's what I call the place's unreality factor.

I lay down on my bed and dialed Anna Willows's number. "Oh, hello," she said. "I was wondering if you'd call back."

"Really?"

"Yes. That disgusting friend of yours told us you'd been robbed."

"And you don't believe him."

"I don't know what to make of that man. He makes the most revolting remarks."

"I was mugged in the parking lot."

"So we've been informed."

"Where's Fulvio?"

"Gone. He left this morning."

"I tried to call him from the hospital, but I didn't persist," I explained. "I had quite a headache."

"Well, Fulvio asked me to call you," she continued. "He expects you to join him in New York within two weeks' time." She gave me his address, an apartment house on Central Park West, and an unlisted phone number. "You're to let him know exactly when. You can call me and I'll make you a hotel reservation."

"And where will you be?"

"In Los Angeles, we're at the Beverly Wilshire Hotel, but only until Thursday. In New York, just call that number. I usually pick it up."

"Secretarial chores?"

"Didn't you know?" she replied, with a touch of bitterness. "I do everything for Fulvio. Right now I'm organizing his departure."

"I thought you said he'd gone."

"He has, but his luggage hasn't. That's my job, one of them."

"I didn't know."

"Well, you know now, don't you? Fulvio really can't do anything without me."

Except sing, I thought, but I kept that observation to myself. "I guess the two of us are going to have to work together then," I said. "You know what he wants me to do for him, don't you?"

"It's absurd," she said. "Fulvio's a sick gambler. He really ought to stop completely."

"I agree," I said, "but he's going to have to decide that for himself. Anyway, I can help him, for a while."

"I think you ought to know that Jeanine is furious."

"I figured she might be. What does Carmela think about all this?"

"Who?"

"Carmela, Fulvio's wife."

"Think about it? She doesn't think anything about it."

"In other words, she doesn't know."

"I have no idea what she knows or doesn't know," Miss Willows snapped, "and frankly I don't care."

"Would you like to get together later?"

"What for?"

"I think we ought to talk," I explained. "We're both now in the business of taking care of Fulvio. I need your help."

"Sorry, I haven't time. I still have a million things to do here. I have to finish packing, I have to pay bills, I have to call New York, all sorts of loose ends. And I'm leaving at ten o'clock for Los Angeles," she said, aspirating the g, an affectation I attributed to singer's diction.

"Well, I guess I'll see you in New York," I said. "Do you think I ought to call Miss Lagrange?"

"I wouldn't," she answered, over a mirthless staccato laugh. "You'll hear from her soon enough."

"About Fulvio's gambling," I interjected hurriedly, sensing that she was becoming impatient with this conversation, "see if you can get him to lay off, or at least to cut down in my absence."

"That's your department, isn't it?" she said, and promptly hung up on me.

With allies like Anna Willows, I wasn't going to need too many enemies. I had already obviously made one out of Jeanine Lagrange, but I felt reasonably sure I could turn her around, once she became convinced I only had her client's best interests in mind. I would overwhelm her with magic and the famous Shifty Lou Anderson charm. It was only the degree of her instant hostility that puzzled me. Fulvio, I surmised, had to be a huge armful for anyone, a big spoiled child, helpless in the real world, but gifted with a single golden talent—his voice. Well, she undoubtedly made enough loot out of it to put up with him, and she would learn to value me.

I went to the bathroom again for aspirin, then called room

service and ordered myself a bowl of pea soup and a small green salad. I was suddenly pretty tired and my head had begun to ache dully again. I made myself stay up, however, and walked over to the table by the window, from where I could look down into the neon-lit canyons of downtown Vegas. A cold wind was blowing in off the desert, pinning pedestrians against the walls of the buildings and blocking any escape from the palaces of pleasure, where the citizens were getting their brains beaten out by the house vigorish.

I sat down and reached for a deck of cards, always my solace in times of despondency or uncertainty. I was waiting for the aspirin to take hold and my order to arrive, after which I planned to go to bed, pop on the television set, and immerse myself in trash. Meanwhile, I thought I'd try a few basic moves. I shuffled, then riffled the cards, sending the small, slick boards, my stock in trade, dancing dazzlingly from hand to hand. I rehearsed the Gymnastic Aces, sending the four one-spots flying out over the table to land unerringly face-up in front of me, then I went into Acrobatic Jacks and Traveling Cards and a few others, just to make sure I hadn't lost my touch. Basic stuff, really, but fun. What I really liked most, of course, was the stock and cull shuffling and dealing itself, with the bottom palms and the blind riffles and all the various shifts designed to bewilder and amaze. I wasn't up to my best, but I couldn't expect to be. Still, even with my head hurting and my stomach rumbling, I could make the cards dance to any tune I played. They didn't call me Shifty for nothing.

I was into a little Three Card Monte, the simplest, friendliest, and deadliest of all small-time gambling propositions, when my order finally arrived. I tipped the waiter and had him set my tray down on the bed, where I could eat and simultaneously glue myself to the screen. After he'd gone, I put the cards away and it was then that I noticed the little brown envelope. It was lying on a corner of my bureau on top of the rest of my mail, mostly bills from L.A., which the front desk must have sent up that morning. It was addressed simply to "S. Andersan" (sic) and carried no return identification.

I opened it and read, written in ink in small black capitals across a single sheet of paper: "ACCIDENT CAN HAPPEN BUT BE CARFUL." It was unsigned.

SIX

♦

Cats

"Louis, I have been wanting to meet you so much," she said, pronouncing my name in the French fashion, as in King Louis. "Ever since Tristan and I saw you at the Magic Castle."

"When was that?" I asked.

"Nearly two years ago, I believe. It was in early spring."

"That's right. I was there for two months. Why didn't you say hello?"

"I don't know. There were so many people that night and you were doing your entire repertoire. You were marvelous."

This is the sort of encomium that tends to make me puff up like an amorous partridge, especially when it emanates from such an attractive source. She was small and sleek and very beautiful, with large dark-green eyes under a fringe of thick black curls, and she had a dark complexion that seemed to glow with health. Her smile was measured, very precise, as if holding something of herself back, and her voice was soft and velvety, lost somewhere at the back of her throat. She reminded me of a big cat, which should not have surprised me. Her name was Simone and she was the distaff end of an act called Tristan and Simone, then headlining at the Stardust. Their illusions involved large carnivores—a lion, a couple of tigers, leopards, a black panther—and they were reportedly sensational. I had never seen them, because I had always been working myself on the nights they performed, but I had, of course, heard a good deal about them. "I must come and see you now," I said. "I've been told you're terrific."

49

"Oh, that is so nice of you. Will you? I would love it."

"I could come tomorrow night, if you like."

"Oh, please do," she exclaimed, clapping her hands together. "I will leave you a ticket. Oh, you *must* come!"

"I will. I'm looking forward to it."

"And on Thursday afternoon we are giving a party. It is Tristan's fortieth birthday, but of course he will not let us mention his age."

"That's understandable. I'm about to reach that unhappy plateau myself."

"Will you come? I will tell you my address."

"I'd love to."

"Many of our friends in magic will be there. It would not be complete without you." She put a small, firm hand on my arm and squeezed it. "I love to watch you. It is like a ballet. You will be there?"

"I can't imagine what could prevent me." I was very conscious of the fact that her hand was still on my arm and I was praying she would not take it away too soon. I felt renewed by it, as if she had a healing touch. "Have you ever been to Lourdes?"

"The miracle place? Why?"

"Nothing. Just speculating. But the last of my headache is gone."

I think she caught my meaning, because she smiled and withdrew her hand. "Please do some more," she said. "I could watch you all night."

"Well, it's Vince's turn now," I said. "Have you ever seen him? He's wonderful."

"Yes, I have seen him," she said, "but it is you I wish to see."

I think I actually blushed. I know I'm a fine close-up artist and all that, but to be singled out like this with such praise by another performer, and especially such a lovely one, is hard to resist. We were alone, outside the door to the convention hall of the Savoy Inn, and I realized that she must have followed me out into the lobby after my stint and waited for me to come back from the men's room. Usually, at these weekly late-night sessions of the Darwinian Society of Magic, which have been held once a week for a number of years now in various locations around Las Vegas, a bunch of us just show up to talk, perform, and enjoy one another's work. Las Vegas is the world capital of magic, because the city provides plenty of jobs, not only for prestidigitators like myself, but for the big important acts like Tristan and Simone. The Darwinian Society, founded a decade or so ago by Gary Darwin, then a part-time magician working as a bellman at the Riviera, gives us all a chance to get together on an informal basis. Vince took me to a meeting years ago, when I first came to town on an engagement, and whenever I'm in Vegas I'm usually among the first to arrive and almost always the last to leave.

"Are you not going to do anything else for me now?" she asked, looking up at me adoringly out of those lustrous green eyes. "Please do your Ring on a Stick one more time for me. It is so delightful."

"I can't, really," I explained. "Vince is a great magician and I don't want to insult him by not watching him work. I think we should go back inside."

"Of course, I understand," she said, putting her hand on my arm again. "But you will come and perform only for me one day. Do you promise?"

"I promise." At that point, if I had been on crutches, I would have thrown them away for her. I might even have tried walking on water. I took her hand and squeezed it. "Come on."

She stood up on tiptoe and kissed me quickly but firmly on the lips. "It was thrilling," she said, then turned and fled before me back into the sanctuary of the hall, where Vince was explaining and demonstrating a two-handed variation he had worked out on the Erdnase Shift.

"Of course, my friend Shifty here is the real broad tosser," he said, as I took a seat toward the back of the room, "but I thought this was an interesting variation and I'd like to show it to you."

I knew all about the Erdnase Shift and its variations so I allowed myself to glance idly around the room as Vince worked. There must have been forty people there, including a number of faces I hadn't seen before, of amateurs and friends, probably. I couldn't immediately spot Simone, but I did locate Tristan's great mane of golden hair. He was sitting on an end chair in the second row, looking large and very muscular; his shoulders and back bulged under a black turtleneck sweater. When he shifted slightly in his chair in order to peer more closely at Vince's demonstration, I found Simone again. She was sitting directly in front of him, looking very small under the pressure of his right hand, which was gently massaging the back of her neck. The action reminded me of the way cats are stroked, firmly but gently, with a lot of emphasis on behind the ears. I remembered something else I had noticed about her during our brief encounter in the lobby, when she had squeezed my arm—the unadorned gold band on the fourth finger of her left hand. It didn't diminish my admiration for her in the least, but it did set me to speculating on possibilities and risks.

"You don't want to go betting heavy on fillies," an old track crony had once warned me, during a particularly painful episode with a lady a few years ago. "They don't run true to form and they're liable to spit it out in the stretch. Pass the action, kid."

Vince wound up the evening restoring demolished cigarettes. It's one of his most amazing, if least appreciated, accomplishments. He takes crumpled butts and gracefully returns them to pristine condition, seemingly just by passing his fingers lightly over them. He can do this in front of your very eyes, from no more than a couple of feet away, and it is a small miracle of dexterity. Seeing it is like observing the work of an eighteenth-century miniaturist, but it can only be truly appreciated by an audience of five or six at a time. It never fails to hook me and so it drew me, as always, into the front row of viewers. There are some moves only Vince Michaels can do superbly and this is one of them. It brought him our enthusiastic applause.

As the gathering was breaking up a few minutes later, I looked around again for my admirer, but she and Tristan had gone. Out in the parking lot, I asked Vince about her. "I don't know very much," he said. "I've only seen their act once, but it won all the awards here last year. It's pure show biz, but there's real magic there. Especially from her. She's the box-jumper and she has to get in there with these cats. It's pretty spectacular."

"Is it a happy marriage, Vince?"

"Uh-oh, Shifty, what are you up to?" He stopped me by the hood of his car, his little round face peering up at me through the gloom. "What kind of a question is that?"

"She's a fervent admirer," I said, "that's all."

"That's not all. I know you, Shifty." He looked worried. "How fervent?"

"I picked up some blips on my radar screen, all right?"

"What does that mean?"

"She kissed me."

Vince did not answer right away, but leaned back against his car and scratched his head. "Well, you hear things," he finally commented.

"What things?"

"Mostly about him. He's supposed to go both ways."

"With or without her consent?"

"I don't know, Shifty. They've been married six or seven years. He's a lot older than she is." He paused, as if to put the pieces together in his head before proceeding. "I think they met in a circus in Europe. He had an animal act originally and she was a trapeze artist."

"Both German, I gather."

"He is. His last name is Krueger. But I don't know about her."

"She has a little accent, but I couldn't figure out what it was. Central European, maybe. It's hard to tell."

"Can I give you a piece of advice, Shifty?"

"Shoot. You will anyway."

"Forget it. The word is he has a temper."

"So?"

"Well, you've seen him, haven't you?"

"The act itself? No."

"Shifty, he's as solid as a cement block. He can throw a full-grown leopard ten feet and does."

I laughed at him. "Vince, I was just asking."

"You have a real talent for getting into trouble, Shifty," he said. "It's bad enough about the horses—"

I cut him off by producing a deck of cards out of my pocket. "Listen, Vince," I told him, "about the shift, let me show you something." Magic could distract Vince from any preoccupation, even impending disaster, so we pulled off some last effects for each other, out there in the night on the hood of his car, a few more miraculous moves to marvel at before bedtime. At least it succeeded in shutting him up. For some reason, I didn't want to hear any more from him about Tristan Krueger. I still had the sweet flavor of Simone's lips on mine.

The act began simply enough, with Simone isolated by a strong spotlight on a darkened stage. She was dressed in high heels, black tights, a ruffled white shirt, and a sequined black bolero. Then the panther appeared. Sleek, coal black, its fangs drawn back in a wicked smile, it crept out from the wings and coiled itself like a snake around her ankles. Simone did not move until Tristan materialized, seemingly out of the air above her. Attired only in a long-tailed leopard-skin jacket and dark purple pants, his oiled, muscular torso gleaming in the stage lights, he appeared to float above them, even as he smilingly executed several impressive-looking, elaborate passes in the air over their heads. The orchestra was blaring away at some sort of Russian dance, and at its climax, on a tremendous clashing of cymbals and tolling of bells, Simone and the black cat vanished in a puff of red smoke. Smiling broadly, Tristan bounded lightly to the stage, arms outstretched, to acknowledge our applause.

It was only the beginning. There were routines involving an enormous lion and a couple of leopards, during which, exactly as Vince had described it, Tristan at one point picked up one of the leopards and tossed him up onto a platform nine or ten feet above his head. The animal remained there until Tristan made him vanish and materialized Simone, who smiled and waved cheerfully at us.

The climactic illusion involved a seven-hundred-pound Siberian tiger, which was rolled out to center stage in a small cage perched on a table. The huge cat paced agitatedly back and forth and took a couple of tentative swipes at Tristan as he draped a cloth all around him. With the cage completely covered, the magician then raised four panels attached to the table and fastened them at the corners. The cage was raised on chains above the stage and Tristan whipped the cloth away to reveal that it was now empty. At the same instant, the panels below unfolded to reveal Simone again. She bounded lightly down, walked over to a trunk that had somehow appeared on stage, and opened it to reveal the missing tiger. She leaped up on his back and rode him off, as Tristan followed, grinning and waving. When they came out to take their bows, Tristan wore the black panther around his neck like a scarf, while Simone swung out over the audience dangling from her heels on a trapeze. As she swooped over my table, she smiled and blew me a kiss.

I had to admit it was a terrific act. Ordinarily, I'm not a fan of the big illusions. The magic is constructed and consists basically of variations, some of them admittedly elaborate, on stunts that have been around for centuries. What you see isn't really what you see and, as the saying goes, it's all done with mirrors. What good stage magic consists of is showmanship. Still, there are acts that have to be admired for their panache, if for nothing else, and there's a bit of envy in the snobbishness of close-up artists like me toward the Doug Hennings and the Siegfrieds and Roys of the profession. And in the case of Tristan and Simone, there was real magic involved. After all, as Vince had pointed out, at some point in every one of their routines she had to snuggle into some very tight quarters with big, unreliable carnivores for minutes at a time. Nothing could have made me get into a trunk with a tiger or let that sinuous menace of a panther drape itself over my feet, so who was I to put down this sort of magic? It's the style of an act that banishes logic. And if the illusion is dazzling enough, then it qualifies as real magic.

I went backstage to see them afterward. Simone, still in her skimpy costume, skipped down the hallway to meet me and threw her arms around my neck. "Louis, did you like it?" she asked. "Wasn't it wonderful?"

"Yes, it was," I said, looking nervously around for her partner.

"It was wonderful wonderful tonight," she said, kissing me on the cheek this time. "I think that is because you were there. Come." She took me by the hand and led me back toward her dressing room.

"Where's Tristan?" I asked, as we skirted a bevy of nearly naked showgirls on their way back from the grand finale, a noisy fandango of flesh and feathers.

"Oh, he is with the cats," she said. "Usually it is me. They always need a lot of attention after a performance. But you will see him tomorrow."

Their dressing room was a suite that had been especially built for them at stage level and near a stairway leading down to the cages on the floor below, where all the animals were kept. "Of course we must take them all home with us every night," she explained, "and bring them here for the performances only. We are a traveling menagerie." She laughed and took my hand. "Come on."

We passed through a large outer room full of trunks and crates of costumes, as well as some of the props used in their act, then walked into a slightly smaller room equipped with makeup tables and mirrors, as well as some comfortable chairs and couches. The walls were decorated with posters and photographs of the act during various stages of performance, but I had no time to appreciate my surroundings. Our appearance was greeted with a hissing snarl from the far corner, where a small, rather fragile-looking cage contained a full-grown black panther, presumably the one used in their routine. I stopped in my tracks. "Oh, come now," Simone said, "that's only Milù."

"He doesn't seem enchanted to see us."

"That is only how he says hello," she explained and walked over to the cage. She squatted in front of the cat and began to talk to him in a soft, purring voice, then reached in between the bars and stroked him along the neck and behind his ears. The gesture reminded me of the way Tristan had handled her the night before, an affectionate and tranquilizing way of petting a large animal. "He is a darling," she said. "I adore him. Usually, when we are alone in here, we let him out. He is our pet. He is like a dog." The panther had subsided to the floor of the cage, but his yellow eyes were focused unblinkingly on me.

"He doesn't look like a dog," I said. "He doesn't sound like a dog."

"You have to know him. Isn't that so, Milù?" She gave him a couple of more pats, then turned back to me. "We bought him from a dealer in North Africa. We have had him ever since he was a tiny kitten. He is such a dear. Would you mind if I let him out now?"

"Yes, I would."

"Oh, dear," she said. "Poor Milù. Nobody appreciates him. He is very sweet with people, but we have to keep him away from the other animals. Of course the lion fights with the tiger, too, and the leopards are very difficult." She giggled and came toward me. "Now can I give you a drink or some wine?"

"No, thanks, Simone. I really just came by to pay my respects. You have a terrific act."

"Oh, Louis, that is so nice of you, coming from such a great magician. Tristan will be flattered."

"Well, please tell him, won't you?"

"But of course." She was in very close to me again and I could smell her, a delicious blend of highly carnal perfumes, both natural and artificial. "You are sure you will not stay?"

"I have to get back to my room in time to look at a TV show," I explained, realizing as I did so how absurd that sounded.

"TV?"

"You know Fulvio Gasparini, the opera singer?"

"Oh, yes, of course."

"Well, he's on Johnny Carson tonight," I said. "I promised him I'd watch it."

"Why, Louis?"

"I'm sort of working for him. I mean, I will be."

"In magic?"

"In a way," I said. "His money is disappearing and I'm supposed to help him keep it."

"That is very strange."

"Not really, Simone. He's a gambler, but he doesn't know how to gamble."

"How very sad. Are you a gambler?"

"Only occasionally, but I know how. What I do best is wager on horses."

"I am finding this very confusing."

"I'll explain it to you sometime."

"Tomorrow, perhaps. You *are* coming to our party?"

"Oh, certainly. I wouldn't miss it."

By this time she had backed me up against the door. I was

hoping I could get it open before Tristan and his muscles came through it, but I needn't have worried. "There is no danger," she said. "Tristan will be with the animals for at least another twenty minutes. Please kiss me."

I leaned down with the noble and cowardly intention of giving her a brotherly peck on the cheek, but her arms went around my neck and her mouth quickly found mine. It didn't take long to develop into the sort of embrace that in a public place might have resulted in an arrest. At one point, I came up momentarily for air and found myself gazing directly across the room into the large, yellow eyes of the panther. The animal seemed fascinated by our entanglement, but I had no time to comment on my impression. I descended back into the manifold pleasures Simone was providing for me, like a diver plunging back into a multicolored tropical sea.

By the time I got back to my hotel room and popped my set on, Fulvio Gasparini was in full cry. Because of the painfully fragile condition I was in, I can't seem to remember exactly what he was singing, some sort of a weepy Neapolitan song, I think, about mothers and too much sunshine. The *Tonight Show* audience loved it. When he concluded on a lens-shattering high note and beamingly opened his arms to acknowledge the applause, Johnny Carson himself rose from behind his desk to greet him. Fulvio bobbed and bowed and waved his way into a seat next to Johnny's first guest, a toothsome starlet from one of the network's soap operas.

I was in such an enfeebled state that I retain only scattered impressions of the ensuing conversation. I do know that it did not rival in significance the tête-à-têtes between Reagan and Gorbachev, but it had its moments. For one thing, Fulvio seemed to have adopted a public posture designed to reinforce the general public's idea of ghetto Italians. He was charming and childlike and entirely untrustworthy. He spoke about his family and food and love as if he had invented them. He was also funny in a predictably ethnic style, with much mangling of grammar and expansive gesticulating to emphasize his more obvious clichés about the virtues and foibles of his native land. And his accent seemed thicker than I remembered it, with every other word ending in an open vowel. All he needed, I realized, was a hand organ and a monkey on a leash to make the picture complete. Toward the end of this performance, just after Fulvio had delivered a small panegyric on his wife and the joys of Latin family life back on the estate near Napoli, the starlet asked him if it was true, as someone had once said of him, that God had kissed his throat. *"Sì,* that is perhaps so," Fulvio agreed, "but look at you!" He beamingly turned in his chair to indicate her obvious assets to the viewers. "God, He kiss you all over!"

The audience roared and then Carson asked Fulvio to favor them with an encore. The tenor bounced to his feet and headed back toward the stage, where Achille Pipistrello sat at the keyboard of a concert grand looking as if he had been sucking on a sourball for two days. *"E lucevan le stelle,* from *La Tosca,"* Fulvio announced, taking his place in the crook of the piano, but not looking at his accompanist. He started to sing, taking the first phrase up in a light half-voice that was thrilling to listen to and made me sit up in anticipation. I even forgot about Simone for a few seconds, but the ring of the telephone shattered the mood.

"Louis? Is it you?" she whispered.

"Who else? Simone, where are you?" I turned down the sound.

"I am home now."

"Are you alone?"

"In the house? No, but he cannot hear me."

"Simone, this is mad."

"I know, Louis, I know. But I want you so much."

"Simone—"

"I know it is our destiny, Louis. I know it."

"I don't know much about destiny, Simone, but—"

"I must have you," she said. "I must."

"Well, I'm sort of available, but—"

"I will turn you inside out with passion," she said. "I will tear the flesh from your bones."

"That sounds painful. Simone, I—"

"I must go now," she whispered. "Goodbye, Louis. I will see you tomorrow. Dream about me."

And she hung up, leaving me to stare blindly at my television screen, where Fulvio was now smiling and waving and bobbing and dancing on his way offstage. I didn't dream at all that night, as I had expected to, but I slept very badly.

SEVEN

◆

Passion

They lived in an expensive residential neighborhood on the outskirts of town, several miles from the Strip and its gaudy pleasures. From the street, the place looked much like any other—a large, rambling ranch house lying low against the desert heat behind a sloping, well-watered green lawn. Its only distinguishing feature was a small sign in front of the entrance that said, "Beware of the Cat." Inside, however, and behind the building, nothing could have been more abnormal, though it took me a while fully to appreciate the layout.

The party had been going on for an hour or so by the time I arrived, just before two o'clock, and there were a couple of dozen guests inside, at least twice that many more out on the patio, where through a picture window I could see Tristan, colorfully attired in spotted black-and-yellow shorts, a tigerskin apron, and a red chef's hat, smilingly presiding over a barbecue. About thirty yards across from him, a full-grown lion rested placidly under an oak tree to which he had been tethered by a clothesline, and beyond him, directly opposite a large octagonal swimming pool, I could see a row of cages in which a couple of tigers and several leopards paced restlessly. A high wall encircled the rear of the premises, but I found myself wondering, as I went in search of a drink, how the neighbors felt about living next to a private zoo full of dangerous carnivores, some of whom were obviously allowed to run around practically loose. And where was Milù? Caged, I hoped.

I found the bar in the den, which contained floor-to-ceiling

library shelves distinguished by an absence of books; they har-
bored only ivory, jade, and alabaster animal statues, framed photographs of Tristan and Simone performing all over the world, and a
number of impressive-looking trophies won by the couple during
their rise to stardom. The bar itself had been set up against the
opposite wall over some sort of bodybuilding machine that looked
like a medieval torture rack. Several ferocious-looking African
masks had been mounted on the walls, and a long, vicious-looking
bullwhip rested in a corner beside an empty cage. I was alone in
the room, except for the bartender, a plump, soft-looking black
youth, who seemed uneasy in these surroundings. He poured me a
glass of California Chablis with a noticeably shaky hand.

"You haven't been here before, I gather," I said.

"No way," he answered. "And I'm not comin' back neither. You
seen what they got in this place?"

"You mean the animals? I guess they're pretty tame."

"I guess. I ain't gettin' near 'em. You seen that black mother?"

"The panther? Where is it?"

"They got it caged up now back in one of them bedrooms back
there," the young man said, "but when I got here to set up, shit,
the fuckin' thing was runnin' around loose. I like to piss in my
pants. I come in the front door and there he is, he's just settin'
there starin' at me. Hell, I took off like there was a rocket up my
ass. I was halfway back to town when they come get me. Shit, man,
you gotta be nuts lettin' some wild thing with all them teeth just
run around your house. How come they ain't all scarred up and
stuff?"

"I guess they know what they're doing. They train these animals,
you know."

"Yeah? Fuck that shit. They get hungry enough or mad or
somethin', they'll eat your ass. Them things belong in cages, man.
You seen that lion they got out there?"

"Yes, I have."

"You seen that little bitty rope they got round that mother's
neck? Hell, he could snap that like it was string. I'll be glad when
this party's over, man."

"I guess you're pretty safe in here."

He did not seem convinced. "I shoulda brought my thirty-eight,"
he said. "That way one of them fuckers comes after me, I got a
chance. I don't want to get chewed up by no cat, man. And it ain't
only the animals, these people here are weird. Look in there,
man." And he pointed to a closet door.

I walked over and opened it. Inside, hanging from various hooks and on the shelves, was a fairly impressive collection of leather gear, restraints, masks, chains, more whips, and several smaller instruments of torture. "How does that grab you, man?" the bartender asked. "Ain't that sweet?"

I shut the door. "I guess they like to play games."

"Games? Some games, man. When they close this bar up at five o'clock in here, I'm gone. And I ain't comin' back, never."

"I can understand that," I said, heading for the door now, as several other guests appeared seeking refreshment. "By the way, the black panther's name is Milù, in case you ever meet up with him again."

The new arrivals, a couple of six-foot showgirls and their much shorter, middle-aged male escorts, were placing drink orders, so I don't think he heard me and I eased myself out of the room. I'd been shaken up myself by the contents of that closet and I wondered what Simone might have to say about it. I even speculated at that point whether I should have come at all, but I decided to relax and enjoy myself, a philosophy (or perhaps a lack of one) that has steered me precariously this far through life. The fact is, I wanted very much to see Simone again.

As far as I could tell, she was not in the house, so I made my way outside and looked around for her. It occurred to me that I didn't know any of the other guests, most of whom, I gathered, were from the show at the Stardust or connected with it at least tangentially. There were tall girls and medium-sized girls and short girls and lots of gay chorus boys, and then I recognized a number of Vegas headliners—singers and comedians and variety performers—all of whom had the lacquered look of people who like to sit under sun lamps and who wear their toupees and false eyelashes to bed. I was surprised by the absence of other magicians, because on the whole we're a cozily clannish lot and like to hang around together. Tristan and Simone's act barely qualified as true magic in my book, admittedly a small and prejudiced one, but they billed themselves as conjurors and I had expected some of their guests to be in the profession. I didn't worry too much about it, however, and figured some would eventually show up, although I knew the party had to end no later than six, which would give everyone there just enough time to prepare for the evening performances. I went over to say hello to Tristan.

"Ah, Shifty, *mein freund,*" he boomed at me, as I came up to congratulate him. "It was so nice of you to come. *Ya,* I am forty

years old now. Incredible, no?" He bared what looked like fourteen rows of perfect ivories at me and rippled all sorts of muscles I
didn't even know existed. "You have some meat now, no?"

"Yes, sure," I said.

"Good!" he exclaimed and heaped up a plate of ribs and ham-
burgers for me that could have fed a starving African village for a
week. "You eat! Salad *und der* fruit *und* cheeses over there!" He
waved his barbecue fork in the vague general direction of the tree
under which the lion sprawled. "You don't worry about Wotan, he
is like a big dog. Is good?"

"Is good," I agreed, wondering what Wotan, obviously the lion's
name, had to do with lettuce and dessert. "So where's Simone?"

But he didn't hear me, because his gaze had suddenly fastened
hungrily on some obviously much more appealing scene behind
me. I turned around and saw a tall, sinewy young man with long
dark hair and a mustache walking toward us. He was wearing black
leather pants, a broad black belt studded with small silver knobs,
and a shirt slashed open to the waist to reveal a hairless chest, on
which rested a large jeweled crucifix. He was smiling broadly and
had eyes only for our host. I let him pass and then drifted out into
the crowd.

I skirted Wotan, who, I could now see, was stretched out
directly behind a picnic table loaded not only with fruit and cheeses
but an enormous layered birthday cake, and eventually joined a
group of young dancers sitting on the grass and chattering aimlessly
about movies. Over their heads, I could see Tristan, who had
abandoned the barbecuing chores to a hired minion, deep in intimate conversation near the leopard cages with the new arrival. His
arm was around the younger man's waist and there seemed to be
little doubt that their relationship had edged past the platonic. I
decided to glean what information I could out of my group. "Who's
the guy with Tristan?" I asked.

"Him? Oh, that's Felix," one of the girls said. "He dances in the
MGM show."

"Friends?"

"I guess," the girl said. "If you call that friendship."

"He's kind of cute."

"Oh, shit," the girl said. "You gay, too? Where are all the men in
this damn town?"

"Shooting craps," I said. "Splitting aces. Excuse me."

I got up because I had just spotted Simone. She had emerged
from the house and was standing on the edge of the patio. I had the

distinct feeling that she was looking for me. She was dressed in high-heeled sandals, white toreador pants, and a white silk shirt that showed off her tan to terrific advantage. She looked as desirable to me as a winning Pick Six ticket. I smilingly made my way toward her.

"Louis," she said, as I came up to her, "where have you been?"

"I got here half an hour ago. Where have *you* been?"

"On the telephone," she said. "My sister in New York."

"Anything wrong?"

"No, not at all. Just chatting. Come." She took my hand and led me back into the house.

"Where are we going?"

"I have something to give you."

I deposited my still-loaded plate on an end table in the living room and followed her. I wondered what the other guests might think, but nobody seemed to pay much attention to us. We passed the den, where a small throng had gathered around the bar, proceeded down a corridor, then turned right into another section of the house, which was obviously much larger than it looked from the street. A door separated this part of the structure from the main living areas. Simone shut it behind us, then turned and leaned with her back against it. "Kiss me, Louis," she said. "Please."

The light in the hall was dim, but I could clearly discern her eyes; they stared hungrily at me and I had the feeling she could see better in the dark, like one of her cats. I did as I was asked and again found myself starring in an X-rated clinch that could have been shown uncut in any Pussycat theater. "Good God, Simone," I said, when I was finally able to come up for air, "what are we doing?"

"This is my gift to you, Louis."

"What is?"

"Me."

She pushed me through an open door and pulled me down onto a king-sized bed. It was very dark in the room and I had the disquieting sensation that we were not alone, but I had no time to sort out my impressions or to think about anything, really, except the carnal excitements of the moment. Somehow Simone had managed to slip swiftly out of her clothes and it took her another ten seconds to help me remove mine, after which we proceeded to make love with the sexual abandonment of a couple of frenzied gibbons. I had never experienced anything quite like it, but the tempo was too frantic for me even to begin to figure out what was happening or why. I took everything she offered me and held on like a man on a trapeze, until at last I went up in a shower of multicolored exploding lights and fell to earth with the spent indifference of a high-wire performer toppling into a net.

I lay there on my back, staring blindly at the ceiling, as she headed for the bathroom. When she opened the door and turned on the bathroom light, I heard a soft coughing sound from a corner of the room, under the window. I sat up at once and found myself confronted by Milù. He was in a long cage that extended almost the full length of the room, but he was sitting up, his large yellow eyes again focused on me. "Hey, why didn't you tell me he was in here?" I called out, pulling a sheet up around me, admittedly an absurd action.

"Because it makes no difference," she answered.

"Well, it does to me."

"Ah, Louis, I have no secrets from Milù."

I rolled out of bed on the side farthest away from the cat and reached for my clothes. "What are you doing?" she asked, as she stood in the doorway, her skin glistening in the reflected light. "Where are you going?"

"Simone, this is just a little bit crazy," I tried to explain. "I'm making love to you in a room with a black panther watching our every move, I'm sure with considerable disdain, while out on the patio your musclebound Teuton is celebrating his birthday. Maybe he's cutting the cake right now and wondering where his wife is."

"You talk wonderful," she said. "I am in love also with the way you talk. Why do you not talk to me while we are making love?"

"Who can talk?" I answered. "It's all I can do to keep up with you."

She giggled, rather sweetly, like a pubescent schoolgirl. "Oh, Louis, you have so much to learn about me. I will have such fun teaching you."

"Can we have the lessons somewhere else? I mean, what if Tristan walks in on us?"

"That is not going to happen, my darling. This is my part of the house. Tristan has the other part."

"Ah, I see," I said. "Then your marriage—"

"It is what we Europeans call one of convenience," she said. "You have nothing to worry about, Louis." I was dressed by this time, except for my loafers, but she came up to me and put her arms around my neck. She was still naked and her flesh felt like cool satin to my hands. "Now, take me again," she whispered.

"Simone—"

"Now, Louis, right now," she hissed. "Just the way you are, right now." She tore my pants open and wound her legs around my waist, hanging from my neck by her arms. I was reminded again of the way the panther had coiled around her feet during their act, but I had no time to linger on the memory. I made love to her a second time that afternoon, standing there with most of my clothes on, while she rode me like the winning jockey in a million-dollar race. Milù's frightening yellow eyes never wavered in their scrutiny of us. The cat was a born voyeur.

That was the beginning of it. I had no idea where it would end, of course, or how, but I didn't care. I had never in my life experienced anything quite like Simone. She was an inventive, and insatiable sexual athlete, the sort of woman every male adolescent fantasizes about. She wanted to make love two or three times every single day and she didn't care where, how, or when. In fact, she took a perverse liking to bizarre situations and settings. We coupled in her dressing room, in hallways, in bathrooms, in cars, in her swimming pool, in a steam room, in a Jacuzzi, on the lawn in front of her house, and on one less-than-memorable occasion under a table in a corner of a French restaurant in the Hilton, where we were interrupted by a startled busboy and had to retire hastily from the premises.

I quickly realized that Simone not only reveled in such bizarre behavior, she needed it, and I was in a state of such permanent arousal with her that at first I meekly went along with every whim of her endlessly inventive libido. "You are wonderful, Louis," she told me, after a spectacularly arduous session in near-freezing weather on a playground jungle gym at 3:00 A.M. "With you it is possible to do anything and everything anywhere. I love you, Louis."

I wasn't sure how I felt about her. Love, really, had very little to do with it. I was physically inflamed by her, to such a point that I forgot about everything else in my life, including magic. Every time I saw her or thought about her, the blood surged up behind my eyes, blotting out everything except physical desire. She had what I considered a perfect body—small, but strong, supple, beautifully proportioned—and she used it to provide pleasure for herself with a lack of inhibition and guilt that I found wholly commendable, especially since I had become the beneficiary of it.

I didn't have to worry about Tristan either. He and Simone lived almost entirely separate lives in their own wings of the house and I could come and go pretty much as I pleased. Although I didn't move in with her, we made no secret of our involvement and on one occasion we even had a drink with Tristan and Felix, his current inamorato, on the patio one afternoon, after returning from a sexual conflagration in my quarters at the Three Kings. Tristan and Simone were genuinely fond of each other, she told me, but they had not slept together since the first year of their marriage. "Tristan has always been gay," she explained. "He made that clear to me from the first and I accepted it, even though I thought I could change him. For a while, I thought I had changed him, but then I realized that he was having men even during those few months he was also being a husband to me. So we have gone our separate ways, you see."

What united them and kept them together, of course, was the act. "I was engaged in a circus in Europe, I was one of the trapeze artists, and Tristan worked with all these animals," she told me in the car one morning, on the way back from an outing in the desert. "I was fascinated. He was not afraid and he did not mistreat the cats, but he had no real rapport with them. He could make them do all these things, you know—sit up and pose and jump through flaming circles and everything—but until he met me he could not get beyond these very usual actions. I changed all that."

She had been hanging around the cages and helping out. "I seemed to have a way with them," she explained. "I could do things with them that Tristan could not do. The animals trusted me, especially Wotan, who was the star of the show. He is so big, you know, that people are impressed, even though he is old and like a big dog now. Even then he was very tame, but you could not pet him or anything. When I started to work with him, after Tristan asked me to become his helper, I was able to get him to do many things lions will not do. Do you know that he goes swimming with us? Lions hate the water, you know. Wotan hates it, too, but he does not wish to be left out, so now, in the summer, he jumps into the pool with us. He roars like mad and he is so funny."

"What about the magic part of it?"

"Oh, that was Tristan's idea," she said. "We had heard about Siegfried and Roy, who are absolutely wonderful with their animals, and the great success they were having in magic, so Tristan decided we should do the same thing. He left the circus and took lessons and we worked on our act for a year. We had to borrow a lot of money, but then we tried it out in Germany first and right away it was a big success. Then we had a tour of South America and now here it is, just four years later, and we are doing so well."

"You've got something Siegfried and Roy don't have."

"What is that, Louis?"

"You."

"You naughty boy, what do you mean by that?" she said, squeezing in close to me and running her hand up the inside of my thigh.

"Simone, we're going sixty-five," I said. "Let's not let passion flower in here."

She giggled, but fortunately decided temporarily to leave me alone. "So what did you mean by that?" she asked again.

"You're the spice in the act," I tried to explain. "You're beautiful, you're sexy, and you're obviously fearless. It imparts a certain panache."

"You must always talk to me this way," she said. "You are a wonderful talker, Louis. Isn't that right, Milù?" And she leaned over the backseat, where the panther lay stretched out, to scratch behind his ears. In the rear-view mirror I could see him raise his head and yawn, which Simone had assured me was a sign of contentment. I had to accept that estimate on faith alone, since Milù and I had achieved absolutely no rapport. All I saw was a mouth bristling with formidable incisors and those yellow eyes straight out of Transylvania.

I regarded Milù, in fact, as the only serious handicap to our affair. Simone loved that cat and could hardly bear to be separated from him. She usually allowed him to run loose in her end of the house and she took him everywhere with her, even on shopping expeditions, though she always left him in the car. "It was so funny once," she told me. "Someone tried to steal our car. I leave it open, you know, and this man climbed in and started up the engine. He obviously did not see Milù in the backseat. But then Milù sat up and looked at him, you know, and this poor man almost had a heart attack. I came out of the store to see him running across the parking lot and screaming so much."

I could sympathize with him. Although Simone had assured me that Milù was not only tame but had been declawed, so that his love taps and casual swipes would not be lethal, I couldn't work up much enthusiasm for him. I felt reasonably safe with him only with Simone around and I insisted she lock him up whenever I came over to the house, which wasn't often. Three times a week, however, she drove him out into the desert in the early morning and let him run free for half an hour or so, which is how I happened to find myself in the same automobile with them. Otherwise, I stayed as far away from him as I could. My feeling about wild animals in general is that they belong in the great outdoors. Mother Nature, as a witty piano player named Oscar Levant once observed, is no mother of mine.

I was so wrapped up in my arduous romance with Simone that I forgot about such mundane matters as time passing and making a living. How long had I been involved with her? A week, ten days, a year? It didn't seem to matter; I was totally mesmerized. Then, one morning, at about eight o'clock, my telephone rang. I was still staying at the Three Kings, even though I hadn't worked since I'd been hit over the head. Vince had told me I could bunk in with him, but I wasn't worrying about money or anything. I was adrift in a sort of sexual Sargasso, in which I had lost all drive and all contact with reality. All I could think of and all I cared about was Simone, or, more precisely, her supple, inventive body. My caller sounded at first like a voice from the distant past. *"Mago,* what is it that you are doing?" he asked. "When is it that you are coming?"

"Ah, Fulvio," I said. "I've been sort of busy here."

"It is that I am needing you, *caro,"* the tenor said. "I have horses of my own now, there are decisions to be made. It is over two weeks and I am busy in the opera house with this *Otello.* The soprano is a mountain of *merda,* but I am making her to smelling good. You are supposed to be here."

I assured him that I would be on my way in a matter of two or three days. I had been inadvertently delayed, I told him, and I invented excuses. "I'll be there by the weekend, I promise," I said. "I have to take my car back to L.A. and pick up my clothes."

"It is that I am losing much money," he complained, "because my wizard is not with me. These horses they have here in New York are goats. You must come."

"Well, I have been," I answered, not untruthfully. "That, in fact, is my problem."

"Cosa? I not understand you."

"Nothing, nothing. Just making a small, private joke."

"I will tell Anna to make the reservations for you and she will telephone to you," he said. *"Va bene?"*

"Yes, yes," I said. "I'm sorry I didn't let you know. How is Signor Pipistrello?"

"A catastrophe, an evil one. He is making me to kill him one day."

"Please say hello to him for me."

"I do that, my wizard. No more *ritardi* now, okay? I see you this weekend. *Ciao.*" And he hung up on me.

His call had the salutary effect of a quick, cold shower. I sat there for the next half-hour weighing my options and I finally realized I had none to put on the scales. I had less than two thousand dollars left in the bank, no work waiting for me in L.A., and no prospects. I called Simone.

"Louis, where are you? You are late. Milù is waiting for his run."

"I'm sorry. I had a phone call from New York."

"New York?"

"I have to leave in a couple of days."

"Leave? You are going to leave me?"

"I have to, Simone. I'm running out of money."

"Money? What is money? You are thinking only about money?"

"No, but it's one of the things I think about."

"That is cruel of you, Louis," she said. "I can see I mean nothing to you."

"Simone—"

Then she screamed. "Oh, my God! Not now! Louis, come quick! Please!" And she dropped the receiver on the table or the floor.

"Simone? Simone!" I shouted into the silence. "What is it?"

I didn't expect a reply and I didn't wait for one. I scrambled into my clothes and headed for the door.

EIGHT

◆

Animal Acts

I suppose I could have called the police, but it simply didn't occur to me that anything could be seriously wrong. I assumed that there was trouble of some sort with the animals. Anyway, when I pulled up in front of the house, about fifteen minutes later, nothing appeared to be amiss. I parked in the driveway and ran up to the front door, found it locked, then hurried around behind Simone's wing where there was a side entrance, the one we used to come in and out of the premises with Milù. It was open and I incautiously let myself in.

"Simone!" I called. "Simone, where are you?"

No answer. I stood still for a moment and listened. Nothing. The house, this part of it at least, seemed to be asleep, with the shades and curtains drawn and the hallway practically in darkness. I guessed that something must be going on out in the back with the cats, so I hurried down the corridor toward the living room, from where I'd be able to look out through the glass doors or the picture windows. I had just reached the den when I heard that awful snarling hiss directly behind me. And I turned to find myself confronted by Milù.

The black panther must have been in the bedroom. He crouched in the hall now, no more than twenty feet from me, flat along the carpeting, those distressing yellow eyes fixed on me, his tail flicking from side to side. I could see him gathering his feet under him to spring and I knew I had no more than a few seconds to act.

"Milù, stop that!" I shouted at him, trying to gain some additional time and hoping that someone, anyone in the house would hear me. "You behave yourself! You stop that!"

The panther's head seemed to flatten itself along the floor, the yellow eyes narrowed into slits of lethal menace, and then he came for me. I shouted for help and ducked inside the room. Milù's charging spring carried him past me, though he half-turned in the middle of his leap and took a snarling swipe at me as he went past. If he'd had his claws, I'd have had no chance, but without them his balance was a little off and it took him longer to recover from the miss. I remembered the bullwhip by the cage against the wall and grabbed it just as Milù came scrambling around the corner after me.

I had never swung a whip before in my life, but my first effort, a desperate, instinctive, slashing blow, caught the animal across the skull with a satisfying crack and curled itself around his neck. Milù screamed and sprang to one side, his front paws tearing at the leash and jerking it out of my grasp. I leaped across the room, opened the closet door, and slammed it shut behind me just as the cat came for me again. His body hit the door hard and I kept it closed with both hands on the knob, while he backed off, snarling with frustration.

I don't know how long I waited, perhaps only a minute or two, but it seemed like an hour. I could hear the cat still out there and imagine his malevolent gaze fixed on the closet door, behind which I cowered, my hands glued to the knob. I remembered that the closet contained other whips, as well as a few odd instruments of torture, some of which could have come in handy, if I had to attempt an escape on my own, but I thought it far more prudent at this point to stay right where I was. Sooner or later, Simone would come to my rescue, even if only inadvertently. This nasty beast would have to be fed or something, but I was not about to risk again becoming part of his diet.

Then I heard Tristan's voice. "What is going on?" he barked. "Milù!" And then he added something in German.

"Tristan, it's me!" I shouted from inside the closet. "Look out!"

Tristan swore in German and then began calling for Simone. I opened the door a crack and saw him, dressed only in shorts, holding a bar stool out in front of him as he backed slowly out of the room. The panther was concentrating on him now and again gathering his feet under him, but he seemed a little more undecided about attacking than with me. He lay flat against the floor, his tail lashing from side to side and snarling his displeasure, but the legs of the stool must have seemed like antler's prongs to him and he was dubious about launching himself against them. Then, as Tristan reached the doorway, I heard Simone.

"Tristan, what is it?"

"Milù. He attacked your boyfriend!"

"Louis?" She appeared behind her husband. "Louis!"

"In here!" I called out. "Look out for him!"

"You stupid—" she began, then pushed Tristan aside and anxiously confronted her lethal pet. "Milù!" she said. "What are you doing?" She crouched down to gaze directly into the cat's eyes. "Milù! Oh, somebody hit you! Milù, my darling! What are you doing there? Nobody wants to hurt you. Why are you behaving this way?" She continued to talk to the cat, keeping up a steady, increasingly soothing monologue, until at last the animal began to relax. He had apparently forgotten entirely about me, for which I was grateful, and became quite docile again. After a couple of more minutes of this, Simone was able to coax him past her husband, who, I noticed, kept his stool warily out in front of him, and out into the hallway. The panther crept along behind her, while favoring Tristan with one last open-mouthed snarl, and disappeared toward Simone's bedroom.

I opened the closet door but lingered inside, as Tristan came back into the room. "What happened?" he asked.

"Well, I called Simone this morning and we were talking and then she screamed," I explained, "so I thought something had happened and I rushed over here. The front door was locked and I ran around the side. That door was open and I walked in. I guess Simone was out back. Anyway, Milù is not exactly a fan of mine."

"He is not a fan of no one, only Simone," Tristan said. "Of course you surprised him *und* he does not know you, so it was natural, really. You must be more careful."

"I will be."

"In the act, we sedate him, you know."

"I didn't know, but I could have guessed."

Felix, looking willowy and dark in a long, black Oriental robe, entered the room. "What *is* going on?" he asked. "Is everyone okay?"

"We have some trouble with Milù," Tristan said. "It is all right now."

"What *are* you doing in that closet?" Felix asked.

"I'm not sure I want to come out yet," I said.

"Oh, but you must! I did that years ago and it was such a relief!"

"Actually, I'm sort of fascinated by this closet," I said, finally emerging again. "I must ask you about it someday, Tristan."

"Toys," he answered. "Simone will tell you."

"Toys? But I adore toys!" Felix said. "Let me see!"

He started for the open door, but Tristan cut him off and slammed it shut. "Not now, Felix," he said, turning again to me. "You say Simone screamed *und* that is why you came over this morning?"

"Yes. I called her from my hotel and she—"

"Louis!" Simone snapped, striding angrily into the room. "Louis, you hit him!"

"You bet I hit him," I said. "He was going to tear me apart."

"He was playing. He only became angry when you hit him."

"Come on, Simone. He was not playing. Or if he was, it was for keeps."

"He has a cut on his head." She turned to Tristan. "He cannot work tonight."

"We will do without him. Perhaps Loki—"

"He is not ready. It is too dangerous."

Tristan nodded. "Yes, you are right."

"Who's Loki?" I asked.

"One of the leopards," Tristan said. "We have been training him, but it takes much time. We try to have at least two animals for every part of the act, you know. Like Wotan, he is getting old—"

"We must call the vet at once," Simone said. "That cut is quite deep."

"I'm sorry, Simone," I told her, "but if I hadn't hit him, he'd have killed me."

"You are stupid," she said. "You should not have done it."

"Done what? I was talking to you on the phone and suddenly you screamed," I protested. "I was worried about you, for Christ's sake!"

"Oh, dear, a quarrel," Felix observed. "I hate scenes."

"Then leave!" Simone snapped.

"Well . . ." Felix said and walked huffily out of the room, like an offended prom queen.

"Simone, why did you scream?" Tristan asked.

"I thought Boris or one of the leopards had gotten out," she explained. "They were cleaning the cages—"

"I did not hear nothing."

"I did. So I shouted and ran out of the room." She turned on me again. "I am very angry at you, Louis."

"Well, I'm sorry. I had no way of knowing. I thought maybe Milù turned on you or something."

"He would never do that, never. Milù and I are one."

"You are crazy," Tristan said to her. "He is dangerous. I tell you so often not to trust him so much." He looked at me and shrugged. "She think he is a person. He is not a person. He is an animal."

"And he has all of his teeth," I observed.

"Milù is special," Simone insisted. "You do not understand. I am very angry, Louis, very." And she walked swiftly out of the room.

"Well, I guess I'll make myself disappear," I said. "I'm sorry about the trouble."

"It's all right," Tristan answered. "But you know, it is funny."

"What is?"

"I don't understand her myself sometimes," he said. "She worry too much about the animals. Of course I worry, too. Wotan is old *und* he is like a big dog now, so it is necessary to keep him apart. One time he *und* Boris, the Siberian tiger, they began fighting *und* that was very bad, but we have been more careful since then. That is why it is funny she do this." He smiled and suddenly clapped me on the shoulder hard enough to make me reel. "Never mind. You pay no attention, Shifty. She get over it. *Und* you know? I am glad you do that. I hate that focking Milù. One day I kill him. . . ."

I did not see Simone again before leaving Las Vegas, but not because I didn't try to contact her. After I had made arrangements to check out of my room and packed my bags, I called her several times, but she wouldn't come to the phone. Tristan was apologetic about it. "You see, Shifty, *mein freund,* she is crazy about that Milù," he explained. "You cannot reason with her about this. You must be patient. You must give her a few days, *ya?*"

"I don't have a few days, Tristan," I said. "I have to leave, either tonight or early tomorrow."

"That is not good, Shifty."

"It's a question of money. I'm going to work for Fulvio Gasparini."

"Oh, that is fine, *ya.*"

"How about if I come by later this afternoon?"

"We have to go early to the theater with the animals tonight," he objected. "You see, with Milù out, we have to change the act a little. Perhaps you can come after the show?"

"I'll try."

"Good. I tell her. But, Shifty?"

"Yes?"

"When she get angry, Shifty, it takes often a long time. How long you will be away?"

"I don't know," I answered. "Six months or so. I'll be in New York for a while, then there are some engagements abroad. We'll be back in the spring, I guess, and then we'll see."

"I tell her all this, okay?"

"Okay. Break a leg tonight, Tristan."

"I have never understand what this means," he said.

"It means 'good luck.' "

"I know, Shifty, but it is a strange way to say so."

"I agree. Anyway, you know what I mean."

"*Ya.* Good-bye, Shifty, *und* you break a leg also."

After this conversation, I decided the best thing for me to do was get out of town as quickly as possible. I called up Vince to say goodbye to him and he told me he had bumped into Dawn at the supermarket that morning. "She's wondering what happened to you," he said.

"I'm sort of wondering myself," I answered. "What did you tell her?"

"Nothing much. Just that you were involved with someone."

"Oh, I feel badly about Dawn, even though we really are just friends," I said. "I showed up and then just disappeared again."

"She said it was the most consistent part of your act."

"It *is* time for me to leave, Vince. All the women I know here are angry at me."

"She knows who it is, Shifty."

"She does? How?"

He laughed softly. "The story about you and the lady at the Hilton has been making the rounds," he explained. "It's a small town, you know. God, Shifty, under the table?"

"You don't know the half of it and you wouldn't believe the rest of it, if I told you. Her goddamn black panther almost ate me alive this morning."

"Are you into animal acts, Shifty? Dawn said it was a kinky scene, but I had no idea—"

"Come on, Vince, I'm not a degenerate," I objected. "No, the cat attacked me. I was lucky to escape intact."

"I gotta hear this."

"I'll tell you about it sometime. What else did Dawn say?"

"That they're into orgies, I guess, stuff like that. You didn't get involved in any of it?"

"No way, Vince. I'm not much good at orgies. I went to one

once, about ten years ago, in Hollywood, this big mansion up in the hills, and they asked me to leave, because I was laughing so hard. I mean, it's funny enough when two people make the beast with two backs, but when it's in a monkey cage it's ludicrous."

"Well, according to Dawn, your friends have a very busy cage going, with a lot of bizarre action, including SM."

"I guess I believe it. I have to."

"Oh?"

I told him about the closet in the den and its contents. "But I never saw any of it," I assured him. "They lead pretty separate lives. He's mostly gay, I guess, and she's, well—superactive. Actually, I'm exhausted."

"Let's have a drink," he said. "I want to hear more about this."

"I can't, Vince," I explained. "I have a lot to do tomorrow and I told Fulvio I'd be in New York in a couple of days."

"Dawn also said that Simone used to hang around with a hood."

"Yeah? Who?"

"Some guy involved in the rackets, but it was a while ago, I guess. Maybe when they first came out here."

"Well, Simone needs a lot of action. Why not a gangster?"

"She must be a nympho, Shifty. That's what I think."

"I don't know, but it was terrific while it lasted."

"You sure it's over?"

"I can't wait around to find out, Vince. I'm going broke."

"Ah, Shifty, it's always the same story with you," he said. "You have too many different things going in too many areas—women, the horses, and now this opera singer. Why don't you just stick to magic, the one thing you do really well? You could be the best in the world."

"No, you are, Vince," I told him. "My trouble is, I don't believe in a life after death. I'm going to play my guitar in the sun while it shines. I'll be seeing you, Vince. Thanks for everything."

Wotan checked out around the same time I did, although I didn't find out about it until afterward. He and Milù had been left behind that afternoon, when Tristan and Simone departed for the Stardust to work on the alternate routines with Boris, Loki, and the other cats. The lion was old and was now being used only early in the proceedings, so the plan must have been to rehearse the new business for the part of the act normally featuring the black panther, then go back and pick up Wotan in time for the show. He couldn't be kept too long in his small cage below the stage, Simone had told me, because he wasn't used to it and would become too irritable to work with. They left him alone, as usual, out in the backyard.

Sometime between five and six, the hour they usually left for the casino, the lion wandered into the house. He didn't find anyone, but he did notice that someone, perhaps the maid, had left the front door open. He poked his nose out, sniffed the cool late-afternoon desert air, and lumbered out onto the front lawn.

Probably nothing would have happened, if a nearsighted, sixty-eight-year-old ex-stripper named Jessie Palmer hadn't been in the habit of walking her Pekingese at that hour. Miss Palmer lived three blocks away and used to vary the routes of her morning and evening walks with her dog, so it turned out to be pure bad luck that she happened to turn the corner of Tristan and Simone's block just as Wotan emerged from the house.

Even then nothing might have happened, because Miss Palmer, peering myopically through the gloom, mistook Wotan for a very large dog. "Jesus, you're a big one," she reportedly said, as she came strolling down the sidewalk. "Look, Muffy, look at the nice doggie!"

Muffy was as blind as his mistress, but he could smell one species from another. What we had here, he decided, was a big and potentially obnoxious cat. Muffy was not heavily gifted with brains, but he was brave. He broke away from his mistress, ran yapping up to Wotan, and planted himself directly in front of him, where he continued to bark angrily, with occasional darting snaps at the lion's ankles.

"Muffy, baby, don't do that!" Miss Palmer admonished him. "That's not friendly. You'll frighten the big bugger."

Wotan had never liked dog acts. There had been several on the same bill with him during his years in show biz and they had always turned out to be noisy and intrusive, making it impossible for him to snooze, his favorite pastime, between entrances and exits. Muffy must have struck him as merely another annoying manifestation of the genre and he wasted no more than two or three minutes before remedying the situation. One newspaper account I later read of the incident indicated that the lion had stepped on the dog, like a housewife squashing a cockroach underfoot. I think what must have happened, however, is that he merely took a swipe at him. The net effect, in any case, was the complete destruction of a very nearsighted Pekingese, a calamity that unleashed the furies in the dog's outraged mistress.

Appalled by the fate of her idiot pet, the aging ecdysiast rushed at poor Wotan and bashed him over the head with her handbag. "You big bully!" she shouted at him. "What do you think you're doing? Why don't you pick on somebody your own size?"

Wotan retreated, sat down, and emitted a plaintive roar, probably his way of pleading for understanding and sympathy. After all, he hadn't started this fracas; all he demanded out of life was enough raw meat to keep him alive between naps and a little peace and quiet while snoozing. What had he ever done to deserve this humiliating assault? He roared again, and the sound of his protest not only aroused the neighborhood but caused Jessie Palmer to drop her handbag. "Holy shit, it's a goddamn lion!" she screamed and began running up the block, waving her arms. "Help! Help! There's a goddamn lion loose! Help! Help, somebody!"

Jessie Palmer had a voice like a fire gong, capable of penetrating concrete. Several neighbors poked their heads out into the street and one man stepped out into his driveway holding a shotgun. Two housewives telephoned the police, who dispatched a patrol car to the scene. Long before it arrived, however, Wotan had departed. Alarmed by all the noise and confusion around him, the lion had first tried to get back into the house, but had found the front door closed against him, probably by a gust of wind. He had then set off at a rheumatic jog down the street, his sole purpose undoubtedly to escape the senseless uproar in his wake. By the time the police arrived, five or six minutes later, the lion had disappeared. Jessie Palmer, surrounded by a knot of sympathetic neighbors, was sitting on the lawn in front of the house, holding what looked like the head of an orange dust mop in her lap, and sobbing like a bibulous banshee. "He killed him!" she wailed. "The big bully! He killed him!"

It took the officers a few more minutes to piece the whole story together, by which time Wotan had apparently made his way into the more sparsely populated outskirts of the city. Calls began coming into the central police switchboard reporting the appearance of a full-grown male lion on the move in the north part of town. More patrol cars converged on the area and helicopters equipped with searchlights began a block-to-block hunt for the marauding beast. Television and radio programs began to broadcast warnings to residents and by nightfall a state of siege gripped much of residential Las Vegas. When Tristan and Simone, who had heard nothing until then, showed up a little after seven to pick up their performing feline for the evening show, they found their whole street in tumult. "Oh, my God," Simone exclaimed to the officer standing in front of their house, "they will kill him! He is helpless!"

"Helpless, my ass!" Jessie Palmer wailed at her. "Look what he did to Muffy, the son of a bitch!"

Tristan and Simone jumped into their car and, escorted by two police vehicles, set off in search of their missing lion. By then it must already have been too late. Wotan had been cornered in the carport of a condominium, after having been spotted a few minutes earlier in somebody's backyard by the young, impressionable new bride of a blackjack dealer at the Sands named Henry Moon. Mr. Moon owned a .357 Magnum powerful enough to blow an elephant apart. Roused to heights of heroism by the high-pitched decibel count of his wife's discovery, he had tracked Wotan across the street and into the carport, where the lion had tried to hide behind a metal dumpster. One last plaintive roar, unquestionably a plea for sympathy and succor, was punctuated by the bazookalike blast of Mr. Moon's vicious heater. Wotan never knew what hit him. When Tristan and Simone reached the scene, it was to find Henry Moon, smoking cannon still in hand, smilingly holding court for the neighborhood over the inert body of their performing cat like a Hemingway hero in the green hills of Africa.

I'm not sure what else happened after that, but I do know that Simone kicked Mr. Moon very hard in the crotch, doubling him over and that Tristan sat down, put the lion's head in his lap, and cried. "He was so gentle, so sweet," the performer declared to the assembled onlookers. "Why do you do this? He would not harm nobody, not even a mouse." No one contradicted him, perhaps because no one at the scene had yet heard about the dismemberment of Jessie Palmer's Pekingese.

I first heard about the tragedy on the news as I was crossing the state line and I even toyed with the idea of pulling off the freeway long enough to call Las Vegas, but I realized I'd probably be unable to get either Tristan or Simone on the phone, especially if they'd gone ahead with their performance that evening. Anyway, what could I have said to them? I did telephone Vince much later that night, after I got home, and he filled me in on some of the details, more of which I gleaned from newspaper accounts the next day in L.A.

At about noon, I called their house and Simone picked up the phone. No sooner had she heard my voice than she began to scream at me. "It's all your fault!" she said. "You did it! You did it!"

"What are you talking about, Simone?" I shouted back. "I didn't leave the front door open! I called to tell you I'm sorry, that's all!"

She was sobbing with rage and grief. "You bastard!" she said. "I knew it!"

"Knew what?"

"I should have listened to Gianna. I shouldn't have had anything to do with you!"

"Gianna? Who's Gianna?"

But she had already slammed the phone down.

NINE

♦

Sacred Monsters

My flight to New York from L.A. was an hour late, so I dropped my bags off at the hotel, which was a couple of blocks east of the Lincoln Center complex, and walked over to the opera house. Anna Willows had left word at the artists' entrance that I was expected and she herself came out to meet me. She was dressed in gray slacks and a blue turtleneck sweater and holding a clipboard. She looked tired and harassed. "You're late," she snapped, as she came through the door.

"Sorry about that," I said. "We were slow out of the starting gate in L.A. and couldn't make up any ground in the stretch."

"Fulvio's been asking about you all day. He's driving me up the wall."

"How is he?"

"He's fine. It's the rest of us who are suffering. Come on." She turned and led me briskly through a maze of corridors into the interior of the house. "At least if he sees you're around, it might calm him down."

I paid little attention to where we were going, because I was intent on finding out what was happening. "I would have come yesterday, but I couldn't," I explained. "What's wrong? Has he been losing?"

"Of course. He bets and he always loses. And one of his own horses broke a leg or something yesterday. It just makes it worse."

"Makes what worse?"

"Everything," she said. "We're two days away from the dress

81

and Fulvio not only detests Caterina, he and Luther are getting into it."

"Who are they?"

"God, don't you know anything?"

"Not much. I'm a horseplayer. I thrive on ignorance."

"Caterina Pantaloni is the Desdemona and Luther Wildwood is the director and designer," she explained.

"And Fulvio doesn't get along with them."

"He and Caterina despise each other, that's all," Anna said. "They've been feuding ever since they recorded the *Ballo in Maschera* together two years ago in London. Of course, Fulvio's right about her. She's a horror, she can't sing on pitch, and she screams her top notes."

"I can see that would be cause for alarm. And this Luther?"

"A pretentious English faggot who overdirects everything and knows nothing about singing. He thinks the opera is all about him and his ugly sets and costumes. He wants Fulvio to do things that are absolutely wrong."

"And Fulvio won't."

"You're beginning to catch on." We turned a corner and she put a hand out to stop me. "Okay, now remember, there's a rehearsal going on," she warned me. "I'm going to sit you down to one side and please just stay there. I'll make sure Fulvio knows you're here, but don't move around except maybe during the breaks. You're not supposed to be in here at all, but Fulvio's arranged it. Or rather I did. Just wait in place till I come and get you."

"What could happen? They only shoot horses."

"Don't be funny, please," she said. "And don't, for God's sake, open your mouth in here."

"In a roomful of opera singers? Who'd hear me?"

She poked her head through the door. "It's a break," she said, then led me into the huge auditorium and sat me down ten or twelve rows back, but well off to the side. A crew of about twenty people was bustling about the stage, putting the final corrective touches on what I assumed was Otello's castle. It was a terrific-looking set, very solid, but eroded and worn, exactly like an ancient seaside fortification. "That's Luther's popcorn set," Anna whispered. "It's made of styrofoam and every time they move it bits and pieces of it fall off. They keep having to sweep the whole stage and that also drives Fulvio crazy."

"Where is he?"

"Back in his dressing room. He won't stay in the hall whenever they fiddle with the set," she explained. "He's afraid one of the bits will get stuck in his larynx." I laughed. "Don't laugh. You weren't around the night the tenor inhaled his mustache in *Rigoletto*. It's not funny."

"It depends on your point of view."

"Now don't move," she said, putting a restraining hand on my shoulder. "I'll tell him you're here. If there's enough time, he may want to speak to you." And she hurried away down a side aisle toward the dressing room.

It wasn't hard to spot Luther Wildwood; the designer and stage director was trailed by a small personal escort of attendants and admirers of every conceivable sex. He was a small, slender man with thinning brown hair, who was obviously engaged in a gallant but hopeless rear-guard action with advancing middle age. He wore tight, tailored gray slacks, a dark-blue shirt open to mid-chest, and a yellow sweater draped over his shoulders like a cape. Suddenly leaving his retinue behind, he bounded up on stage and began to fuss with two of the stagehands over how a tattered banner controlled by wires could be made to look as if it were blowing in the wind. He made a small but vivid drama out of the problem and I could tell he was obviously a star in his own right. I began to look forward to the inevitable confrontation with Fulvio.

What I was seeing, I gathered, was merely a staging rehearsal. The orchestra and conductor were absent from the pit and only an accompanist was on hand. The chorus, a sleepy-looking group of mostly middle-aged people who looked like fugitives from a tour bus, had been milling about the set, but they were now dismissed. Wildwood clapped his hands together and called for the love scene involving Desdemona and the Moor that ends act one, then left the stage. "Places, please!" he called out. "And *silenzio!*"

Fulvio strolled in from stage left. He was dressed in a brown terrycloth jump suit and white tennis hat that made him look like an enormous ice-cream cone. He did not seem pleased and stood there, arms folded, staring glumly down toward Wildwood's group, now bunched behind the director about a third of the way up the center aisle. "Fulvio, from the beginning, please!" Wildwood said.

"Alone?" Fulvio asked. "This is love duet or solo?"

The soprano now appeared stage right and strolled indifferently toward him. She was a tiny, round woman of about forty, with legs like Doric columns, a prognathous jaw, and a soaring beehive hairdo. She was dressed in black, with a double strand of pearls around her neck, and looked about as amiable as a wolverine. She took up a position beside Fulvio without either touching or looking at him. It seemed an unlikely coupling and I began to wonder how Wildwood would be able to make us believe these two odd-looking characters were in love with each other, at least without making us laugh.

I needn't have worried. The minute they began to sing, even at half-volume, which was all they would permit themselves to do in rehearsal, I forgot all about their appearance and attitude toward each other. I knew about Fulvio's voice, but Pantaloni was a revelation. She made a sound of such sweetness and potential power that it could have melted icecaps. Anna Willows, I decided, was merely drenched in envy. I sat there enthralled for several minutes, as Verdi's magnificent score obliterated everything else from my mind. At the end, as Fulvio went up to a soft high note over the soprano line and allowed it to soar like a magical bird above my head, I had to force myself not to applaud.

It didn't seem to please Wildwood, however. No sooner had the singers released together and turned to move upstage on the closing notes of the duet than the director came running down the aisle. "No, no, Fulvio, Caterina," he said, "you must turn before, as we agreed. At least two measures earlier. And you walk up toward the castle on the closing phrase, so that Otello picks up Desdemona and carries her in on these last notes."

"Well, of course I will do it," the soprano said. "It is *he* who will not move." She indicated Fulvio with the toss of a shoulder, as if ridding herself of a noisome insect. "I cannot lead him. He must move first."

"Is wrong," Fulvio said. "Is not time to move."

"Now, Fulvio, we've been all through this before," Wildwood said. "You agreed to try it my way, at least once."

"I decide is wrong," Fulvio said. "Is crazy."

"But don't you understand the concept, Fulvio—"

"Concept is *merda*," the tenor interrupted him. "I am singing the A soft and holding for thirteen beats. You think is easy?"

"*Madonna mia*," Miss Pantaloni said and walked briskly offstage right.

Fulvio shot her a look that could have cut her in half. "She is soprano, she knows nothing," he said. "I not sing this note soft and move, *mio caro*. You wish to try, you come up and sing the high note. And I am right. Verdi is not saying to move. Verdi is saying to move *after* the note, not before."

"Fulvio, we are trying to do something a bit innovative here," the director explained. "We want an Otello who is more forceful, more impulsive, more animal in his desires. He must always *take* what he wants *when* he wants it. Don't you see?"

"Otello is not animal, Maestro. Verdi is not writing this music for animals."

"Quite right," I heard Anna's voice whisper. I had not seen her come back, but she must have returned sometime during the duet and sat down behind me. "It only makes sense if you think of Desdemona as Madonna. If Luther gets his way, Otello will wind up asking, 'Where's the hankie, honkie?' "

It became clear very quickly that Luther was not going to get his way. The director was obviously struggling to keep his temper while continuing to explain his point of view to the tenor, but Fulvio was having none of it. "I no sing this A soft and turn upstage, no, no," he declared. "Better I stay *a casa, caro mio.* Is not Marvelous Marvin Hagler here, *cocco.* Is Otello, who is noble Moor, you understand?"

I thought Wildwood might begin to scream. His cheeks had become pink and his whole body was shaking with suppressed frustration and anger, even as he struggled to remain calm and reasonable. "This guy's going to have a stroke," I whispered to Anna.

"No, he won't," she answered, with a good deal of very evident satisfaction. "Luther can throw quite spectacular tantrums of his own, but he knows better than to try that on Fulvio. The audience isn't coming to look at his sets and costumes or to admire his brilliant direction; they're coming to hear Fulvio sing. Fulvio's the sacred monster here, not Luther."

Anna was right. After several more futile attempts at persuasion, Wildwood gave up and returned to his observation post in the auditorium, followed by his worried-looking, clearly outraged staff. He refused to have any further direct contact with Fulvio, who was now instructed by one of the director's minions, a cadaverous hermaphrodite named Algie, to resume the run-through from the start of the duet. Caterina Pantaloni reemerged from the wings and took up her position beside Fulvio without looking at him, while everyone else in the theater tiptoed about, anxious not to touch off the explosion everyone expected. "I've been at rehearsals that left blood on the walls," Anna whispered. "Luther better not confront him again."

Suddenly quite tired from my long flight, I sank back in my seat and let Verdi take over. Too bad you couldn't get a little action on the opera, I reflected. You could become addicted. . . .

I had been delayed in leaving L.A. because of the accident to Hugo Mandelbaum. He had become an unwelcome presence in my life again as a result of my visit to Happy Hal Mancuso's office, where I'd gone to pick up my last paycheck from the Three Kings and some income tax forms; I'd probably be out of the country in April and I wanted to pay early, especially as I had money coming back to me. I also needed Hal to get me out of my two cruises in March without burning that small bridge behind me. "You're an idiot," Hal snapped at me. "I give this thing with the opera singer six months."

"Hal, you're probably right," I told him, "but it's going to be interesting."

"So is bankruptcy. So is death." He looked gloomily up at me from behind his desk like a doctor regarding a terminally ill patient. "You want to rent your place while you're gone? I figure you'll need the money."

"To whom? Some client of yours?"

"Hugo. He needs a place when he comes to L.A. He's too cheap to pay for a good hotel room."

"How often does he come?"

"Once a week, usually. He's got a girl singer he thinks he's in love with."

"Hugo, in love?"

"Listen, even bacteria fall in love. I think I can get him to pay you six hundred a month. That should cover your expenses."

"What about my stuff? Will he take care of it?"

"What's to take care of? Old *Racing Forms* and magic posters? What else you got in there?"

"My furniture, Hal. My magic books, a lot of my clothes."

"What's Hugo going to do, sell them? All he wants is a place to take this gal, Shifty. The lady's married to a record executive. She isn't going to leave him to settle down with Mr. Good Taste."

"My God, what do you suppose she sees in him?"

"Who knows? Who cares? Maybe she's into humiliation and disease. Yes or no, Shifty? I'll make sure he pays you."

That's how I happened to find myself once more enmeshed with Hugo Mandelbaum. I had to stay over an extra day so he could fly in from Las Vegas the following morning to see my place, pay me a month's rent in advance, and pick up a key. He arrived about noon, dressed in an emerald green leisure suit and Gucci loafers, took one look at my one-room digs, and said, "You actually live here?"

"What's the matter with it?"

"It's okay, if you're an ant."

"I'm in an unappreciated profession, Hugo, and I bet on horses," I said. "I believe in keeping the overhead low."

His eyes scanned my walls, decorated chiefly by blowups of race horses in action and old magic posters, took in the piles of old *Racing Forms* and programs in the corners of the room, and he said, "It's a toxic dump site. You need federal aid."

"It's clean," I said. "The price includes a Mexican maid who comes in and tidies up once a month."

"Does she give head?"

I ignored that one.

"Say, do you know the only thing a Jewish princess goes down on? The escalator at Neiman-Marcus."

"Do you want the place or don't you?"

He flung himself onto my queen-sized bed and bounced on the mattress a couple of times. "Testing the lay of the week," he said. "Say, Shifty, how come it takes so much longer for a woman to have an orgasm?"

"I don't know, Hugo."

He laughed. "Who gives a shit?"

"Yes or no, Hugo?"

"Yeah, I'll take it," he said, bouncing upright again. "Here's your first month's rent." He handed me a check and I gave him a set of keys. "When are you leaving?"

"Tonight, if I can get out of here in time."

"Terrific. I'm going back to Vegas, but I'll drop some stuff off later this afternoon. That okay?"

"Sure. Now let me introduce you to Max Silverman," I said. "He's the manager here. Only don't tell him any jokes. Max doesn't like jokes."

"What's the matter with him? Is he deaf?"

"He's pretty old, Hugo," I explained. "He reads Russian literature and plays the violin. Give him a break."

We found Max out by the mailboxes. Dressed, as usual, in his tattered bathrobe, black beret, and slippers, he was sweeping out the hallway and gathering up discarded junk mail. I introduced him to Hugo and explained the situation to him. "So where are you going, Shifty?" he asked.

"New York, Max. I'll be away a few months."

"You got a job?"

"Sort of."

"Good. Maybe it'll keep you away from the horses for a while."

"Not really, Max." I decided not to explain the exact nature of my new work to him, because it would only set him off. Max had a rooted conviction that my life would improve dramatically if I never went near a racetrack again. "I'm in sort of an advisory capacity."

Max snorted. "So now you're a tout," he said. "Shifty—"

"Hey, Max," Hugo cut in, "give the sucker a break. What are you, his mother?"

Max gazed at Hugo as if actually seeing him for the first time; he did not enjoy the view. "So what are you?" he asked. "A pimp?"

"Pretty sharp, Max," Hugo said, grinning. "No, I use the nookie, I don't peddle it."

Max's kindly old face froze and he turned away from Hugo as if he had just had to witness a horrifying accident. "There was a fellow looking for you this morning," he said to me. "He was looking at the tenant list."

"Who was it?"

"I don't know," Max said. "Some little stocky guy in a brown suit, looked like a cop, maybe. I told him you were here."

"No name, Max?"

The old man shrugged. "He said something, but I didn't catch it. I guess he'll be back."

"It can't be important," I said. "I've paid my bills. Anyway, send all my mail to Hal's office, Max. He'll take care of it, okay?"

"Okay. Be well, Shifty." He took my hand in both of his. "You're a good kid. We'll miss you."

"Hey, Max," Hugo said, "did you hear about this guy who goes in for a medical checkup?"

"Hugo—" I began, but I might as well have tried to derail a bullet train with a penny.

"So the doc tells him, 'I need a full medical workup on you. I want a specimen of your urine, your semen, and your feces.' 'That's easy,' the guy says. 'Here, take my shorts.' "

"Is this man a friend of yours?" Max asked and shuffled off without waiting for an answer.

Hugo and I went our separate ways, but he came back before I did, sometime in the middle of the afternoon, with a suitcase and a couple of extra pairs of slacks on hangers. As he was leaving the apartment, somebody stepped out of the shadows of the hallway behind my place and zapped him. He must have been unconscious for quite a while, because Max found him and he was still out. His money was missing but nothing else, not even his gold chains. In fact, he was wearing them when I stopped by Cedars Sinai, the nearest hospital, to see him. I had come back to pick up my own bags to head for the airport and Max told me what had happened. "He probably was telling a joke," the old man said, "and the guy who did it couldn't stand it anymore. Maybe it was a woman. I hope so."

Hugo had been taken to the intensive care unit at Cedars and they wouldn't let me in to talk to him, though he waved feebly at me from his bed near the door. His head was heavily bandaged and his face looked gray, but one of the nurses, a pretty young redhead, told me he could talk and knew where he was. "He's probably going to be just fine," she said. "He's got a bad concussion and we're going to keep him at least overnight here to make sure there's no fracture or anything. You can see him tomorrow, Mr. Anderson. He'll be in a private room, if the doctors release him from ICU."

"I'll be in New York tomorrow. You sure he's okay?"

She smiled a little grimly. "He tried to feel me up. I think he'll live."

"He'll live. The minute he starts telling dirty jokes, send him home."

I still might have made my plane, but I was told that I had to stop by the police station and make a statement. By the time I got out of there, the rush-hour traffic delayed me and I missed my flight. I booked myself out the following morning, checked into a motel near the airport, then called Hal to tell him what had happened.

"I think Max was right," he said. "It was probably a critic."

"You know what's funny, Hal?" I said.

"What?"

"The guy who hit me in the parking lot in Vegas did it the same way."

"It's usually the head they go for, Shifty. That's where the brains are. In Hugo's case, they should have hit him in the mouth."

"No, that's not what I'm talking about, Hal," I insisted. "The guy who hit both of us took away our money. No wallets, no jewelry, no watches, nothing."

"So?"

"So what if it was the same guy? Maybe he was after me again and not Hugo."

"That's real dumb. Wouldn't this guy know by now what you do for a living? You telling me he followed you from Vegas to nail you again? That's crazy."

"He got three grand out of me the first time, Hal."

"It doesn't make a lot of sense, Shifty."

"No, it doesn't. That's why it's interesting."

"Forget it, Shifty. Go do your crazy thing in New York. When you tap out with the screamer, I'll be here. Good luck."

The rest of the *Otello* rehearsal that first afternoon passed without incident and afterward Anna took me backstage to see Fulvio, who was still steaming from the confrontation with Wildwood. He was stretched out on a small sofa that his bulk all but obliterated, so that he seemed to be floating on air, and he had a towel wrapped around his neck to guard against sudden drafts. Even my appearance did little to lighten the mood, though the tenor did favor me with a quick smile and stretched out a hand toward me. "Ah, my wizard," he said, "is good that you have come at last. Everything is going wrong, *mio caro*."

I apologized for being so late. "A friend of mine was in an accident," I explained.

"So is always something," Fulvio declared. "Here is one accident after one other. This director is *stupido* who knows nothing about singing. He knows nothing about nothing. And you see the soprano, no? One night I strangle her for real in the last scene."

"Fulvio, it's going to be all right now," Anna Willows said. "They're giving you what you want, aren't they?"

"What I want is this should be Verdi's *Otello*," the tenor said, "not story of Mr. T. You have seen the costumes? Is disgusting."

"It looked and sounded terrific to me, Fulvio," I said, "but then what do I know about opera?"

"You are here for the horses, *mio caro*. Is also disgusting."

"What is?"

"I am spending very much money and nothing is happening," he said. "One of them break a leg in the morning, another have bad cold, the others is not running yet, but they are eating very much and they are needing medicines. Anna—"

"Yes, Fulvio?"

"You give him my papers and you tell Geraldo he is coming."

"I've left the credentials at the hotel for him."

"Is good," Fulvio said. "My wizard, you go see what is happening, yes? I have the *Otello* to think of. Tuesday is the dress rehearsal, then Friday the *prima*. After that we go racing, maybe Saturday. You talk to Geraldo."

"That would be Monkton."

"*Sì*. He is nice man, they say very good trainer. Only with me nothing is happening."

"What does Miss Lagrange have to say about all this?"

Fulvio grinned and cocked a warning index finger at me. "She think is great foolishness," he said. "She is angry with me."

"About your gambling, right?"

"About that, yes. And she is *furiosa* about you."

"Maybe I ought to talk to her."

"She wish to see you, I know," he warned me, "but maybe it is better we let time pass, *mago*. Is my money, but sometime she think it is hers. I wish you to worry about the horses. And you study hard, *mago*. I am not winning even one race here. Every day I am losing."

"You're betting at OTB, I figure, or with bookies. That has to stop, Fulvio."

"*Va bene, va bene*," he exclaimed impatiently. "I only bet what you tell me, all right?"

"Yes, because if you don't do what I say, Fulvio, I can't help you."

"I understand, my wizard, believe me." He put his hand tenderly to his heart. "I am in your hands."

There was a light knock on the dressing-room door and Anna opened it. Algie, looking visibly distressed, was standing in the hall holding some bits of paper in one hand. "Mr. Wildwood wanted me to give you these," he said, offering them to Anna. "Some notes of his on the rehearsal."

"*Cosa?*" Fulvio called from his couch. "*Chi è?*"

Anna stepped to one side and Algie edged nervously into the room, like a terrified sparrow cagily eyeing a bread crumb near a sleeping cat. "I have some notes from Mr. Wildwood about the rehearsal," he said.

"Notes? He has notes? What notes?"

"Here, these," Algie said, showing them to him.

"*Dio mio*," Fulvio exclaimed, "*che stronzo!*"

"You can leave them with me," Anna said, taking them from the boy. "Thank you."

Gratefully, Algie turned to go, but Fulvio stopped him. "Wait!" he said. "You tell Signor Wildwood I am not doing his *Otello*, I am doing the *Otello* of Verdi. The public is not coming to look at the sets or the clothes or to die with pleasure because we are acting sex drama. The public is coming to hear Fulvio Gasparini sing Verdi, you understand?"

Algie merely nodded, his gaunt face a study in the anatomy of terror.

"And you tell the Pantaloni *strega* that if she step in front of me one more time during our duet," Fulvio continued, "I strangle her then and we not sing the last three acts. *Va bene?*"

Algie nodded again and bolted through the door, which Anna closed firmly behind him. "Really, Fulvio," she said, "that's a little much. It's not his fault."

"Poor Verdi," Fulvio said, waggling his hands over his head in despair, "he is in the hands of the *squalidi!*"

TEN

◆

Horsemen

I rented a car and drove out to Belmont Park, where Fulvio's horses were stabled, very early the next morning. At that hour it was an easy drive, with the streets of New York still empty of traffic and the city looking deceptively elegant from the height of the Triboro Bridge. A pale, cold sun threw the skyscrapers of Manhattan into bold relief, as if they had sprung suddenly to life in the imagination of an artist rather than as ruthless expressions of corporate power. I hadn't been in New York for any length of time for seven or eight years, but I hadn't missed it. What I remembered were not its glories, but its horrors, few of which I had had time to savor since my late arrival the previous afternoon. I was hoping I could divide my time pretty much between the opera house and the racetrack, a parlay I figured would keep me as far removed as possible from the cheerless hassle in the city streets.

When I turned in at the horsemen's gate, the guard in the booth waved me to a stop and came waddling over, flatfooted and benign-looking in a creased brown uniform, the gold braid shining dully through the early-morning mist. I showed him Fulvio's credentials and asked where Gerald Monkton's string was stabled. "Barn 33," the guard said. "Say, ain't he got a horse running today?"

"I wouldn't know. Not one of ours, anyway."

"Well, it don't matter," the guard said. "He ain't had a winner all meet, so there's no reason to think that'll change, is there?"

93

"I wish I could help you, friend," I said. "I'm new in town. He's in a bad streak?"

"Most always," he said, grinning. "Take that road there and go down almost to the end. You can't miss it." And he waved me through.

I drove slowly along a narrow, winding road flanked by large trees, under whose naked branches, on either side, were the horse barns, dark green, low, and secretive-looking in the pale light. I could hear the soft stamping and coughing of the horses. Here and there dim lights burned in the windows—the grooms at work—and men walked silently along the road, shoulders hunched against the cold. At every intersection I slowed practically to a stop, looked both ways between the rows of stables, then started slowly forward again, never driving faster than ten or fifteen miles an hour. Even at that speed a horse could become frightened and bolt or begin breaking down the walls of his stall.

Barn 33 was almost the last in a long row. I parked and headed for the tack room at the nearest end, where a tall, wiry black kid was sweeping up outside one of the stalls. "Hi," I said. "Mr. Monkton around?"

"He ain't here yet," the boy said. "He usually come about nine."

"That late? Who takes care of the horses?"

The boy stopped sweeping and looked at me with curiosity. "We do," he said.

"You train them?"

"Aw, no, nothin' like that," the boy assured me. "No, Mr. Sanchez, he take care of that."

"Who's Mr. Sanchez?"

"He work for Mr. Monkton."

"And where do I find him?"

"He took some horses over to the training track," the boy explained. "He be back."

"I see. Say, my name's Lou Anderson. My friends call me Shifty." I shook his hand; it was large, limp, and sweaty to the touch. "What's yours?"

"Walker," the boy said.

"You been here long?"

"About two months."

"I'm with Mr. Gasparini. You know him?"

"I seen him a coupla times."

"How many horses you got here?"

"About twenty. We got a few over to Aqueduct."

"Which ones are Mr. Gasparini's?"

"They all over."

"I'll just look around, okay?"

"Sure," the boy said, "that's okay."

I strolled along the shed row, past several other, older stablehands at work, and eyed Monkton's string. None of the animals impressed me much, but then I'm not a real horseman; my game is betting on them. Still, I can spot a real champion when I see one, because they all have an intangible air about them, a quality compounded of power, grace, courage, and a touch of arrogance. A top Thoroughbred wants to run, it's bred into him, and he's as competitive as any human athlete; he'll kill you to win. It's not an especially admirable attribute, in horses or men, but it's what you look for when the money's up. Nice guys finish last, the immortal Leo Durocher once said; nice horses, you could add, run out of the money. Not always, but much of the time. I didn't see any killers in Monkton's barn.

"Do you have a list of Mr. Gasparini's horses?" I asked Walker, when I found him again, this time mucking out a stall.

"I dunno," the boy said, looking a bit sheepish. "Mr. Sanchez, he have one."

"Which way's the training track?" I asked this dynamo.

Walker waved vaguely toward the end of the barn. "Thataway," he said, " 'bout half a mile."

I was feeling lazy and it was very cold, so I got back into my car, drove over to the training track, and parked fairly close to the outside rail. I joined several other watchers about halfway up the stretch just as a ghostly horse and rider galloped by. "Come on, Mommy, behave yourself," the man next to me said, watching the motion of the horse going past. The filly was running smoothly but under tight restraint, with her head to one side, fighting the bit. "Crazy bitch," the man muttered, eyeing the stopwatch in his hand as the horse neared the five-eighths pole.

"She looks good," I volunteered.

"Oh, she can run some," the man said, "but she's ornery. She like to broke down the starting gate the other day."

"She wants to run, maybe."

"She don't know what she wants," the man said. "She don't know what this is all about yet. Some of them never learn." His gaze remained fixed on the filly and he clicked the stopwatch into action as she began to lengthen stride at the half-mile pole, with the boy now curved up over her neck and letting her run some.

It was becoming lighter and in the distance, above the tops of trees, loomed the empty grandstand of the main course. The air was crisp and clean, the only sound being the rhythmic drumming of the hooves as a couple of dozen horses and riders moved at varying speeds over the dark-brown surface of the track, still damp from a recent rain.

After the filly had run a half-mile, the trainer beside me clicked his stopwatch again and grunted. "How'd she do?" I asked.

"Forty-eight and three, but she was just breezing," he said, his eyes still on her as the boy eased up. "She's still about a month away, too fat and much too mean."

"What's her name?"

"Goonavere."

"You mean as in Queen Guinevere, King Arthur's lady?"

"I guess. I don't name 'em." He cast a quick, appraising eye over his animal as she came trotting past him on her way back to the stable. He looked up at the rider, a tall, bony Latin American boy with high cheekbones and a concentrated, unsmiling face half-hidden under a red-and-white crash helmet. "All right, Juan?"

"She move pretty good, Mr. Quinlan," the boy answered, slowing the filly to a walk. "It's still wet out there and I didn't ask her for much. She seem all right."

"Yeah, it's a goddamn swamp underneath," Quinlan said. "No sense takin' any chances. Thanks, Juan."

The boy clucked to the filly and rode off, standing high in the stirrups like a champion jock. "He looks big for a jockey," I said.

"He can make the weight, but he ain't no jock," Quinlan declared. "He's like me when I was ridin'. I had good hands and there wasn't nothin' I couldn't get on, but I wasn't no race rider. Never had the feel for it."

I took a closer look at him. He was short, but sturdily built, with a square, rosy-cheeked face, thick, wavy reddish brown hair going to gray, a good-humored mouth, and the small, canny eyes of a cardshark. "You were a jockey?"

"For about three years, in my teens," he said. "Then I got to eatin' pretty good. You ain't a horseman, are ya?"

I smiled. "Not me. But I like to bet on them."

"You a tout or somethin'?"

"No, just a horseplayer. I have an interest in a few horses with a friend of mine. He's a singer, Fulvio Gasparini."

"Never heard of him. What's he sing?"

"Opera, mostly."

"Godamighty, I can't stand that stuff."

I stuck out my hand and introduced myself. "I'm just poking around this morning."

"Andy Quinlan," he said. "Some people call me Red."

"Which do you like?"

"It don't matter a damn to me. What's this Shifty deal?"

"I'm a magician and I'm good with cards," I explained.

"Remind me not to play poker with you," he said. "Well, I got some errands to run. Nice talkin' to ya."

"Red, I'd sure like to pick your brains a little," I told him. "I just got here and I'm kind of feeling my way about."

"Well, I'll be over to the kitchen in about half an hour, if you want to come by."

"Where are you stabled, in case I miss you?"

"Barn 33."

"Really? Monkton's barn?"

"He don't have all of it. I'm down at one end, with four stalls."

"That's who trains for us."

"That so?" Quinlan said. His expression did not change, but he had the look in his little eyes of a man holding aces while listening to a guy obviously chasing an inside straight. "Well, see ya later." And he strolled leisurely away from me back toward the barn.

I decided not to look for Sanchez until I could have another conversation with Quinlan and maybe steer him around to the larger subject of Gerald Monkton, so I stayed at the rail for another twenty minutes or so to watch the horses, until my ears started to sting, then got back in my car and nosed about until I found the backstretch cafeteria.

It was a little after eight when I walked in and the place was crowded; the workouts were mostly over and there was still time before the vans had to be loaded for the afternoon's card at Aqueduct. Track employees, trainers, stablehands, exercise boys, jockeys, and their agents sat at the tables and milled about the counter under blown-up photographs of famous old race horses and vanished human heroes of the turf. The room was heavy with smoke and laughter and loud talk, but I had no trouble finding Quinlan. He was sitting by himself at a small table near the door and nodded to me as I came in. I procured myself a cup of coffee and joined him.

"Couldn't find the damn vet," he said, as I sat down. "Them guys sure want to get paid on time, but you can't get 'em when you need 'em."

"You got a sick horse?"

"There's always somethin', believe me. I got an old gelding, he can run some, but he's got a little abscess we gotta clear up. Always somethin'. But I guess you know that."

"Yeah, I've heard the tale before."

"So tell me, how come you and this opera fella—"

But our conversation was interrupted by the arrival of a fat, short man in a long blue overcoat down to his ankles. "Hey, Red," he said, gazing down at us from a corner of the table, "what'd you have out there today? Anything I ought to know about?" He had heavy-lidded eyes blown up behind thick glasses, with a black wool cap perched on the back of his head and a pair of enormous binoculars around his neck. "Did I miss anything?"

"Hello, Art," Quinlan said. "You want to clock my workouts, you'd better get your ass out of bed in the mornings."

Art allowed himself to smile, a reaction that obviously did not come easily to him. "Come on, Andy," he said, "I'll get it from somebody else anyway."

"Nothin' to tell you, Art," Quinlan said. "Track's still pretty wet. I didn't ask 'em for anything."

"Okay. I'm not wrong about that colt you're running in the fourth today, am I?"

"I don't know. What'd you say about him? I never read your sheet."

"You ought to. Might get yourself some winners. I said he showed nothing. Put him in at fifteen to one. Am I wrong?"

"He worked okay the other day."

"He blew out in one-o-one. I wasn't too impressed."

"Then why ask me?"

"You weren't holding him, were you?"

"You figure it out."

"Well, you don't work your horses fast, but I figure he ain't much."

"His daddy, Sing Sing, could run some," Quinlan said, "and the mare had speed."

"You never ran him at two. What happened?"

"Popped osselets in both ankles," Quinlan explained. "I had to fire him and turn him out for six months. Then when I had him training pretty good again, he popped a split. I fired him again, had to. He's gonna be a useful animal, Art, maybe win a few races. I sure hope so. I got about forty thousand dollars tied up in him."

"So you own a piece of him, right?"

"I went in with Welch."

"I hear he's giving you a hard time."

The trainer shrugged. "He likes to win. So do I. Anyway, I'll have Dragon ready pretty soon."

"Dragoon? How's he coming along?"

"Fine. He runs real good fresh, you know."

"Yeah," Art said, with satisfaction, "I caught him a couple of times last fall. At good prices, too. They just don't believe that horse."

Quinlan smiled. "If I had two more like him," he said, "I'd be in business."

"You like anything today?"

"Hell, Art, you know I never bet."

"Yeah, and the sun don't come up in the morning either." Art smiled again, this time looking like the small fat kid who owns the only ball and bat in the game. "I'll see you, Red." He sauntered away from us and stopped by another table.

"A clocker?" I asked.

"Art Mendola," Quinlan answered. "He's got a tout sheet."

"Not a horseman either."

Quinlan laughed. "He don't know a horse from a beetle, Mr. Anderson."

"Please call me Shifty."

"Sure."

"What's your colt's name?" I asked. "The one who's running today."

"Anchor. If he breaks good, he can run some."

"I'll bet him."

"Don't bet much. He drew the inside and I don't know how he's going to like that wet dirt in his face."

"Does he have any speed?"

"Some, enough to get position. He'll be all right."

"Thanks," I said. "I don't know much about New York racing, so I'm going to take it easy. But then I'm not a big plunger either."

"Good way to go broke, Shifty. I've been there, too."

"Do you mind if I ask you about Monkton?"

"Nope." He glanced at his watch. "I got a coupla minutes. What do you want to know?"

"Is he a good trainer?"

The horseman took his time answering that one. His hands curved around his cup and he slowly lifted it to his mouth, took a long sip, and deliberately set it down again. His eyes, narrowed almost to little slits, glanced quickly about the room. "Good?" he finally echoed my question. "What do you mean by 'good'?"

"Does he win races?"

"Some."

"Am I asking the wrong questions?"

"Nope."

"Anything else you want to tell me?"

Quinlan thought it over, while he raised the coffee to his lips again. "Monkton don't make the horse, Shifty. He's got that Ignatz."

"Who?"

"The Mexican who works for him."

"Sanchez?"

"Yeah, they call him Ignatz."

"That's a funny name."

"Well, I don't know how they spell it. It's somethin' like that," Quinlan elaborated. "Anyway, he's the one with the horses. That ain't what Monkton's good at."

"What is he good at?"

Quinlan permitted himself a tiny smile that narrowed his eyes still further. "Talkin' to owners."

"I guess that's a talent."

"Wish I had it," the trainer said. "I'd be a rich man today." He stood up. "Well, Shifty, nice talkin' to ya."

"Yeah, thanks, Red. By the way, how do you talk to owners?"

"I tell 'em the truth," Quinlan answered. "Most of 'em don't want to hear it." And he walked away, moving slowly on his feet, like an aging fakir over a bed of nails.

After he'd gone, I fished the *Racing Form* out of my coat pocket and took a look at the fourth race. I couldn't find Anchor listed in the entries, but I did come upon an animal named Encore, owned by Jack Welch and trained by Andrew Quinlan. The man obviously had a genius for creative mispronunciation. Anyway, I liked what I saw in the *Form*—a pattern of nice, evenly spaced works and a good speed rider named Ted Bates up. I decided I'd risk a small wager on him and maybe bet on him for Fulvio as well. I don't know why, but I had good feelings about Red Quinlan.

I never did get to meet Gerald Monkton that first day, because the trainer never came by to check on his horses. When I eventually got back to Barn 33, I found the string being tended to by a large, middle-aged man with a dark, pockmarked complexion and a scraggly mustache. Dressed in dirty khakis, an old padded windbreaker, and scuffed boots, he looked like an unsuccessful bandit, not exactly Turf Club fodder. When I introduced myself to him, he gave me a callused, sweaty hand to hold and his gaze strayed unhappily away from me, as if I presented an almost unbearable complication in his life. "Señor Monkton, he not here," he said. "Maybe he come later."

"Where would I find him?"

"Maybe this afternoon, at the track."

"Well, I guess he'll be in the Turf and Field Club, right?"

Sanchez nodded, still not looking at me. "*Sí.*"

"I'm not sure I can get in there," I said, "but I'll find him eventually. Do you have a phone number for him?"

Sanchez nodded again. "Oh, yes."

"Then maybe I'll call him. Could I see our horses, please? Your boy didn't seem to know which ones they were."

"Oh, sure." He shouted out something in Spanish to one of the grooms at work in a nearby stall, then took me on a quick tour of Fulvio's animals.

I made notes on them and jotted down some quick impressions, then caught up to Sanchez again as he was getting ready to check the bandages on one of the horses he'd brought back from the track earlier. "Listen, what about the horse that broke down the other day?" I asked.

"Oh, the French filly," he said. "Yeah, she got a bone chip. Señor Monkton, he ship her out to the ranch."

"Where's the ranch?"

"Down south."

"Any other of Mr. Gasparini's horses there?"

"I don't know. You ask Señor Monkton."

"Okay. Anyway, thanks. You've been a help."

"All right," he said, not looking at me and moving down the row of stalls to survey another of his charges.

"By the way, is your first name Ignatz?" I couldn't resist asking.

"Ignatz?" He looked back at me in surprise. "Ignacio."

"Oh, sure. I should have known."

I went back to my car to spend half an hour in solitude with my *Racing Form,* then drove out of the barn area and nosed about the streets in the vicinity until I found a diner with a public phone. I was certain it was still too early to call Fulvio, but I had no compunctions at all about rousing Miss Willows. She was awake but unenthusiastic to hear the sound of my voice. "I don't think Fulvio can come to the phone today," she said. "He goes straight from here to a costume fitting and this afternoon there's a fourth-act run-through."

"That's okay," I said, "but he'll want to know what our action is."

"Yes, I see."

"Do you have something to write on?"

"Of course."

"Good. Then please tell Fulvio that he's betting two hundred dollars across the board in the fourth race on a horse called Encore, a name he'll appreciate, I'm sure. And a fifty-dollar Exacta box in the seventh on the four and five. Got that?"

"I suppose so."

"He'll want to know, so please tell him."

"Did you meet Gerry?"

"Monkton? No, he wasn't around, but I talked to Sanchez."

"Who?"

"His foreman. I may look up Monkton this afternoon. I'm going to Aqueduct for the races."

"Should you do that?"

"That's what Fulvio's paying me for," I explained. "I don't want him betting at the OTB, because they rip you off there with the added take-out and he's been losing. Besides, I'm not going to be seeing much of him, am I, until this *Otello* opens?"

"He'll want to talk to you, so I'll call you."

"Good."

"And Jeanine wants to see you."

"I want to see her, too."

"Do you? That should be interesting."

"Actually, I'd like to get it over with."

I drove to Aqueduct, sat in the grandstand all afternoon, and made no effort to find Monkton. I'd decided that there were things I needed to look into before actually meeting him, so I sat in the grandstand by myself, watched the races, and made our bets. We finished one–three in the Exacta, but by then it didn't matter; Red Quinlan's maiden had enriched us. Encore went off at twenty-two to one and ran a closing second, after breaking alertly but being shuffled back along the rail and forced to come wide into the stretch. He paid $16.40 to place and $7 even to show.

On the way out of the track, after the ninth, I found myself on a down escalator behind Art Mendola, who was still attired in his morning costume, but with the stump of a spent cigar now growing like a diseased mushroom out of his mouth. "That maiden of Quinlan's ran pretty well," I observed.

Mendola looked back at me, but with no indication that he had ever seen me before. "The son of a bitch," he said, "he's always pulling that shit on me."

"He didn't tell you the horse couldn't run, did he?"

"Some trainers I can read like a book," he said. "Quinlan don't give nothin' away. I never know when the bastard's firing."

"Maybe he doesn't know either."

"He knows," Mendola said, "he knows, the son of a bitch."

"He's a pretty good trainer, huh?"

"He's a good horseman," the tout corrected me, "one of the best. If he played the game right, he'd make some big scores."

"What about Gerald Monkton? You know him?"

"A bum," Art Mendola said, "a phony bum with a heart as tiny as all indoors."

"Nice talking to you, Art," I said, as we hit bottom and he shuffled morosely away from me toward a row of parked limousines. He didn't answer.

ELEVEN

♦

Long Views

I wasn't prepared for Jeanine La-
grange. I went up to see her the morning after my first winning day
at Aqueduct, expecting to be introduced to some sort of formidable
ice lady, and I found myself confronted by one of the most attractive
women I'd ever met. Although I was reasonably certain that she
was older, she looked about thirty. She had a slender, well-
proportioned figure with long legs that made her seem taller than
she was, an impression accentuated by elegant black pumps, a
beautifully tailored dark-gray business suit, and a short, upswept
hairdo of thick, dark curls topping a long, intelligent-looking face.
She wore no lipstick and very little makeup, but her naturally dark
complexion enhanced a startling pair of large, very dark green eyes
with dismayingly long lashes. When I was ushered into her office
by her secretary Gregory, the cheerful young gay I'd already spo-
ken to several times on the phone, she rose and came around from
behind her curved desk to greet me. She shook my hand firmly and
asked me to sit down on a loveseat across from her. "I'm very glad
you could come," she said. "I realize now that we should have met
some weeks ago."

"I'm not sure that we'd have enjoyed that," I said. "You haven't
been exactly friendly on the phone."

"I'm sorry," she said. "I was simply protecting my client's interests. Fulvio attracts a lot of very dubious people."

"And I'm certainly as dubious as any."

She smiled. "Well, your name . . ." And she shrugged, waggling
one hand next to her face, a very Latin gesture.

"You're not American, are you?" I asked.

"Oh, no. I'm Italian."

"Really? You speak perfect English."

"I was very young when we came over here. And I have a certain facility, I suppose."

"I'll say. What part of Italy?"

"Near Naples. But please, let's not talk about me, Mr. Anderson." Her phone rang and she picked it up, then stood up and headed quickly for the door. "Excuse me one moment."

During her absence, I gazed idly around. The room was large and airy, on the top floor of an old office building directly across from Carnegie Hall and with a terrace looking down over Fifty-seventh Street. The walls were decorated with concert posters advertising the wares of a number of Lagrange clients, including Fulvio, a blowup of whose beaming, bearded countenance occupied most of the wall directly behind the desk. The furniture consisted of a few elegant and comfortable pieces, the most impressive of which was Jeanine Lagrange's desk, crescent-shaped and piled high with papers neatly stacked into various categories. It was a no-nonsense office, functional and devoid of frills and amenities, except for a single tall, waxy-looking tree rising out of one corner, between two sets of shoulder-high filing cabinets.

I was looking down over the street when she returned, shutting the door firmly behind her. "Sorry," she said. "I have a contract going out today, a messenger waiting, and I forgot to sign my covering letter. There is too much going on here."

"I do have the feeling you're pretty busy."

"If you only knew," she commented, sitting down behind her desk again.

"By the way, Lagrange isn't an Italian name, is it?"

"I was married once," she explained, "to Jean Claude Lagrange, the conductor."

"Oh."

"You haven't heard of him."

"No, I'm afraid not."

"I wish I hadn't," she said, flashing me a quick, dazzling smile. "I was not exactly cut out for marriage, you see. When I opened my own agency and began representing many other artists besides Jean Claude, he became a little irritable."

"Just a little?"

Another smile. "Just very much. You understand?"

"I think so."

"But now, Mr. Anderson—"

"Shifty, please."

"Such an odd name."

"It's a question of habit, that's all."

"Yes, well . . ." She frowned and looked briefly away from me, as if making a neat little pile in her head of exactly what she had to say without having to risk another distraction. When she turned back to look at me, she appeared concentrated and severe, more like the woman I had first had to deal with on the phone several weeks earlier. "Do you know, Shifty, what is at the heart of the Fulvio Gasparini phenomenon?"

"He can sure sing up a storm."

"That's only part of it," she said, "because so can many other very gifted artists. No, it is something more. Let me explain. Fulvio is all heart. You hear him sing and you fall in love with him, not because he is good-looking or anything like that, which he is not, but because he is standing there before you—this big, warm boy of a man—and he is singing *only* for you. Do you understand what I'm driving at?"

"Sure. It's the same quality Pavarotti has."

"Precisely. Pavarotti is great, but he is now over fifty. Fulvio has his whole career still before him and he is fabulous. He has such a gift for life that he makes people feel wonderful about themselves. He sings to their deepest feelings about themselves. Do you see what I mean?"

"You don't have to sell me on Fulvio, Jeanine," I said. "I believe you."

"What he has is very, very special," she said, looking away from me now and drumming the fingers of one hand idly on the desk top, as if to define for herself a way to get to the point. "I think that what I'm trying to tell you is that I'm very concerned about him."

"About his gambling?"

"Yes, exactly." She stopped drumming and turned back to me. "Fulvio is sick. He has this terrible compulsion to lose his money. You wouldn't believe how much he has lost over the past couple of years alone."

"I think I would believe you. I've seen him in action. In fact, that's how we met."

"I know the whole story," she said. "He has this crazy idea now that you are going to save him."

"I think I can help him."

"Oh, come now, Shifty, you must think I'm a fool." She sat back in her chair to look at me, a slight but this time not very pleasant smile on her face.

"Whatever I may think of you, Jeanine," I told her, "I would never make that mistake."

"How can you help him?"

"I took this job with him, if you want to call it that," I explained, "on one basic condition—that he would listen to me and do only what I tell him to do. That's the agreement. Didn't Fulvio make that clear to you?"

"What does it matter what he said? All gamblers lie, to others and to themselves."

"Quite true. But that's why I'm pretty hard to fool. If Fulvio won't let me help him, I'll pack up and go. It's as simple as that."

"Why don't I believe you?"

"Because you think I'm a diseased gambler like him," I guessed. "And you think I'm in this just to milk money out of him and take off."

"And isn't that precisely what you are doing?"

"No. Do you want to hear what I think about all this? I've done some heavy cogitating about it."

"Of course. Please enlighten me."

"Okay. First of all, I understand your concern," I said. "Fulvio is a hooked gambler, no doubt about it, and you're quite naturally worried that he's going to go down the tubes financially."

"Many artists have, Shifty. I could name you a dozen."

"Of course. Many quite ordinary citizens have blown their whole lives gambling. We know that. And you're afraid it will overwhelm your client and take the place of everything else."

"It will. It already has."

"Really? I haven't noticed that. My impression is he places the music first. I saw him in Las Vegas and I was at a rehearsal my first day here. We talked horses a little, but all he could really think about was the role. I gather he's been having his problems with Wildwood."

"Luther is a very brilliant director, but he sometimes needs his behind kicked."

"I think Fulvio's doing that superbly."

"I didn't know you were an expert on opera as well."

"I'm not, but in my field I'm a very disciplined performer and I can recognize the genuine thing when I see it."

"You are comparing what you do to Fulvio's art?"

"Sure."

"That's ridiculous."

"To you, maybe, but not to me. How many hours a day does Fulvio devote to his music?"

"Several, at least, when he's working. Or he should."

"I practice four to six hours a day, Jeanine."

"It is not the same."

"I don't make the money Fulvio does. That's the only difference," I insisted. "You don't know anything about magic, so who are you to judge?"

I had not convinced her, but I did succeed in slowing her down a little. She looked long and hard at me, as if trying to bore into my very soul with those fierce dark-green eyes of hers. They reminded me of Simone's, but they were even more exciting in their concentrated intensity. I had a sudden carnal urge toward her, but I quickly squashed it. After Simone, I was in no shape for another adventure of any kind, even though I had to admit to myself that Jeanine Lagrange was quite definitely a woman to be taken seriously in every way. Since I had managed to stand my ground with her, I decided to press my advantage a bit. "And since you've made it clear to me that you think Fulvio's in big trouble with his gambling, in what way am I going to be damaging to him?"

"Because you'll encourage it and he will become ever more deeply involved," she answered quickly. "How can you possibly help him? You happened to win for him and he thinks you are lucky. By the time he loses twice as much as he has been losing and he understands you are simply another degenerate like himself, it will be too late. That is my concern, in a nutshell, as you might say."

"Well, I guess it's up to me to prove you wrong," I argued. "Let me start by explaining something to you."

"Certainly."

"I'm a horseplayer, not a gambler.'"

"There is a difference?"

"Oh, yes. You see, in casino gambling you are playing against the house. The percentages in every game are mathematically rigged against you. Sooner or later the casino must take your money. The night Fulvio met me I got hot and the next day, at roulette, our luck held. But I know you can't win in the long run."

"Then you are here under false pretenses."

"Not at all. When Fulvio told me he was crazy about horses, I was sure I could help him."

"You must lose there, too."

"No, that's where you're wrong, Jeanine," I corrected her. "You see, in horse racing the house cuts the pot, just like a man operating a poker game. After that cut, it's you against the other bettors. The house doesn't establish the odds, the bettors do."

"Why do they all lose, then?"

"They don't. A tiny percentage wins. It's tough, because you're bucking a formidable tiger, which is the house vigorish."

"I beg your pardon?"

"The vigorish is gamblers' terminology for the house cut, Jeanine, which in racing is very high, usually around seventeen percent, but higher in the so-called exotic bets—Trifectas, Exactas, Quiniellas, Pick Sixes, doubles, and so on. Do you follow me so far?"

"Not in detail, but the general outline is clear," she said, sitting back and gazing thoughtfully at me with her hands folded under her chin. "Go on."

"Okay, here's the heart of what I'm driving at," I said, with far more confidence than I actually felt. "In racing, the house is indifferent. The track doesn't care how the pots are split, it already has its share. So the rest of it is ultimately divided among the smarter, tougher, more disciplined players. It's not easy, but you have a chance. In casino gambling, you have no chance. Now—"

"So you are saying that if Fulvio does what you tell him to do, you can make him win," she cut in. "You want to channel his madness into your area of expertise."

"Yeah, that's about it," I agreed. "If Fulvio walks into a casino, I can't stop him, but I can at least gamble intelligently for him and cut his losses. If he'll stick to horse racing, I might even make him a winner."

"Are you a winner, Shifty? Why aren't you rich?"

"I don't do it full-time, Jeanine," I explained. "Like Fulvio, I have an art I'm primarily dedicated to. I consider this job temporary. Between engagements, you might say." I smiled at her, but she did not smile back; the dark-green eyes remained unconvinced and skeptical. "Look, you have nothing to lose," I finally pointed out.

"How so?"

"He's going to bet his money with or without me. He stands a better chance betting with me."

"If you lose, he'll lose more than he's losing now."

"Not possible, Jeanine. Sure, we may hit a bad streak," I said.

"In fact, we'll have losing days, plenty of them. You can't have a real opinion at a racetrack and not let yourself in for a lot of aggravation—losing photos, horses in trouble, bad rides, even some dishonesty. But if Fulvio sticks with me, I can help him, which is all I ever promised, him or you. What can you lose, Jeanine?"

She did not answer right away, but continued to regard me thoughtfully, as if I represented a peculiarly shaped piece in a large puzzle she was working out in her head. She sighed, then stood up and walked over to the window. "I don't know where this will end," she said, as much to herself as to me. "Fulvio is the greatest singer in the world and I am the best manager in the world, but this defeats me, I'm afraid."

"While you're at it, may I ask you something that's been puzzling me?"

"Certainly," she said, turning back to look at me again, her face in shadow, with the light from the window behind her. "What is it?"

"Why did you encourage Fulvio to invest in race horses?"

"I? Encourage?"

"Well, didn't you? You're his manager, after all," I said. "He wouldn't be spending hundreds of thousands of dollars on these expensive animals without at least discussing the matter with you, would he?"

"We have discussed it, yes."

"So I have to assume you advised him to invest in them."

"I took what you might call a long view."

"Which is?"

She did not immediately answer, but returned to her desk and sat down again. "I really don't think I should have to account to you for my actions," she finally said. "Fulvio's investments are a private matter between us. They are none of your business."

"Okay, but I'm going to tell you what I think about it."

"I would welcome that."

"Betting on horses to win is chancy enough," I said. "Investing in expensive racing stock with the idea of turning a profit—"

"I researched all that," she interrupted me. "There are tax advantages."

"Yes, I know that, Jeanine," I said, "but the smart course would have been to invest in stallion shares and broodmares. It's boring, but that's the long view in racing. Putting money into horses at the track in the hope they'll win big purses is like playing the lottery. It's nothing but a numbers racket. You have one chance in ten thousand, if that."

"Why?"

"Because blood lines are a constant and have a market value," I explained. "If a horse is well bred, by a good sire and out of a top mare, the animal has a value, even if it never wins a race. The way to make money in this game is to breed and sell, because good breeding doesn't guarantee that a horse can run. And they are costly to keep in training. When they break down or get sick, there are vet bills. And these animals eat a lot."

"My understanding is that many owners and stables do very well," she said.

"What you read about in the papers are the successes," I pointed out. "You never hear much about the failures—the million-dollar yearlings who get hurt and sick or just can't run. Believe me, it's a tough game."

"I was against the idea, but it can't be tougher than mere gambling."

"It's the riskiest gamble of all."

She sighed. "Well, I suppose I must respect your opinion," she said, "but I did not advise Fulvio to go into this. When he insisted, I got him the best advice I could."

"Gerald Monkton?"

"No, but he was recommended."

"By whom?"

"Now, really. I don't think I should go into all of this with you."

"Why not? Isn't that why you wanted to see me?"

"We have strayed from the main point," she objected, "which is, purely and simply, the gambling aspect."

"Well, that's what we're talking about, I thought. How many horses does Fulvio own?"

"I don't have the exact figure in front of me."

"You mean you don't know?"

"We've given Mr. Monkton a certain amount of capital to invest," she explained. "He must remain within certain parameters."

"Fulvio must be very, very rich," I said.

"I do not discuss the financial status of my clients with anyone," Jeanine admonished me. "But I can tell you that no one in the world of opera today, not even Pavarotti and Domingo, commands larger fees. And I will tell you something else, Mr. Shifty Lou Anderson, I know exactly where we stand, you and I."

"You do? I wish I did."

"I am going to keep a very close watch on you," she said. "If I think you are endangering Fulvio's well-being, you will find me a formidable adversary."

"If Fulvio doesn't make money, I don't make money," I said. "That should reassure you. I'm going to give him the best gambling advice he's ever had."

"We shall see."

I stood up. "Anyway, it's been an education," I said, smiling. "I wouldn't presume to give you advice, Jeanine, but I wouldn't book Fulvio into places like Las Vegas again."

"Next time I can get him half a million dollars a week," she snapped.

"And your percentage comes off the top, right?"

Startled, she recoiled slightly, as if I had suddenly jabbed her with a good left hand. "What are you implying?"

"What you make isn't tied to his gambling losses, Jeanine," I said. "I have a bigger stake in his not losing than you do."

"How dare you?" she asked, standing up, her face white with fury. "How dare you?"

The intensity of her reaction astonished me. "I don't know," I said. "How do I? My own mother could never answer that question." I got up and eased myself toward the door. "It's been fun visiting with you."

I quickly let myself out of her office. One of my strengths as a performer has always been knowing when to get off.

"What you say to Jeanine you make her so angry?" Fulvio asked me on the phone that evening.

"I don't know, Fulvio," I answered. "I guess there's just something about me that pisses her off."

"No, is serious, *mio caro*."

I explained my point of view to him. "I think she got angry," I concluded, "when I pointed out that she really doesn't have a rooting interest in whether you win or lose."

"*Come?* Is Jeanine who handle all of my business."

"Her commission comes off the top, that's what I mean."

"She is very good manager, *mago*. If she say is good investment, I do it. She don't like my gambling."

"That's clear enough. Fulvio?"

"*Sì?*"

"Whose idea was it to buy all these horses?"

"Jeanine, of course."

"It wasn't your idea?"

"She come to me with this plan and she tell me she have found a trainer for me. Is good tax business, she say, much better than betting."

"She found Monkton?"

"Some friend of hers. Jeanine knows nothing about horses, *mago*. But listen—"

"Yes?"

"Be nice to her. When we win much money, she will be nice to you. I tell her to leave you alone."

"Thanks, I'd appreciate that."

"Now, my wizard, why we have not bet today? I was waiting for you to call."

"I figured you were busy and I'm still feeling my way, Fulvio. I couldn't find a good bet."

"You find one the other day."

"We were lucky."

"And tomorrow?"

"Tomorrow's Tuesday, Fulvio. The track is closed. I only go when it's open."

"Ah, *sì*, of course." He laughed, his voice threatening to shatter my eardrum. "When this *Otello* is over, then we have a good time, *va bene*?"

"Sure. And by then maybe I'll know something. How are rehearsals going?"

"Is all right, *mago*. You will see tomorrow at the dress. You are coming? I tell Anna."

"Of course. I wouldn't miss it."

"*Bene*. I am in a sea of *stronzi, mio caro*, but I will sing such an *Otello* Verdi will rise from his tomb to kiss me. *Ciao*." And he hung up.

I got up off the bed and fished out my notes on Fulvio's horses, then I put in a call to Jay Fox in L.A. He wasn't in, so I decided to order something from room service and wait for him to get back to me. I had the *Racing Form* to read, so it wasn't as if I had nothing to do with my time.

TWELVE

♦

Untouchables

"Where have you been?" Anna Willows hissed in my ear. "I've been trying to reach you all morning."

"I'm sorry, I've been moving."

"Moving? Where?"

"Out of that overpriced fleabag you put me into."

"Where are you?"

"I found an okay motel way over on the West Side," I told her. "I can't afford these New York prices."

"How dreary," she said. "Anyway, I wasn't sure you'd gotten the message. Fulvio's been driving me mad."

"He must be nervous."

"Oh, God, you don't know the half of it," she whispered. "He's always like this before a dress or a first night. And then Gerry's been calling."

"Monkton?"

"Yes. He heard you'd been around the stable. He wants to meet you."

"Well, maybe tomorrow. I'll be going to the races for sure," I said. "Pepperdine, one of Fulvio's horses, is running."

"How do you know?"

"I saw the entries."

"Shit, now Fulvio will want to go. He won't be able to and he'll be impossible all day."

"Why can't he go? He's not singing tomorrow, is he?"

114

"He can't risk it," she explained. "If he gets too excited and shouts, he could hurt his vocal cords. Or he could catch a cold. No, he won't go out till after the first night. But he'll take it out on me."

"That's tough," I said, pretending to a concern I really didn't feel, "but when you're a star someday . . . "

"Oh, up yours," she said, slumping into a seat two down from me. "I hate this. I wish it were over."

I didn't. In fact, I was pretty excited, since this was the first dress rehearsal I'd ever attended in an opera house. At Fulvio's insistence, it had been closed to all but a couple of hundred close friends of the cast and family members, who sat scattered about the huge auditorium, well away from working company staff members, including Luther Wildwood and his entourage. I was sitting on the left side this time, two-thirds of the way back, but with a great view of the whole stage and with my Zeiss racing glasses draped comfortably around my neck. "Fulvio's so nervous," Anna said, as much to herself as to me. "If Caterina screws him up again, he'll kill her."

"Well, you wouldn't mind that, would you? Aren't you covering the role?"

"Not officially, but what does it matter? That bitch has never missed a performance in her life," she grumbled. "She has a throat of iron and sounds it."

The conductor, a chunky young bullfrog of a man with a great mane of Ethiopian curls, made his way through the orchestra pit and mounted the podium. As the house lights began to dim, I saw Achille Pipistrello sitting off to one side a few rows in front of me. He looked just the same, perhaps even grumpier, yellower, and more cadaverous than when I'd first met him. "Where's Pipistrello been?" I asked, leaning toward Anna.

She shot me a look of mild disgust. "He travels with Fulvio, but we don't see as much of him in New York, thank God," she said.

I wondered why, but I didn't have time to ask, because by then the house lights were out and the bullfrog suddenly raised his right arm and brought it crashing down into the middle of a Verdian hurricane. I was immediately overwhelmed and could think of nothing else the entire act. If this opera isn't a masterpiece, then I've never heard one, and the cast sang magnificently. Fulvio, especially, was in splendid voice. He made his initial appearance at the top of a ramp, presumably leading to the storm-tossed harbor of Cyprus, and belted out an opening phrase that mesmerized me with its purity and power. I couldn't imagine why it had taken me so long to discover opera; I'd always enjoyed the fragments of vocal music I'd heard all my life, but I'd never had occasion to really get into it. Not enough money, not enough time, and then, of course, all those years in Los Angeles, which has always been an operatic wasteland. Twenty minutes into this *Otello*, I knew that my life had changed, that from now on I'd be an opera buff, thanks to Fulvio. Odd, I reflected, where a passion for horses could lead you . . .

I became completely lost in the musical drama of the jealous Moor, his sappily innocent bride, and the incarnation of evil Verdi had created in the role of Iago, being sung in this edition by a good-looking young American baritone with a great dark voice like a cathedral bell. Only toward the end of the act did I become aware that something a bit out of the ordinary was apparently going on between the protagonist and his trusting wife. Fulvio and Caterina Pantaloni were singing mellifluously of their undying love, but neither seemed to be paying the least attention to the other; they faced front and sang out to the audience, like a couple of AIDS victims afraid of infecting each other. It jarred somewhat, even though the music carried us along and they were warbling beautifully. Then, quite suddenly and for no apparent reason, Caterina stepped directly in front of Fulvio, her arms flung out imploringly toward the upper balconies. "What's she doing?" I whispered to Anna. "Has she got relatives up there?"

"The bitch," Anna answered. "Fulvio will kill her."

He didn't. In fact, he began by trying to counter her movements so as to stay clear of her, but she persisted in repeating the maneuver on every one of her phrases, thus effectively blocking him from the chin down every time he opened his mouth to sing. Finally, Fulvio must have decided to put an end to it. At the point in the duet where he asks her for a kiss, the tenor simply picked the soprano up by her waist and set her firmly to one side; then, on her music, he strolled nonchalantly past her, completely obliterating her with his bulk, on his way back into the castle and slammed the door in her face.

"Oh, Christ!" Anna exclaimed and bolted out of her seat toward backstage, as the house lights came up.

The conductor, ashen-faced and wild-eyed, turned on the director, who by this time was himself rushing down the aisle toward the scene of the action, trailed by his groupies. Jeanine Lagrange, whom I hadn't noticed before and with a worried-looking Gregory in her wake, was also on her way from another part of the auditorium, and all around me people were bunching up in agitated knots to discuss this crisis in human relations. It left me entirely indifferent; I was sure the dilemma would be resolved soon enough without me and I stayed where I was. My head was full of Verdi's music and nothing else mattered much to me at that point, not enough to make me want to concern myself with anything else. Opera stars were supposed to be outrageous, I reasoned, so let them fight it out among themselves. In the opera house, Fulvio didn't need my help; he was a winner at any price.

The only other person who seemed unmoved by this crisis was Achille Pipistrello. The old man remained in place, his hands resting stolidly on an ivory-headed cane tucked between his bony knees. After about fifteen minutes, during which the hurried comings and goings from front to backstage and the continued absence of the conductor from the pit indicated a further delay in the proceedings, I got up and went down to say hello. "Ah, the wizard," the old man said, as I shook his hand. "So you did come."

"Fulvio didn't tell you?"

"I have not seen him."

"Is something wrong?"

The old man shrugged. "Wrong? What is to be wrong?"

"Aren't you with Fulvio anymore?"

"Oh, yes, yes, of course. But here in New York it is not necessary that I am with him. He is inside the opera house, where there are many other musical assistants."

"Oh, so you only travel with him."

"And when he has a new role to learn or an old one to study again."

I sat down on the arm of the seat in front of him and waved toward the stage. "What do you think of this?"

"It is much foolishness, my friend," the old man said. "It is something that will pass."

"I hope so," I said. "I hope it doesn't ruin the performance. This is the most terrific thing I've ever heard."

"Yes, poor Verdi. Poor Mozart, poor Rossini," Pipistrello said, "they have to suffer the madness of the sacred monsters."

"What's going to happen?"

"Nothing, Signor Anderson. There will be scenes, there will be tears, there will be shouting, although always well projected and in pitch, oh yes. Then there will be a solution found and all will proceed as normal as before."

"This is normal?"

The old man smiled at last. "Nothing is normal in the opera house," he said. "Normal is outside. In here it is all *fantasia* and tears. But what does it matter, eh? It is Verdi who counts, not these little children with their *capricci*."

"Their what?"

"The scenes that children make." He smiled again, then glanced beyond me and around the auditorium. "But about you—did nothing happen?" he asked.

"Happen? What do you mean?"

He shifted slightly in his seat, as if suddenly uncomfortable in his underpants. "Perhaps I make too much of it."

"Oh, so it *was* you," I said. "I thought so. It *was* your note."

"You could tell?"

"I guessed, when you misspelled 'careful.' There's an *e* in it."

"Ah, I have not studied English, you know."

"I'd like to see you," I said. "Can we get together?"

Again he looked around, then reached swiftly into his wallet, pulled out a card, and gave it to me. "If you wish." But he did not seem overly delighted at the prospect. "Perhaps during the day," he said, "when I am at the workshop."

Behind me I could hear a stirring in the hall. The conductor had reappeared, followed by Wildwood, and I guessed the rehearsal would be resuming soon. Some sort of modus vivendi must have been reached; union musicians and stagehands could not be allowed to languish expensively in place, even on the whims of sacred monsters. I leaned down toward the old man. "What was supposed to happen, Achille?" I asked.

The sharp brown eyes bored into mine, but then he shrugged and looked away. "You were late in arriving."

"Well, I *was* mugged. And then—"

"You were attacked?" he asked, jerking his head around toward me.

"Yeah, in a parking lot."

"Agostino," the old man mumbled.

"Who's he?"

"What did he look like?"

"He hit me from behind. I didn't see him."

The old man shook his head. "Perhaps not," he said. "What else?"

"Well, I met this lady—"

"A lady? What lady?" Pipistrello asked, the brown eyes alive with alarm.

"I'll tell you about it when I see you," I said. The conductor had mounted the podium and rapped on his stand for the attention of his musicians, as the house lights had begun to dim again. "I'm sure it was nothing important."

"Perhaps not, no. I imagine too much."

I did not speak to Achille Pipistrello again that afternoon. He left long before the end of the opera, but I was so caught up in the performance that I paid no attention to anything else. Perhaps as a result of their contretemps, both Fulvio and Caterina sang more bewitchingly than ever the rest of the way, especially during the big scene in act three, when Otello assaults his wife and then humiliates her in the presence of the Venetian ambassador. They were both extremely convincing in their distress, especially when Fulvio flung Caterina to the floor. But only in the last scene, when Otello is supposed to strangle Desdemona, did matters really get out of hand again. As the Moor leaned over her supposedly sleeping form, Desdemona suddenly sat up, bounded out of bed, and ran out of the room. She did not reappear until it was time for the murder to be discovered. Anna gasped and someone behind me laughed. "She must have taken poison in the bathroom," a voice whispered.

To his credit, Fulvio ignored her behavior. He simply remained in place, pretended that the scene had gone exactly as it was supposed to, and sang stupendously. I was in tears when the curtain came down and so was Luther Wildwood, but not for the same reason. "How can they do this to me?" he shrieked, as he ran down the aisle toward the stage. "How dare they?"

I saw Jeanine Lagrange and the bullfrog also heading for backstage and I could hear an uproar already in progress behind the Met's massive gold curtain. "Oh, God," Anna said, groaning. She got up and left as well, but I had no interest in witnessing this carnage. My head was full of song and drama, so I made my way through the tense little crowd now gathered in anxious bunches in the aisles and found my way out into the street. Let them deal with it; I was going home to commune with old Joe Green, as a magician friend of mine used to refer to the Italian genius.

I had moved out of the hotel Anna had booked me into, a trendy little hostelry catering mainly to out-of-town classical-music lovers, partly because it was too expensive, but also because it wasn't worth the money. The employees were a surly lot, who seemed to consider my presence on the premises an inconvenience, and the room was small, dark, and dismally decorated, with a heavy emphasis on neo-Victorian bric-a-brac. My one window looked out on a monolithic cracker-box apartment building that shut off the daylight, and the street below had apparently been designated by the city for twenty-four-hour engine-revving and horn practice, with early-morning interludes of siren-sounding. I decided that for half the money I could have a motel room over by the river that was no less hideous but at least had no pretensions to sustain and seemed to be patronized by the New Jersey wash-and-wear set. My room there was larger, quieter, and admitted some daylight, even though, decoratively speaking, it left a good deal to be desired. Plastic and Naugahyde prevailed, but then, for sixty bucks a night, I could hardly expect the Imelda Marcos bridal suite.

The main problem with my new digs was getting there, which turned out to be not even half the fun. I'd already had my fill of New York taxis, all of which seemed to have been designed by Procrustes and were driven either by surly paranoids or newly arrived aliens in training for Le Mans, so I chose to walk. This whisked me into an obstacle course designed to test Darwin's theory of survival of the fittest. I had to thread my way cautiously for fourteen blocks, first past parallel rows of festering brownstones inhabited, I presumed, by muggers' training teams, whose members idled on their front stoops between raids, sizing me up as I passed. Whole blocks had apparently been set aside in emulation of Hamburg's famous red-light district, with miniskirted hookers lining the sidewalks while their pimps hovered within knifing distance. Welfare hotels teemed with the marginal survivors, whose hordes of untamed progeny ran loose about the streets, getting themselves an education in the subtler aspects of pursuing the American dream, instantly on sale there from their friendly neighborhood dope peddlers. In every doorway the losers slumped—bums, bag ladies, panhandlers, lunatics, and the merely homeless—the invisible dead and dying to whom, for some reason, nothing from Ronald Reagan's resurgent corporate America seemed to have trickled down. Too bad. What we clearly needed, I found myself thinking, was a Swiftian solution to the dilemma of the poor. Why couldn't we just eat them?

By the time I reached my motel lobby, which was guarded, I now noticed, by a uniformed young black with a gun, I felt as if I had survived some sort of Hogarthian nightmare. "Is there a way to get here by helicopter?" I asked the pale young man behind the desk.

"From where, sir?" he answered, looking puzzled.

"From anywhere. Do you think I can do this every day?"

"I'm sorry, sir, but I don't understand."

"Never mind," I told him. "You've got a nice place here, if I didn't have to get to it by walking through somebody's colon."

I might as well have been babbling in Urdu, for all the reaction I could get from this wimp, so I picked up my messages and mail and went up to my room, bolting the door behind me.

There were two bills, a chatty postcard from Vince Michaels, and a note from Hal informing me that Hugo had decided not to sublet my apartment after all, since he now felt, understandably enough, that he couldn't trust the neighborhood. There was a message from Gerald Monkton asking me to meet him for lunch in the Turf and Field Club at Aqueduct the following afternoon. And there was a call from Jay Fox, asking me to return it at home.

The Fox sounded in excellent form when I got him on the line ten minutes later, from which I gathered he had been winning. "Oh, yes, Shifty," he confirmed, "it's been a very profitable week." And he proceeded to regale me with a detailed account of how he had put over a winning show parlay on Friday, running a twenty-dollar bill up to over a thousand through six races. "That was just the start of it," he concluded. "I took that grand and hammered it into three by Sunday night. I'm in a good swing, Shifty. What are you up to?"

I told him about the *Otello,* but he didn't seem impressed. "Nothing succeeds in opera like excess," he observed. "What about the horse action there?"

"So far I've made one bet and we cashed it," I said. "I'm moving cautiously, Jay. Fulvio's pretty much tied up until the opening on Friday and I'm getting myself an education. They play some games here in New York I haven't quite figured out yet."

"Well, don't go overboard on Monkton," he warned me. "That's what I'm calling you about."

"I figured. What did you find out?"

"He's a very low-percentage trainer," the Fox said. "He has good stock and he enters a lot of races, but he doesn't win. He looks like the kind of trainer I call a magician. Their horses look good on paper and at the track, but they invariably make them disappear by the eighth pole. You want the stats?"

"Sure."

"Okay, last year he entered two hundred and twelve races, mostly in New York, and won eight, none of them stakes. How does that grab you?"

"It doesn't. You wonder how these guys stay in business."

"That's easy, Shifty. They steal."

"Maybe he's independently wealthy."

"Okay, about your opera singer's horses—"

"Yeah?"

"Not much there," he said. "Battle Flag is an English-bred three-year-old maiden, winless in five sprints here, but he may want more distance. Basingstoke is a five-year-old plodder who's won a few races at one and a half to two miles on minor tracks in England. He hasn't run here yet, but they don't write many races at those distances in the States. Mazarin is a French six-year-old gelding who's won a Group II and several Group III races in France, but he's been having leg problems, they say. Pepperdine's got speed, but usually breaks slow, rushes up, and spits it out in the stretch."

"Grand."

"The other three you mentioned—Tumbles, Iolanthe, and Mad Margaret—haven't run yet."

"Pepperdine's in tomorrow."

"Well, don't risk anything on her."

"Not a dime, Jay. I'm meeting Monkton for lunch."

"That should be interesting. You know something else?"

"What?"

"The guy used to be a winner, back in San Francisco, where he started out," Jay said. "Of course, all he had then was cheap claimers. But he was always in the top five in the standings, he was live."

"Well, maybe he's just in a bad swing," I said. "That happens to everyone, right?"

"Sure, Shifty," Jay said. "Jesus came back, so why can't Gerald Monkton?"

THIRTEEN

◆

Homework

Red Quinlan was sitting on a bench out in the wintry sunlight, smoking and talking to his groom, a stocky black kid named Jefferson. "They cool out fine, Mr. Quinlan," the boy said, as I came up behind him. "You want to do 'em up now?"

"Yeah, Jeff, I think we'd better," the trainer said. "We're running a little short on time today."

"Yes, sir. You takin' the filly?"

"Yeah. You can put the bandages on Bundle. The van'll be here for him at ten." The boy left and the trainer stood up, grinding his cigarette out under his boot heel. "Can't stay away, is that it?" he asked me, with the hint of a smile.

"Nice race your colt ran the other day."

"Yeah, better than I thought he would. I'm going to give him one more sprint and then stretch him out. He'll be fine, if I can keep him sound." He picked up a currycomb, a sponge, some rags, and a pail of soapy water, then headed for Guinevere's stall. "Don't bet the one I got in today."

"Bandolier?"

"Yeah, Bundle. Can't run a lick."

"We've got Pepperdine running," I said. "If she gets out of the gate."

"He don't never work her out of it, so she'll have to learn how on her own," Quinlan observed.

"Has Monkton been around today?"

123

"Ain't seen him."

"I'm supposed to meet him for lunch in the Turf and Field Club."

"We'll be there."

"You?"

Quinlan glanced back at me and grinned. "My owner likes to sit in there," he said. "Makes him feel important." Without hesitating, he stepped into the filly's stall. The animal shifted uneasily on her lead, swung her head around, and focused a large, mad eye on him. "All right, Mommy," the trainer said, coming up on her left and going right to work on her, "all right now, you take it easy. This ain't gonna hurt. Look at you—mud from your ears to your toes." At his first touch the horse shivered and lunged for him, but Quinlan had anticipated the move of her head and was quickly out of reach, already at work on her with the sponge. "Now does that hurt?" he asked softly. "Does it? Oh, I know you. I know you like to be left alone, but this won't take long now."

Talking softly to her all the while, Quinlan continued to work on her, taking care to keep always out of reach of her teeth. Once she swung her rump around and he was forced to grab her tail and leap to one side to avoid a vicious kick. "Hey now," he said, not raising his voice or pausing in his work, "what were you gonna do, Mommy, kill me?" He grinned at me. "She's pretty crazy and she can hate, but she's the kind that can run. Yeah, Mommy, I'll bring you up to a race. I don't care if you do blow your top and I got to catch you with a net. All right, here we go now. . . ."

While he was finishing with her, I walked down two stalls to see how Jeff was getting along with Bandolier. The boy was on his knees, putting the final touches to the protective bandages on the animal's front legs. He was having no trouble at all because Bandolier, small and brown and sleepy-looking, was standing placidly over him, sniffing up his back for concealed sugar. "Christ, just like a cow," Quinlan said, coming up beside me.

"I guess that's okay now," Jeff said, patting the wrappings and looking up for approval. "I'll clean up here, Mr. Quinlan."

"Fine, Jeff," the trainer said. "We're goin' over to the kitchen. I'll be back for the loading."

I started to follow him, but a car pulled up at the corner of the barn and a tall, white-haired man got out and came toward us. He was dressed in a blue business suit and had a moon face, with large brown eyes set over a hard beak of a nose. "Well, Red, how does he look? He got a chance?" the man asked.

"I wouldn't bet on him today, Jack," the trainer said.

"He isn't in against much," the man said, unhappily. "I might put a hundred on him."

"Suit yourself. You'll get a price, if he does come in. All I hope is he gets a sniff of the money."

"Yeah," Jack said, "we haven't had much of that lately." He glanced at me. "I'm Jack Welch. Who are you?"

I introduced myself, but Welch paid no further attention to me. "How's Dragoon doing?" he asked.

"I want to get one more work into him."

"Le Duc?"

"I think he's got one or two races left in him," Quinlan answered. "I want to put him in the sale next week."

"What do you think we can get for him?"

"Well, that left tendon is startin' to go again," the trainer said, "so it depends on how hard they look at him. Twenty, at most twenty-five. Maybe nothin'."

"And the filly?"

"About a month away."

"The colt sound?"

Quinlan nodded. "I think so," he said. "I didn't like the look of a shin last week, but it cleared up. He'll win for us."

"It'd be about time," Welch said. "This is beginning to cost more than I can afford."

"You want a cup of coffee?" Quinlan asked. "We were on our way over to the kitchen."

"Nah, I've got to get back to town," the owner said, heading for his car. "I got city inspectors to cope with. It's one goddamn thing after another. I'll see you at the races." He climbed back into his vehicle, a small, silver Cadillac, and drove gloomily away.

"Friendly type," I observed. "Is he always that cheerful?"

Quinlan smiled, a little tightly. "He likes to win, Shifty," he said. "We haven't been winning."

"How long you been together?"

"Five, six years, I guess. We've never had any big ones, but we've never had any losing ones either."

"What's he do?"

"He's in the restaurant business. He owns a couple of places downtown."

"You ought to do okay, right?" I ventured. "He must know that colt can run, and then you've got Dragoon. Will he wait?"

"I sure hope so," Quinlan said, "because he's all I've got."

We walked the rest of the way to the cafeteria in silence, then, as we reached the front door, he turned to me. "Your man was down to see me last night," he said.

"Who? Monkton?"

He nodded.

"What about?"

"Lay Duck."

"The one you want to sell?"

Quinlan nodded again and squinted at me through narrowed eyelids. "I think he wants to buy him."

"For whom? Did he say?"

"I thought you might know."

"Monkton's got pretty much of a free hand."

Quinlan nodded thoughtfully, then opened the cafeteria door. "Come on," he said, "I'm buyin' in here."

"Can you afford it?"

"Coffee, that's all. What'd you think I was offering?"

"I thought maybe pheasant under glass."

"I don't even know what that is," Quinlan said, "but it sure don't sound good."

I spent the rest of the morning with Quinlan, not only because I liked him, but because he was turning out to be a very useful source of information about the New York racing scene. I've found out over the years that you can't just show up at a racetrack, open the *Daily Racing Form,* and expect to start winning. Like every ballpark, each track is different, with its own biases and its own peculiarities, which have to be understood and carefully considered before risking any money at the betting windows. Even more important, perhaps, is getting some sort of handle on the star players in the game—the jockeys and the trainers. Some do well at some tracks and badly at others. Some favor speed horses, while others point for the longer distances. There are riders who are quick out of the gate and others who are not. Some jockeys will take chances to win, some won't. Some trainers work their horses fast in the morning, others don't. There are hundreds of such factors to consider in connection with handicapping any given race, and the bettor who simply plunges blindly in, relying solely on readily available statistics, is an almost certain loser. You have to pay your dues at the track, as in life, and only the inspired student of the sport can hope to walk away with the money. If I have any argument with Jay Fox, it's over his complete reliance on the numbers, because I also believe that fantasy and instinct and luck are important, perhaps even crucial to success. But to give the Fox his due, somebody taught Picasso how to draw before he turned the art world inside out. I needed Red Quinlan, if I were to have any chance of making a winner out of Fulvio.

After the van had departed for Aqueduct, with Bandolier and Jeff aboard, the trainer finished up his chores, changed into a fairly disreputable-looking blue-checked sports jacket, added a garish tie, and asked me for a lift. "My wife's meeting me over there," he explained, "and she can drive me back. It's on our way home."

"She come to all your races?"

"Mainly she comes to help keep Welch off my back," he said. "I got too big a mouth on me and he could sure get me started."

I could see he was nervous, as well as unhappy about "Bundle's" chances in the race, so on the drive to Aqueduct I kept the talk light and told him a couple of amusing stories about failed betting coups that got a chuckle or two out of him. He seemed abstracted, however, and, as we turned into the horsemen's gate, he said, "I got somethin' to tell ya."

"About what, Red?"

"Your man Monkton."

"What about him?"

"Well, I shouldn't tell ya nothin', see, but it just ain't right. Only you didn't hear it from me."

"Okay."

He waited until I'd pulled into a parking space and then squinted warily at me. "You heard me tell Welch we was hopin' to get twenty-five thousand for Lay Duck, right?"

"Yes, I did. You said he had one or two races left in him."

"Yeah, he's gettin' ready to bow again and this time it'll be the end of him," Quinlan said.

"So?"

"So what Monkton did, he came around and offered me forty grand for him. Said he'd write me a check right then and there."

"And did he?"

"Yeah. I got it in the bank. Welch is gonna be real happy when I tell him."

"Why didn't you tell him this morning?"

"There's a condition to it. I got to put the horse in the sale."

"What for?"

"Monkton's guaranteeing me forty," the trainer explained, "but the deal is he gets to keep the difference, if the horse sells for over forty."

"Who'd pay even that much for him?" I asked. "It figures any good trainer would know what the horse is worth, right?"

"Right, Shifty."

"So no one's going to bid that much."

"You better come to the sale and see."

"When is it?"

"Next Tuesday mornin', at Belmont."

"What are you going to tell Welch?"

"He'll be happy to get the forty and he ain't goin' to the sale."

"I don't get it, Red. Monkton's going to get stuck."

"It's not his money, Shifty."

"You mean it's ours?"

"You better come to the sale."

"I will. And thanks."

"For nothin'. You see, Shifty, we got guys here at this track, ain't a horse moves in or out of their barns without their gettin' their palms greased."

"I guess you aren't one of them."

"I'm a horse trainer, not a goddamn thief." He got out of the car and walked angrily into the main grandstand area, with me hurrying after him.

Gerald Monkton was waiting for me in the Turf and Field Club at a table directly over the finish line. A tall, slender man of about forty, with a manufactured tan and a carefully coiffed head of iron-gray curls, he was elegantly dressed in gray flannel slacks and a dark blue cashmere blazer. His eyes were hidden behind tinted Pierre Cardin bifocals, perhaps to protect him from his own dazzling smile; he had large, even, brilliantly white teeth, all of which were lit when he rose from the table to greet me. "Mr. Anderson," he said, shaking my hand vigorously, "so glad you could come. Please sit down."

"Thanks. I hope I didn't keep you waiting."

"Not at all. You know we have that filly running today."

"Pepperdine? Yeah."

"I'd have had to be here anyway." He signaled for the waiter with the casual aplomb of an emperor beckoning to a slave. "We're in the fourth," he said, "so we don't have a lot of time."

"I was over at the barn," I volunteered. "I thought I might see you there."

"I left pretty early," he said. "I had some things to do in the racing office. It's one thing after another in this business and not much of it has to do with the racing itself." He smiled again and I thought I might have to get my own dark glasses to protect myself from the glare. "I'm sorry I missed you."

"Well, I always enjoy the backside," I said. "And I had Red Quinlan to talk to."

Monkton chuckled patronizingly. "Oh, Andy's a colorful sort, all right," he said. "Too bad he hasn't been having much luck this year."

"He doesn't have a lot of horses."

"True. Still, there's no reason he shouldn't do better than he does, no reason at all. He's a good horseman."

The waiter materialized and we ordered sandwiches, as the horses in the first race on the card appeared on the track. From our cushy table, high above the action and protected from the elements by plate-glass windows, they seemed remote, like figures observed on a distant screen. Both Aqueduct and Belmont are huge emporiums, with massive grandstands and luxuriously appointed betting facilities for the plungers, but the spectators have been removed from the racing itself. I was used to the intimacy and relative informality of the California scene, where you can still smell the animals and see them up close and listen to all that good talk around the paddock and by the gap, where the horses and riders pass on their way to the starting gate. New York racing is like being on a gambling ship or in the bowels of a casino, where only the betting counts and the sport itself has been relegated to the status of a giant slot machine designed to raise money for the state. "You know," I observed, as the horses moved away from us around the clubhouse turn, on their way to the starting gate, "someday they'll just eliminate the live stuff altogether."

"What do you mean?"

"They'll computerize racing images on closed-circuit screens," I explained, "and run off preprogrammed races for the bettors."

"You don't believe that, do you?"

"I didn't believe a movie actor could be elected President," I said. "Think of the money it would save. No horses, no jockeys, no stable help to worry about—just the loot flowing in."

Monkton laughed. "Who'd bet on that kind of race?"

"The same people who play the lottery and the slot machines," I answered. "You wait long enough in this great country of ours and somebody will figure out a way to build a better machine. The living are a pain in the ass."

"Jeanine warned me you were quite a character," Monkton said. "She was right."

"Did she call you about me?"

"Oh, yes. That's why I wanted to meet you. I'm not sure what it is you're doing here."

"What did she tell you?"

"That you've been hired to help Mr. Gasparini gamble his money."

"That's about it. He can use all the help he can get. I've seen him in action."

"So what interest do you have in the horses?"

"Well, he'll be betting on them, won't he?"

"I don't know. I suppose so." He glanced away from me a moment, as if to clear his mind of a bothersome suspicion. "I wouldn't risk a lot on the filly today," he warned.

"Not a dime," I said. "Fulvio wanted to bet on her, but I advised against it."

"She has a lot of ability," he continued, "but she's very high-strung. She gets all worked up on her way to the gate. I'm trying to find some way of settling her down. She's awfully well bred."

"What'd you pay for her?"

He didn't answer right away, but looked at me from behind his shields for a few seconds, then smiled a little tightly. "I'm afraid you'll have to get that information elsewhere," he said. "I'm not authorized to disclose it."

"Not authorized? By whom? Jeanine?"

He nodded. "Of course."

"She told me she doesn't know."

"Well then, she doesn't."

"Who does, besides you?"

"I keep very accurate books, Mr. Anderson," he said, not at all amused now by the turn our conversation had taken. "They're open to inspection by any properly authorized person."

"How about Fulvio?"

"Well, of course," the trainer said, obviously startled by my question. "But he's never asked."

"Gerry, if you were investing a lot of money in a very risky enterprise," I said, "and we'd have to concede that horse racing is about as risky an enterprise as you can get, wouldn't you want to know how your money is being spent and what the prospects are?"

"Certainly," he said. "And as I told you, we have nothing to hide here. We're investing in good racing stock and building a strong, competitive stable, which is what I was asked to do."

"Well, I think Fulvio is going to want to know where his money is going. That will be my advice to him, anyway."

"Swell," Monkton said. "Whenever he wants to know, I'll be only too glad to tell him exactly where we stand. Excuse me a moment." He got up and moved across the room to greet a large party of new arrivals, who were just settling down at their table as he reached them. Monkton shook hands, slapped backs, smiled, laughed, and charmed, his teeth blazing away in overtime. Other clients, I figured, then turned my attention to the starting gate, where a short field of undistinguished sprinters was about to contest the first race.

After it was over and I had jotted down a few notes about it on the margin of my program, Monkton returned, followed by the waiter with our order. The trainer seemed disinclined to waste much more of his abundant charm on me, so we munched away in silence, while I studied the *Racing Form*. As the horses appeared for the second race, he stood up. "I've settled the check," he said, "so don't bother about it. I'd better get down to the receiving barn."

"Fine, thanks," I said. "I'll see you in the paddock."

"Swell." He flashed me that smile again, perhaps to make sure he could still turn it on and off at will, then left fairly quickly. I finished my coffee and turned my attention back to the track and the second race. More homework.

Twenty minutes before the fourth race, I went down to the paddock, which at Aqueduct is small and graceless and directly in front of the stands. Sanchez, shabbily resplendent in a scarlet windbreaker, was walking Pepperdine around the tiny circular track in the enclosure with the other horses, trying to keep the filly moving and relaxed. She, however, was having none of it. Wild-eyed and testy, she fought the lead, tossing her head up and down and occasionally swerving wildly to one side, forcing Sanchez to use all his strength to keep control of her. She was wet on her neck and lathered up between her legs, the picture of a fractious nitwit. Above us, several lines of hard-eyed speculators peered down at the activity and one of them, in a voice like a sandblaster, called out, "Hey, Monkton, cut out the foreplay! She's ready now!"

The filly settled down a bit after she got out on the track, but all the way to the post I could see her still tossing her head about while the rider, a journeyman jock named Billy Roark, and the pony boy fought to get her to behave herself. Monkton, who had taken no part in the saddling procedure but had allowed Sanchez to do all the work, seemed unconcerned. In fact, he didn't even have a pair of binoculars to witness what was going on and took his leave of me minutes before the horses reached the starting gate. "I'm going upstairs," he said. "I have to see some people."

"Thanks for lunch."

"No problem. Anytime." And he headed for the elevators.

I watched the race from a post at the rail by the finish line, squeezed in between several of the grooms for the other entries. Pepperdine was the last to load, even though she had drawn the two hole. Apparently, the starter figured she couldn't be allowed to remain too long in the gate or she might go crazy. In fact, just before the start, she reared up, almost unseating Roark. When the gate popped open, she lingered behind, then rushed up between horses and fought briefly for the lead. At the half, she was through and fell steadily back. Roark eased her up at the end and brought her in forty lengths behind the winner. It was as shameful a performance as I'd ever seen, especially at a major track, and I wondered what Monkton would have to say about it.

The answer was nothing. When I returned to the Turf and Field Club, I found the trainer sitting at the table with the party of people he had greeted earlier. He was laughing and joking and turning those devastating teeth of his upon the handsome middle-aged woman beside him. Not once did he look out at the track below to see what sort of shape Pepperdine was now in. The filly could have broken a leg and been carted off in the horse van and he wouldn't have noticed.

I spotted Red Quinlan at a table two rows down from me and I walked over to say hello. "This is Nora," he said, introducing me to a slender, freckle-faced woman with serious eyes and a pretty face prematurely wrinkled from too much sun. "Honey, this is that magician fella I told you about."

Nora smiled and shook my hand firmly. "I'm happy to meet you," she said. "Andrew has told me a lot about you. Are you really a magician?"

"My powers are limited," I said, "but yes."

Nora clapped her hands together. "Oh, please, show us something. I'm trying so hard to cheer Andrew up, but you know how he is."

I sat down and did Ring on a Stick and pulled a sponge ball out of my ear and made some coins disappear and Nora loved every move. "That's wonderful!" she exclaimed. "What else can you do?"

"Can you turn this damn colt of mine into a race horse?" Quinlan asked.

"Red, I can't walk on water either," I said.

"Oh, shoo, Andrew, don't be such a grump," Nora told him. "I'm sure he'll be all right."

"*He* will, honey, but what about us?"

The conversation was interrupted by the arrival of Jack Welch, who had clearly not been having a good day at the windows. "All that goddamn favorite had to do to keep my show parlay going was not try to come in through the parking lot," he observed, as he slumped into his chair. "What the hell's wrong with some of these riders? Haven't they ever heard of coming through between horses?"

"Now, Jack," Nora said, putting a hand gently on his arm, "you'll be all right. You shouldn't be betting every race. You're just incorrigible."

The restauranteur grumpily picked up his *Form*, but he seemed to relax a bit; Nora evidently had the Nightingale touch. "I'm going downstairs," Quinlan said, standing up. "You coming, Jack?"

"Nah, I'm going to dope the fifth. I'll see you after the race." Quinlan started to leave, but Welch stopped him. "Can I risk anything on our pig?"

"Jack, how can you call that nice little colt a pig?" Nora asked, smiling ruefully.

" 'Cause he acts like one."

"I wouldn't bet a dime on him, Jack," the trainer said. "Not today. Maybe down the line a bit, when we stretch him out." And he walked swiftly away from us, as Welch returned to his study of the entries in the fifth.

The owner cashed a sizable Exacta on the contest, which improved his outlook on life, after which he and Nora left to join Quinlan in the paddock for Bandolier's race. I stayed put and watched from my table as Bandolier ran eighth in a ten-horse field, beaten twelve lengths and showing no sign of ability. I decided not to wait for them to come back, as I didn't want to have to listen to Welch's graceless complaints or have to witness any more of Nora's soothing ministrations. Quinlan, I knew, would stay with his horse and make sure the animal had come out of the race sound.

I spent the rest of the day in the grandstand, made one small losing bet for myself in the feature, and concentrated mainly on making more notes against future action. Once again, on the exit escalator after the ninth, I found myself standing behind Art Mendola. The tout was being harangued by an elderly hard knocker, who had obviously been struggling through a tough streak. "It's the shits," the old man was saying' "I can't get a handle on this meet at all. I mean, I ain't losin', I'm even."

"Sure you are," Mendola told him. "You started with nothin' and you ended with nothin'."

FOURTEEN

♦

Secrets

Achille Pipistrello did not return my phone calls, but that didn't worry me. I was hardly ever around myself, so I thought he may have tried to get me back and not bothered to leave a message. I was spending most of my time at Belmont and Aqueduct anyway, acquiring the education I needed to launch my tenor and me onto the seas of high gambling finance. I hadn't even seen Fulvio, though I talked to him every day on the phone at least twice, with progress reports and observations. He, of course, was eager to start blowing his money in large chunks out there, but I succeeded in fending him off and insisting that we wait until he himself could be in attendance. I'd have stood no chance of succeeding in this game plan if he hadn't been facing an opening night at the Met, in one of the most difficult operatic roles ever written. "Fulvio," I told him at one point, "you've got to concentrate on your art. There's plenty of time for fun and horses."

"*Si*, you are right, *mago*," he said, "but I am fighting with the *cretini* here and all is misery. The Pantaloni *belva* is a calamity. Is time for play, *mio caro*."

I didn't go to the track on Friday, the day of the opening, because I had contracted a nasty little head cold, so I stayed in my room, worked on some moves, then, loaded with decongestants and aspirin, I set out in the afternoon to look up Pipistrello. A woman at something called the Castagno Opera Workshop, where I had called him earlier, informed me that he was involved in a *Bohème* rehearsal that had begun at two o'clock. "It should be

135

over by four or four-thirty," she said, "but you never know with Maestro Pipistrello." She laughed. "He's a holy terror sometimes."

"I can imagine," I said. "Please don't bother him. I'll just drop in."

"Is he expecting you?"

"Sort of," I lied. "Anyway, I can always wait."

The Castagno Opera Workshop was located in an old apartment house on the upper West Side, near Broadway. I rang the bell and went in through a once elegant but now dingy, barren lobby, up a flight of worn marble stairs, and through an unlocked front door into the workshop itself. I found myself standing at the end of a long, narrow corridor, facing a pay telephone and a battered bulletin board on which were posted rehearsal schedules, advertisements, and notices of various kinds, including an exhortation, scrawled in pencil across a plain sheet of notebook paper, to participants behind in their fees to pay up. The noise was deafening. In addition to the singing, which was coming from behind several closed doors, a resonant conversation was being carried on by a group of loiterers in the hall. They projected their dialogue, bouncing words off the walls at one another. A door opened at the end of the corridor and Achille Pipistrello stuck his head into the hallway. "It is too noisy!" he snapped. "It is impossible to hear ourselves."

"Sorry, Maestro," one of the loiterers boomed. "We didn't realize. . . ."

Pipistrello recognized me. "Ah, you," he said. "Come in then." He disappeared back into his studio.

As I started to edge past the talkers, one of them muttered, "With that cast he's got in there, he's lucky he can't hear them." Two or three of his listeners snickered.

I passed an open doorway through which I caught a glimpse of a large, matronly woman sitting at a kitchen table. She was simultaneously sewing a costume and talking on the phone, while other members of the workshop swarmed in and out of the room on various errands. Inside the rehearsal space, I found the maestro seated at a battered upright piano facing a circular row of music stands behind which several nice-looking young people stood over their open vocal scores. The room was bare, uncarpeted, free of drapes and other sound destroyers. There were plain wooden and metal folding chairs and, against the far wall, a large bookcase was crammed with scores, sheet music, old programs, scrapbooks, bits of costume material, and props. The walls were also adorned with black-and-white snapshots of opera productions, probably those of the workshop itself, I guessed. "This is a run-through now," Pipistrello informed his singers, as I sat down. "Da capo and try not to stop." He began to accompany a soprano and a baritone through the Mimi-Marcello duet that opens act three.

I found myself once again enthralled, this time by Puccini. The rehearsal lasted about an hour and remained resolutely informal throughout. The singers, who had mostly pleasant if undistinguished voices, strolled in and out of it, paying little attention to musical nuance or to dramatic interpretation. Everybody's main concern seemed to be getting through the score without committing any major blunders. Occasionally, Pipistrello would stop playing and correct a flagrant mistake or one of the singers would ask for a repeat of some particularly troublesome section, but for the most part the rehearsal consisted of the sort of run-through I imagined the cast of a Broadway musical would have quite early in the game, long before the director or the conductor made any serious attempt even to block the action or to set basic tempi. I assumed that no one in the room would be performing in public for quite a while, so I was astounded to find out when the rehearsal was over that this cast would be appearing together in the opera at a public school in Queens the following week. I must have looked astonished, because Pipistrello grinned wickedly at me from his piano stool. "Don't worry," he said. "Maybe they will know it by then."

"I don't know much about opera," I said, "but you're still working from the scores. What about the action?"

The baritone shrugged. "Oh, who cares?" he said. "We'll walk through it once and that's enough. Half the props won't be there anyway the night of the performance, so we'll improvise as we go along. We just have to get through it, that's what matters. It's a tricky little piece."

"You can say that again," the tenor noted. "I'd rather do ten Verdis or Donizettis than one Puccini. All those key changes and different tempi and all that action. Me, I'm just going to stand there and sing and pray to God I don't break on my high notes."

Later, on our way out, Pipistrello explained to me about the workshop. "It's a place not to study," he said, "but to get experience. There is no time for polishing. They have to learn a part and get through it at least once before an audience, it's no matter how."

"Do you conduct these performances or what?"

"Oh, no, my friend, not me," he said. "My task is to get them through it, that is all. No opera company in the world can afford to waste time teaching a singer a part. When you audition for the managers, they wish only to know what roles you have done. The more performances you have had, the better chance you get hired. In opera there is very little time for to rehearse. Sometimes you come in and you sing the part with no rehearsal, even at the Met and La Scala. You do one Rodolfo, you can do another one somewhere else. That is why these young people come here, that is what this workshop does."

We stopped by the open kitchen doorway just as the woman, who was still on the phone, said, "Maria, my Rhadames is sick. You call up Luigi right away and see if he can sing tomorrow night. Otherwise we got to move the *Tosca* up a week or cancel. If Luigi can't, try Franco. He won't pay, but he knows the part."

"Madam, *buona sera*," Pipistrello said, bowing slightly. "*A domani*."

"*Va bene, Maestro*," she answered, with a quick smile. "They know their parts?"

"No," he replied, "they know nothing."

"*Dio mio!*" she exclaimed, looking alarmed.

"They have a few days."

The woman glanced skyward, as if to invoke divine intervention. "*Santo cielo*," she said, "in my time we knew what we was doing."

"Other times, Signora, other systems." Pipistrello bowed again and we left.

"Who's that?" I asked, on the stairs.

"Madam Castagno," he explained. "She run the workshop. Opera is her life."

"And yours, I guess."

"Ah, Signor Anderson, it is a life of frustration and despair."

"Is this how Fulvio started, too?"

"Not here. In Italy," he said, leading the way out into the street. "I was at his debut, in L'Aquila."

"Where's that?"

"The Abruzzi, up in the mountains. It is very beautiful and very cold. Fulvio crack all his high notes."

"What opera?"

"This one, *La Bohème*. They whistle him."

"Whistle?"

"That is like booing here. I sit up all night with him. He cry so much. He want to leave, never to sing again. I force him to stay, to try again."

"And he did, of course."

"Oh, yes, or he would not be singing today. You cannot run from this terrible beast, the public. You must stay, you must face it. So at the second performance, Fulvio is trembling, but in the aria he have a high C, my God, it make the people to scream. After that, he begin his career."

We turned down Broadway. A cold, damp wind was blowing up the avenue, sending bits of the city's refuse scuttling before us and forcing us to hunch into our overcoats against the chill. "Can we get a drink or something?" I asked. "I've got a cold."

"Certo," he said. "Come, there is a place I go to."

We walked a couple of blocks in silence, then turned east along a side street and into a small café a few steps below the level of the sidewalk. It was a cozy burrow dominated by a huge espresso machine and a pastry counter, behind which stood a thin, mustached barman. The small room was almost empty at that hour. We sat down at a corner table and I ordered an espresso *lungo* for the maestro and a cappuccino for myself.

"So you've been with Fulvio a long time," I said.

"Sì, from the beginning, almost."

"You taught him?"

"I coach. I am not *maestro di canto.* No, Fulvio was already studying for three years when I meet him. They are bringing him to me to study the *repertorio."*

"And you stuck with him."

"Yes, they ask me. When they bring him, his voice was already *piazzata.* Placed?"

"I guess."

"Yes. Of course he always have this voice of great natural beauty. It take not much time to place it. He study with Strapponi, the famous baritone, in Milan and then he come to me. He can sing, but nothing else. He sing everything by ear fortissimo. I fix all this. It was not easy, but Fulvio has good instinct. He is artist despite himself, but he is also very lazy."

"Who hired you? His family?"

The old man shook his head. "No, no, Fulvio is orphan," he said. "He is brought up there, outside Naples. The priests discover this voice and they go to Don Pippo."

"Who?"

"Carmela's family," the maestro said, looking nervously around.

"Oh, so they—"

Our conversation was interrupted by the arrival of our coffees, which, I gathered, came as a relief to Pipistrello. The old man heaped sugar into his spoon and dumped it into his cup, then stirred the brew noisily, his eyes all the while restlessly glancing about the room and toward the street. I waited until he calmed down a bit and raised the cup of steaming liquid to his mouth. "Is this making you uncomfortable, Achille?" I asked. "Am I being too nosy or something?"

His little brown eyes now focused on me. "I wish you to ask on these family matters from Fulvio," he said. "He will tell you."

"I will, but I'm just curious," I said. "I really don't know Fulvio all that well and I've seen very little of him since I got here, because of the opera. I want to know about his background, so I can help him."

"Yes, yes, I understand," the old man answered, nodding vigorously and inhaling his coffee with the avidity of a drunk attacking the last of his pint bottle. After draining it, he set the cup down on its saucer with a satisfied little burp. "It is fine," he continued, "but it is also complicated."

"Just tell me a little about him, whatever you can, Achille."

The old man hesitated, then leaned back in his chair and folded his arms across his chest. "I tell you what it is easy to know, *va bene?*"

"Sure, that's fine."

"Well then, Fulvio is orphan, as I say," the maestro declared. "He is raised in this big *orfanotrofio* in Ottaviano, which is near Naples, you understand?"

"Yes, by priests, you say."

He nodded. "*Sì.* When he is fifteen or sixteen, the priests take him to Don Pippo and he sing for him. Afterward Don Pippo pay for everything and he take Fulvio into his care. That is how Fulvio become a singer."

"And is that how he met Carmela?"

"Yes. She is Don Pippo's daughter, you understand?"

"I think so." I smiled, trying to reassure him. The mention of Don Pippo seemed to have made him nervous again. I was trying to take the pressure off him, but without much success. However, I plunged ahead anyway. "What is it easy to know about Don Pippo?" I asked. "Is that his real name?"

"It is Giuseppe Cupiello, but everyone call him Don Pippo."

"What is he, a rich music lover?"

The little brown eyes widened in amazement and he laughed, then choked himself off abruptly, as if he had inhaled a nasty piece of gristle. "Ah, a music lover," he gasped, "that is fantastic! Of course, yes, a music lover!" He swung around in his chair and hacked himself into a folded jackknife. I stood up and pounded on his back. "It is all right," he said at last, sitting up and fending me off. "It is fine." He stood up, blowing his nose into a huge green handkerchief. "I must go now."

"Please, Achille," I said, "don't answer what you don't want to, but you've got to tell me a little more. After all, it was you who warned me to be careful. Why should I be careful?"

The old man leaned toward me, his eyes brimming with the tears his fit of involuntary laughter had brought on. "Don Pippo has very long arms, my friend," he said. "They can reach around the world." He started out and I went up to the counter to pay the bill. When I looked back, he had gone.

I caught up to him a few steps up the street. "Achille," I said, taking his arm, "what's wrong here? What are you trying to tell me? Am I supposed to worry about this guy in Naples? What *is* the problem?"

"It is a part of the problem."

"Tell me, who is Agostino? Does he work for Don Pippo?"

"No, no," the old man said, "it is not that. No, he is a friend of the others."

"The others? What others?"

"Like all great men, Don Pippo has enemies. And so Fulvio has enemies."

"But who are they?"

The old man stopped running away from me and turned now to look at me, his eyes hidden under the brim of a battered brown Borsalino. "My friend, I already know too much," he said. "I have also to be careful, you see. There was a doctor. . . ." But he cut himself off on the very edge of this revelation.

"A doctor? Who? What about him?"

"Before you go to Naples next month, I will tell you more, *va bene?*"

"I guess that would help."

"Until then, you must ask Fulvio to tell you what he wish to, you understand?"

"Okay, yes. But I want to know who Agostino is and who it is I have to watch out for."

"That answer, too, you can find out for yourself, Signor Anderson," the old man said. "I wish to tell you this one thing. He is called the Hammer."

"A hit man?"

"He is for sale."

"Who bought him, Don Pippo?"

"No, you have asked the wrong question. Watch out, my friend. There are enemies all around."

"What are you suggesting I do, leave?"

Pipistrello considered that suggestion quite seriously, his eyes still hidden from me. "Yes, that is best for you, I think," he said. "Leave." He resumed his scurrying walk toward Broadway.

"I'll see you tonight," I said, "won't I?"

But he didn't answer and I watched him go, until he disappeared around the corner, toward the subway station.

I couldn't get through to either Anna or Fulvio before the performance that night, but a ticket had been left for me at the box office. It was way off to the side in one of the upper balconies, but I didn't care. I sat there enraptured while Verdi again whisked me into his musical rendition of Shakespeare's tragedy and this time the performance was unflawed by any sign of hostility between the tenor and his soprano consort. Both Fulvio and Caterina sang and acted superbly, and they received a dozen curtain calls from the ecstatic first-night audience. On my way backstage, during the last of the ovations for the principals, I passed Luther Wildwood leaning against the wall, just inside the stage door. He was pale and drenched in sweat, but smiling. "Luther, Luther, it was your genius," the hermaphrodite was squealing in his ear. "It was your magnificent concept, your sets, your costumes that made this such a triumph! Luther, you're so wonderful!"

"Yeah, and you sang terrific," I said, as I passed him. "The audience loved you."

I had practically to fight my way into Fulvio's dressing room, where I found my gambling tenor embracing the beaming bullfrog in the presence of a swarm of admirers packed into the room like politicians around a pork barrel. Fulvio was laughing and nodding and bouncing the conductor up and down like a beach ball. "Ah, Maestro," I heard him say, "these little operettas, eh? We show them, eh? I sing like a god, yes!"

I wedged myself into a corner and waited for the room to empty a bit. Anna Willows, looking smashing in a low-cut black velvet gown and enough pearls to seed an oyster bed, hovered behind Fulvio, smiling in all directions. She retreated into the background after a couple of minutes and began to edge toward the door, as Jeanine Lagrange, again with the faithful Gregory in tow, cut through the crowd toward her client. "Ah, Gianna, *vien qua!*" Fulvio shouted, when he saw her. "Was it not magnificent? Was I not marvelous? You ever hear such an *Otello*, eh? I sing like God Himself, no?"

"Yes, Fulvio, you were truly superb," Jeanine said.

"Oh, my goodness, Fulvio," Gregory said, with a little squeak of ecstasy, "I was simply devastated! You were incredible! You were magnificent! I'm all goose bumps!"

"Eh, you hear that, Maestro?" the tenor said, bouncing the bullfrog up and down in his grasp. "You hear? Even with *la stronza* I make the smash hit, yes! Next year you find me a soprano and we do even better! I kill the people here!"

As the pandemonium around the star continued, I watched Anna Willows gently ease herself out of the room. I stayed in place until, after another ten or fifteen minutes, Fulvio noticed me and beckoned me over. "My wizard!" he sang. "Tomorrow we begin, eh? Now we can start to enjoy ourselves!"

"Fulvio, you have a performance Wednesday night, remember," Jeanine said. "You must not tire yourself."

"I no tire," he said. "The *mago* here, he do all the work. I enjoy myself, that is all! *Mago*, is not so?"

I nodded. "Perhaps you'd like to come with us," I ventured, smiling at Jeanine. "The track is a great place to unwind."

"I don't need to unwind," she snapped. "I don't want Fulvio to exhaust himself."

"You no worry, *cara*," Fulvio told her. "I bet, I laugh, I eat, I forget, but I no shout, *bella*, no. Is not to worry."

"Fine, then," she said. "Fulvio, I'll talk to you tomorrow." Trailed by Gregory and without even another glance in my direction, she sliced her way back through the crowd and out into the hall.

"You no mind her, my wizard," Fulvio said. "She is always so serious."

"So I gather. Have you seen Achille?"

Fulvio grimaced briefly. "The *squalido*? No. He never come here on *la prima*. He know how I feel. He talk to me tomorrow. He tell me how bad I sing. *È uno squalido!*"

"You don't think he liked your performance?"

"He like nothing," the tenor said. "If sun is shine up above, is raining where Pipistrello is."

Our conversation was interrupted by the arrival of a new, pushy gaggle of excited admirers and I was swept aside. I waved good-bye to Fulvio and fought my way out into the relative peace of the corridor, where other groups of relatives and friends were moving in and out of all the singers' dressing rooms. From down below, toward the stage, came the sound of voices and a rumble of activity indicating the striking of the *Otello* set. At the Met, I gathered, work went on practically around the clock.

I headed in the direction of the main stage entrance, but I must have taken a wrong turn. I suddenly found myself in a relatively empty hallway and I realized that I had somehow wound up in an area of small rehearsal rooms. I was about to turn back, when I heard sounds and murmuring voices coming from one of them. I am by nature a snoop, so I quietly eased myself back in that direction and I heard Anna Willows say, "Jesus, not here! Are you crazy?"

The door of the room was a few inches ajar, but I could see nothing. I tiptoed past it and took up a position beyond it, just inside the next doorway, which was open and led into a small, darkened studio furnished with a baby grand, a dozen or so music stands, and a row of folding metal chairs. I stood there quietly and waited. The open door next to me closed, as if someone had pushed it shut, but it quickly reopened and Anna, looking a bit disheveled and tugging her low-cut dress back up over her bosom, suddenly bounced into the hallway. "You're crazy!" she hissed back toward her hidden companion. "I told you not here! Call me tomorrow!" And she hurried away toward the dressing rooms, her hands now working frantically to restore the composure of her upswept hairdo.

Thirty seconds or so after her precipitate departure, Gerald Monkton strolled out into the corridor. Dressed for the occasion in an elegant black dinner jacket, he was smiling and seemed completely at ease. He walked casually after her, looking like the very model of a self-satisfied perfume ad. I waited until he had disappeared from view before I followed him out toward the unfriendly chaos of the New York streets.

FIFTEEN

♦

Playing for Keeps

The morning after the *Otello* first night, Fulvio and I made our own joint debut, at Aqueduct. He and Anna Willows came by the motel for me in a rented limousine, complete with uniformed chauffeur, and we headed out across the city, about an hour and a half before post time. The soprano, wrapped in a sable cocoon, slumped sulkily in one corner, while Fulvio and I hunched over our *Racing Forms* and I explained our betting strategy for the day. "We pass the first race, Fulvio," I said, "which is a short field of bad maidens with an obvious, odds-on favorite. After that, I sort of like the card. Our main action comes in the seventh and eighth, where I have a couple of animals with credentials who ought to go off at decent prices."

"*Cristo,*" the tenor said, looking stricken, "we have to wait so late? Is to die!"

"No, no," I reassured him, "we can take a couple of fliers before then. I was just pointing out the main action spots."

"Ah, is good, my wizard! I am here for to play!"

"Honestly, Fulvio," Anna said, "here we have our first day off in weeks and we have to go to the races! I have so many things I need to do for myself."

The tenor grinned and put a proprietary hand on her knee. "You wait, Anna. We make so much money today you will cry for happiness." He winked at me. "She is afraid we lose," he said. "When I win, she is always happy. She spend my money like a man

145

in a desert drink water. Then she no cry about wasting time, you will see."

Fulvio's arrival at the Turf and Field Club aroused as much excitement as the appearance of a plump fawn in a leopard cage, especially among the maître d's, waiters, and parimutuel clerks, all of whom obviously knew him well and had benefited in the past from his largesse. The minute we stepped into the premises, the tenor began spreading sawbucks around like a farmhand tossing feed to a flock of chickens and we skidded on runners of grease straight to a large table directly over the finish line, within easy stroll of the betting windows. "Ah, is good," Fulvio said, sinking with a great sigh of relief into his cushioned seat and gazing eagerly out toward the track, where the entries for the first race were already on their way to the post. "So *mago*, what we bet here?"

"Fulvio, I told you," I said. "We are not betting this race."

"God, how boring," Anna exclaimed. "All this way to go to the races and we just sit here." She stood up. "Well, I'm going to bet on the gray one with the long tail."

"Give me your money," I said. "I'll book it for you."

"Why you do that?" Fulvio asked, as Anna moved disdainfully away from us toward the betting area.

"Because her horse is the only one in the race with absolutely no chance," I explained. "If she's going to throw her money away, she might as well toss it to me."

Fulvio laughed. "She bet five dollars, is all," he said. "She like it. Sometime her horse win."

"Sure, Fulvio, and sometimes you can pick winners just by throwing darts at a board or reading your horoscope. It's tough enough out here," I said. "If I can't beat the hunch players and the ladies who bet on cute jockeys, then we're wasting our time."

Luckily, and exactly as I had predicted, the odds-on favorite won the first race by about twelve lengths, while Anna's gray, a plodding bum, ran last. "I don't understand what you see in this," she said to Fulvio. "It's so boring."

"Is not boring when you win, *cocca*," the tenor answered. "Right, *mago*?"

"Right."

I proceeded to prove the truth of this statement by whisking us into an enchanted trip through the card. There are days at the track, not many but enough of them to keep me coming back, when the winning numbers simply jump off the pages of the *Form* and dance bewitchingly before your eyes. You go to the window and you bet with supreme confidence on your selection and inevitably it does exactly what it is supposed to do. Miraculously, this was going to be one of those days. I knew it from the first, as surely as I knew, on faith alone, that I had the sun in the morning and the moon at night. My horses ran exactly as if I had rehearsed them for their roles, popping in first across the finish line to the accompaniment of Fulvio's explosive outbursts of joyous laughter. We won three races in a row, passed the fifth, when the odds on my selection dropped too low and it ran second, then cashed again in the sixth and seventh. "Is incredible!" Fulvio exclaimed. "My wizard, you are magnificent! How much we win now?"

I added up the pile of bills in my pockets. "How about twenty-two thousand dollars?" I answered. "You like that figure?"

"Is wonderful! What we do here?"

"Well, Fulvio," I said, tapping the number of the horse I liked on my program, "this is my best bet of the day. It's a mile and one-eighth on the turf, a handicap for mainly allowance horses, and there isn't much speed in here. Tofan, the California horse, is our play, because he figures to be in front and I think he's going to stay there."

Fulvio glanced at the tote board. "Why he is not bet? He is six to one."

"Would you like him better if he were eight to five?" I said. "You don't like six to one?"

Fulvio grimaced and shrugged his shoulders. "Is feature, no?" he countered. "The favorite usually win."

"No, Fulvio, the favorite does not usually win this kind of race," I corrected him. "These are unclassified horses competing, some of them for the first time, under unfamiliar conditions. The favorite here comes from miles out of it and is going to need a fast pace up front to make his run. In my opinion, he's not going to get it. We're going to take the lead with Tofan and set slow fractions and win wire to wire. We're not going to get six to one either. Our animal should be about five to two, but New Yorkers tend not to believe California horses, so maybe we'll get a better price."

"Tofan is a silly name," Anna said. "I'm certainly not going to bet on any horse with a dumb name like that."

"Shut up, you stupid," Fulvio said, amiably. "You no win nothing all day. What you know? Nothing. The wizard here is telling us. Why you not listen? Why you play so stupid?"

Anna stood up, her face red with anger. "Fulvio, how can you talk to me that way?" She walked away toward the restrooms.

Fulvio smiled. "She is a *stupida*," he said. "She lose my money, but I am winning so much." He gazed toward the tote board again just as the odds changed. "Sheefty, look—is what you say!"

Evidently I couldn't do anything wrong; the odds on Tofan had dropped to seven to two. They never went lower and, in fact, went up eventually to four to one, even after I had gone to the window and bet five thousand dollars to win on him. About two minutes before the race, Anna rejoined us, followed by Gerald Monkton. "Look who I found," she said, as she sat down.

"Geraldo!" Fulvio exclaimed. *"Benvenuto.* Sit down. You know the wizard."

"You didn't tell me you were coming," the trainer said, ignoring me and sinking into a chair.

"I called your stable this morning and left word," I said. "Maybe Sanchez didn't understand me."

Monkton turned the teeth on Fulvio. "How's it going?" he asked.

"Fantastic!" Fulvio told him. "We win good, *mio caro.*"

"That's swell," the trainer said. "I think Frank's horse will win this one." He was alluding, I knew, to the favorite, trained by one Frank Merlot, a veteran needle man.

Fulvio looked worried and glanced at his program. "Frank?"

"He means the favorite," I said. "We like Tofan."

"Really?" The trainer's eyebrows arched in disbelief. "I don't think he can go this far."

"Well, that's what makes horse racing."

"Mago, we go save on the favorite," my opera star said, in some alarm.

"Fulvio, please. He's six to five. You can't make money that way."

"I think Gerry's right," Anna said. "I'm going to bet on him." She hurried toward the betting lines as the announcer informed us that the horses had reached the post.

"If she's lucky, she'll be shut out," I said.

"You seem very sure of yourself," Monkton commented.

Fulvio leaned back in his seat with a sigh. "You are right, *mago,*" he said. "I do what you say."

"How much are you winning?" Monkton asked.

Fulvio laughed. "Much money, Geraldo," he boomed. "And now we win more, you will see."

Anna did get shut out and complained about it, but we were watching the race by that time and ignored her. Exactly as I had foreseen, Tofan bounced to the lead a few strides out of the gate and opened up about four lengths on the field as the horses swept around the clubhouse turn toward the straightaway. The board showed fractions of 24.2 seconds for the quarter and 47.1 for the half, a shade faster than I had wanted our champion to go, but he had about six lengths on the field as he turned for home and I felt confident he'd hold on. At the eighth pole, however, he was showing signs of tiring, and the favorite and some other horse began to make a run at him. By the sixteenth our lead had been cut in half. *"Cristo!"* Fulvio exclaimed. *"Porca Madonna!"*

I glanced at him. He was standing up, his binoculars glued to his eyeballs and his face wet with perspiration. "I knew it, I knew it!" Anna said. "Gerry was right!"

"He's going to get caught," the trainer observed calmly.

I began to root, actively and loudly, for Tofan to hold on. "Stay there, baby!" I heard myself say. "Don't let 'em get you! You can do it! Come on, sweetheart, be a race horse! Ho, ho, ho! Keep going, keep going now! Attababy!"

Tofan must have heard me. As his two pursuers loomed up on either side of him, he found one last burst of energy and lunged for the finish line, a clear neck and a head in front as they hit the wire. "My God, my God!" Fulvio exclaimed, falling back into his seat like a felled moose. "Is too much! What happen, *mago?"*

"We won, Fulvio," I said, grinning. "We just made twenty thousand dollars."

"They say it's a photo finish," Anna contradicted me, pointing at the board, where the photo-finish lights were blinking.

"No, no," Monkton said, "you won, clearly. Congratulations." The teeth were on, but his eyes were cool and guarded, focused on me.

"By a neck and a head," I said. "A little too close, maybe."

"My God, my wizard!" Fulvio exclaimed, suddenly rushing around the table toward me. I rose in alarm. The tenor picked me up like a stuffed rabbit in his massive arms and kissed me resoundingly on both cheeks. "You are *magnifico!* You are *stupendo!* My wizard!" He continued to bounce me up and down until I thought my ribs would crack.

By the time he put me down, the race had been declared official, with Tofan finishing first and paying ten dollars for every two-dollar ticket. Fulvio and I were sitting on forty-two thousand dollars in winnings, some of which, in the form of hundred-dollar tips, the opera star began to dispense to the help. "Too bad you didn't invest in the Pick Six," Monkton said. "You'd have made a real killing."

"How do you figure that, Gerry?" I asked. "We didn't have the winner in the fifth."

"Oh, I didn't know. Did you only bet straight?"

"Is there any other way?"

"Next time we bet some Exactas," Fulvio declared, "and we win even bigger."

"No, we won't, Fulvio," I said. "What's the matter? Forty-two grand isn't enough?"

"Is enough, is enough," Fulvio agreed. "My wizard!" He picked up his program. "What we do now?"

"Nothing," I said. "The last race is for New York–bred maidens, impossible to pick. I suggest we go home."

"You crazy! We make one bet."

"No, Fulvio."

"One small bet, Sheefty, please—for Anna!"

"Okay, for Anna." I looked at the *Form* and found a first-time starter named Easy Virtue; it seemed an appropriate combination.

Anna was not amused, but Fulvio was enchanted with my selection. "Is for you, Anna," he bellowed. *"Mago,* you give her the money to bet."

I peeled off a hundred-dollar bill from the huge roll in my pocket and handed it to her. "On the nose, Anna," I said.

"This is ridiculous," she declared. "I'm going to keep this." She dropped it into her purse.

Fulvio laughed. "You *stupida!* Go bet, *mago.*"

"A hundred for us, too, Fulvio," I warned him. "I don't know anything about this filly, except that she works respectably."

"I don't think she has much speed," Monkton said. "I watched her on the track last week."

"Well, so we blow a hundred," I answered. "We can spare it." I knew I was in danger of becoming insufferable in my arrogance, but I knew that nothing could go wrong with our day by that time and there was a quality in Gerald Monkton that made me want to extinguish his teeth permanently. I went to the nearest window and bet a hundred dollars on Easy Virtue to win.

She went off at odds of seventeen to one and, contrary to Monkton's estimate of her ability, she popped the gate and opened up three lengths on the field in the first quarter-mile. By the half she had eight and she coasted home by six, in hand, with the rider not even bothering to tap her with the whip.

Fulvio was laughing so hard he was crying. "Oh, you stupid," he said to Anna, "and you not even bet on her."

White-faced, Anna stood up. "I'm going to the ladies' room," she said. "I'll meet you by the elevators, Fulvio." And she moved quickly away from us.

"Well, Fulvio, you've had a splendid day," Monkton said. "What incredible luck!"

"Is more than luck," the tenor boomed. "Is the wizard here!"

"You can't win all the time, you know," Monkton said.

"My wizard always win!"

"No, Fulvio, he's right," I said. "We had an incredible day, a once-in-a-year kind of day. Sooner or later, we're going to have some losers."

"Always later, not sooner, *mago*."

"Well, congratulations," the trainer said, standing up. "That's a lot of money to be carrying around in New York. Do you want me to put it in the stable account here?"

"Is good idea, Geraldo. We keep some for tonight, eh?"

I gave Monkton most of Fulvio's winnings, but kept my share, which amounted to over six thousand. I definitely liked the feel of it in my pockets and I wasn't about to allow it to be amalgamated into an account Monkton controlled. "I'll send Jeanine a receipt for it," the trainer declared.

"Send it to me, please," I said. "Or better yet, just leave it with Sanchez and I'll pick it up from him in the morning." I turned to Fulvio. "We'd better keep our action money separate from your other assets, Fulvio," I hastily improvised, "or I'll never be able to keep track of what we're doing."

"Ah, *sì*, is good idea," the tenor said. "You do what he say, Geraldo."

"Certainly," the trainer answered. "Again, congratulations. Fulvio, anytime you want to see the horses—"

"Oh, is okay," Fulvio said, waving a hand expansively in my direction. "Sheefty, here, he act for me. You tell him. Is all for taxes, no? Anyway, we win so big, who care about all that, eh? Maybe I sell all the horses now and we just bet on them." He laughed at Monkton. "Don't worry, Gerry, is okay. Tomorrow we think serious, but today we play!"

Actually, we played for three days consecutively, before Fulvio had to go into seclusion again for his second performance of *Otello*. On Sunday we lost, but less than five hundred dollars and only because an eight-to-one shot got nipped by a lip at the wire in the ninth. On Monday we had another good day, nothing like our incredible Saturday, but a solid winning effort. Fulvio left another five thousand dollars in the stable account, this time on his own, because neither Gerald Monkton nor Anna came to the races with us that afternoon. I had a pretty good idea what they were up to, if not where, but I didn't feel I should enlighten Fulvio on that particular subject. We left the track as usual in a small blizzard of Federal Reserve notes, which Fulvio flung in his wake like a passenger feeding gulls from the stern of a cruise ship. He had style, all right, if no practical sense.

We rode back into Manhattan alone in the limousine, except for the chauffeur, who was separated from us by a glass partition. It was the first time I had had Fulvio to myself and I wanted to steer the conversation around to his background. It wasn't easy, because my tenor, like all hooked gamblers, wanted to talk only about action. "Look, tomorrow is Tuesday," I finally said, after a half-hour of chatter during which we had had to relive every triumphant moment of the past three days. "And on Wednesday you have your second *Otello*. Let's forget about the horses for a couple of days. I need to clear my mind."

"Ah, *sì*, I understand," Fulvio said, grinning and patting my knee with his great paw. "We keep your brain fresh, my wizard. Then on Thursday we begin again, *va bene?*"

"Indeed."

The rush-hour traffic into Manhattan was worse than usual and we inched along toward the Queensboro Bridge in a thick sludge of cars, trucks, and buses. *"Dio mio,"* Fulvio exclaimed, "is worse than Naples! *Guarda che robba!"*

I seized the opportunity. "I've never been to Naples," I said. "Tell me about it."

"Is wonderful and terrible," he answered. "Is a city of thieves, Sheefty. You must be careful there. They will steal everything from you."

"Were you born there, Fulvio?"

And so he told me about his childhood in the orphanage, grim but sheltered at least from the misery of the streets. "And I have this *dono di Dio*, this gift of God, my voice," he said, "so even as a boy I am treated like someone, you know? Later, after my voice break and then it become something else, but still so powerful, Padre Rambi, who know me from a baby, he take me to Don Pippo."

"Don Pippo? Who's that?" I asked, feigning complete ignorance.

Fulvio paused briefly before answering, his gaze on the honking herd of cars outside our windows. "Don Pippo, he is like my uncle," he said at last. "He hear me sing and he kiss me with tears in his eyes. And since then he pay for everything for my voice. I could be nothing without him."

"And that's how you met Carmela."

Fulvio swung around to look at me. "How you know that?"

"I forget. Maybe you told me. Or I heard it somewhere."

"*Strano.* You are true wizard," he said. "Carmela, she was child when I sing for Don Pippo, but she fall in love with me even then. She always after me. Then, when I make big success, she tell Don Pippo she wish to marry me."

"Did you want to marry her?"

"I never think about marrying," he admitted. "I am traveling so much."

"So why did you?"

Again the pause, again the glance out the window before answering. "Ah, Sheefty, is Don Pippo's desire I marry Carmela," he finally admitted. "I never think about her because she is *una bambina* when I first see her. But she is all he have, his only child, and she love me so much, I could not say no. Especially to Don Pippo, who do everything for me."

"Does Carmela ever travel with you?"

"No, is not possible, *mago*," he said. "We have two boys, Giuseppe *e* Franco. She has to stay home with them."

"But you're always on the road. When do you ever see them?"

"Well, I try every season now to sing one opera at San Carlo, in Napoli. That keep me home three or four weeks. Then in the summer or fall I spend two months at home. Sometimes, if I am singing in La Scala or Vienna, somewhere not too far, Carmela come with the kids. But is not easy. They are in school. And then there is the property. Is big, it take much time. Carmela, she manage everything."

"Where is your place?"

"Is near Pozzuoli. You know Pozzuoli?"

"No, I don't."

"Is north of Napoli. We have big villa and much land on the sea, to the north. We have pine woods all around and we make our own *mozzarella di bufala*. We have the buffalo, our own herd. Oh, is fantastic, Sheefty. You never taste such *mozzarella* in your life. You eat it an hour after it is made, it melt in your mouth." He placed the tips of his fingers against his lips and blew a kiss into the air. *"Squisita!"*

"I'm looking forward to it, Fulvio," I said. "I mean, I think it's great that we're going to Naples, even though I can't figure out why you need me there."

"There is a *pista*, a track for the horses."

"Fulvio, I won't know what the hell I'm doing there," I warned him. "I wouldn't risk a lira on something I don't understand. You can't expect me to pick winners in Naples, for God's sake."

"No, no, is okay," Fulvio answered, with a big laugh. "Is all crooked there anyway. No, we go maybe once, maybe twice, for the fun of it. But we have gambling. We play some roulette maybe, at my club. You always bring me luck, *mago*."

"It'll be sort of a holiday for me, Fulvio."

"You wait, you have a good time. In Napoli you must be careful, but is fantastic place. And I sing very good there."

"I presume Anna will not be coming with us."

Fulvio smiled. "No, she no come. Carmela would not like."

"And Signor Pipistrello?"

"Ah, *sì*, he always travel with me. Here is not necessary and Jeanine no like him, but there I need him. He is a *peste*, but he know my voice very well."

Our limousine finally inched onto the bridge and we began to make better progress into the city. A light snow had begun to fall and out the window of the car the towers of Manhattan gleamed in the white haze. Fulvio lapsed into silence and stared out toward the river below, where a couple of tugboats were maneuvering a barge upstream. He sighed. "You know, *mago*, I wonder what happen to me if I could not sing," he said softly, without looking in my direction. "I was just big fat kid in an *istituto*. Without Padre Rambi, without Don Pippo, what I become? I am nothing. God has been very kind to me. . . ."

He seemed disinclined to talk any more about his past or his family, so we chatted again about our plans for the end of the week, after the second *Otello*, and then the limousine dropped him off first in front of his apartment building. He turned back to me before going inside. "You work hard, *mago*," he said, smiling broadly. "We make so much money, we take it all away."

"I'll do my best, Fulvio. You know, I'm really looking forward to meeting Don Pippo. Have you told him about me?"

"No, not yet. But don't worry, he know you are my friend."

"How does he know?"

"You will see, *mago*. Don Pippo, he know everything." He waved, pulled his scarf up around his mouth against the cold, and left me.

I would never have gone out that night if I hadn't felt so drained. The three days of play had absolutely wiped me out emotionally, not only because I had had to work so hard to come up with all those winners, but because I had been betting in such large amounts for someone else. Although I obviously had a strong rooting interest in Fulvio's success, I wasn't risking anything, so I should have been relaxed. But the fact that I was responsible for the movement of all that loot through the parimutuel machines made me nervous. Basically, I'm a loner at the track; I don't like to be responsible for anybody else's fate but my own. And I had been spending my evenings handicapping, my early mornings in the barn area, my afternoons gambling, and my nights tossing and turning and worrying. By the time Fulvio's limousine deposited me in front of my motel, I felt as if someone had clamped a small sack of wet concrete against the back of my neck.

I spent twenty minutes under a hot shower and then dozed off on my bed. At about eight-thirty, I woke up with a start. I was very hungry and I needed to get out of that room, to go see a show or a movie, something, anything to take my mind off horses and past performances and betting strategies. As they say around the track, I needed freshening.

I hadn't had a chance to go to a bank and deposit my money, so I had over six thousand dollars in bills of various denominations stashed in hiding places about the room. An imaginative and enterprising thief could have cleaned me out in half an hour, but for some reason I wasn't really worried about being robbed, though I suppose I should have been. Anyway, I got dressed, took a few hundred of my winnings with me, and sallied out into the New York night to treat myself to a good time.

My theory is that the man who attacked me was not, as the police thought, some casual mugger, who just happened to spot me passing by, but a hit man with a purpose. He may even have been waiting in the lobby of the motel for me to come out and followed me until he saw his opportunity. He may have been watching me for days. I'll probably never know for sure, but one of the room clerks told me later that he had noticed a man hanging around. Yes, he thought the guy was short and stocky, with a bull neck and a big round head half-hidden under a black fedora. The clerk noticed him because of the hat, which didn't go with the rest of his outfit—a baggy brown suit and a long, dark-brown overcoat. "Come to think of it," the clerk said, "he looked like a cop. Except for the hat, see? Cops don't wear black fedoras."

Anyway, he went after me sometime around ten-thirty. I had had a good dinner at a small Italian restaurant on West Forty-eighth Street, near Broadway, with the idea of taking in a movie, but by the time I'd finished eating and had had three or four glasses of Chianti I was ready for bed. It had turned into a cool, damp night, with the threat of more snow in the wind, but I decided I'd walk home. I figured it would finish me off and I'd sleep better after a bout of what passes for fresh air in New York.

My attacker caught up to me on Tenth Avenue, about halfway back to the motel. He must have tailed me from the restaurant, though the cops think he was merely some street criminal loitering in a doorway and waiting to pick off a passing pigeon. I think now that my story might have ended right there, on that grimy New York sidewalk, if I hadn't had all that training in misdirection, which is the key to being a successful sleight-of-hand artist. Anyway, I sensed him coming, I almost saw him, and I took a little step to one side.

The blow he had aimed at me grazed my skull, near my right ear, and drove hard into the base of my neck, just above my collar bone. It stunned me and knocked me off balance, so that I staggered out toward the street. I think I must have shouted something, but I don't remember what. Luckily, my involuntary progress took me between two closely parked cars and I half-rolled over the hood of one just as the second blow was delivered. This one missed me entirely, but struck the windshield, shattering it.

I rolled off the hood and landed on all fours in the wet street. My neck and shoulder felt numb and the side of my head was bleeding, where whatever the man had hit me with had torn through my ear and the skin above. I knew he was coming after me again, but somehow I got up in time to lurch out into the avenue, where a speeding panel truck caught me in its headlights. The driver honked, slammed on the brakes, swerved to avoid me, a lucky maneuver, because he got his vehicle between me and the mugger, who was coming out into the street after me. The truck came to a full stop and several other vehicles slowed down behind him, which also may have saved my life. I had no more energy left and had slumped to my knees, an easy victim. My attacker could have quickly polished me off.

The driver of the truck was the first person to reach me. He was a tall, muscular black man, who picked me up under my arms and dragged me back toward the sidewalk. "Hey, man, you okay?" I heard him say. "What's going on here? Shit, he must've stuck you. You're bleeding like a pig, man."

I don't know if I answered him or not. My memory of the next hour or so is very hazy. There was a small crowd around me for a while and somebody went through my pockets, presumably for identification. An ambulance arrived and I was whisked away in it, while one of the paramedics made me lie down, put on a temporary bandage, and a neck brace and sandbags on each side of my head. Then I lay in an emergency room answering a lot of dumb questions about my insurance status for what seemed like an hour, but was probably only a few minutes, after which they got around to X-raying my neck and closing up my wound with five or six stitches. They wheeled me into a cubicle next to a Puerto Rican bravo, who was in much worse shape than I was, and abandoned me.

I went to sleep. I don't know for how long, but again it may have been only a matter of minutes. I couldn't tell, because somebody had stolen my watch. Somebody had also taken my money, but at that point I didn't care. My ear and neck were now throbbing and I was too sore to worry very much about it. After about another hour or so, a New York City cop came by and took down a report. He was about thirty, small, thin, with blue jowls and eyes hidden under a single eyebrow that stretched from temple to temple. He seemed about as interested in my case as a bank manager in the plight of the urban poor. "Okay, that's it," he said, after writing it all down.

"Another routine mugging, huh?" I said.

"Yeah, looks like it."

"Somebody else took my money and my watch."

"There may have been two or three of them," the cop explained. "They probably picked your pockets when you was on the sidewalk. You didn't see the guy who hit you, right?"

"No, but I guess the driver of the truck did."

"Like I told you, he says the guy he saw was white, heavyset, maybe five-six or -seven, and wearing a brown suit with an overcoat. You don't know the guy, right?"

"Right."

"But we don't know if he was the one who hit you either."

"In other words, you haven't got much to go on."

"Right. Consider yourself lucky."

"Why?"

"He must have hit you pretty hard," the cop said, "with a pipe maybe."

"How about a hammer?"

"A hammer? That's funny. It's more like a sap of some kind. Anyway, he hit you pretty good. He could have killed you."

"Yeah, I guess he could have." I then told the cop about the incident in Las Vegas and the second one in L.A. involving Hugo Mandelbaum. "I think it was the same guy."

"Yeah? Not likely."

"Maybe I've gotten paranoid."

The officer stood up to go, clearly ready to leave. "Yeah, that can happen," he said. "You'll be hearing from us, if we make an arrest."

"I won't hold my breath."

"No, I wouldn't do that," he said. "Maybe you ought to stop walking around alone at night."

He left and I went back to staring at the ceiling. It was 4:00 A.M. before I got back to my motel room. This time I took a taxi.

SIXTEEN

♦

Sniffles

"Jesus, what happened to you?" Red Quinlan asked, when he saw me at the barn on Wednesday morning.

I told him what I'd been through. "It looks worse than it is," I added. "They had to put some stitches in my ear and this bandage around my head to keep it from falling off."

"Your head?"

"My ear."

"You look like one of them Egyptian mummies."

"Thanks, Red, very flattering. Anyway, that's why I couldn't make the sale. I stayed in bed yesterday."

"Yeah, I looked for you." He walked over to his car, picked up a couple of sacks of carrots, and deposited them next to several barrels of grain supplements at the corner of his shed row.

"So where's Le Duc now?" I asked.

He nodded toward the far end of the barn, where Sanchez, Walker, and another of Monkton's grooms were working. "He moved the horse down there last night. Did you look at the *Form* this morning?"

"Yes, I did. Eighty grand?"

Quinlan nodded again. "Yep." He didn't seem at all pleased by what had happened, even though he had managed to unload an unsound horse on another trainer at about twice the animal's actual value. He ripped open one of the bags of carrots, dug out a couple of handfuls, and began feeding them to his charges.

159

"So tell me what happened, Red."

"The bidding opened at fifty-five," he said. "Some crony of Monkton's. Monkton raised and they bumped each other up."

"Why didn't they keep going?"

"It was bad enough," Quinlan said. "Ain't a horseman at the sale didn't know what was up. They went about as far as they could go. Hell, even if Lay Duck was sound he ain't worth forty."

"So Monkton pockets forty thousand of his own on the deal."

"Well, his buddy got some of it, but that's about right."

"And the new owner's name is Fulvio Gasparini."

"Wouldn't be surprised."

"What are you so unhappy about, Red?" I asked. "Welch has got to be ecstatic and you unloaded a cripple."

The trainer turned around and looked at me in amazement. "What the hell's wrong with you, Shifty?" he said. "That's a nice, honest animal. Always gave his best. He'd run for you on three legs, if he could. He don't deserve this. When Monkton's through with him, there ain't gonna be nothin' left of him. I hate to see that. I guess you wouldn't know about that."

"I'm sorry, Red, I just didn't understand," I assured him. "I didn't know Monkton mistreated his horses, too."

"He don't," Quinlan said, "but he ain't never around, and that big Mexican, that Ignatz, he don't know a race horse from a burro. He just does what he's told. I can't blame him, 'cause he don't have no stake in what goes on, he just works for a paycheck. But you can't handle horses like they're just pieces of meat. You gotta pay attention, you gotta care about 'em, Shifty. This guy Monkton is just about typical of everything that's wrong with racing today." He turned his back on me and resumed feeding carrots to his eager animals.

I decided that silence was prudent at that point in our relationship, so I walked up to the tack room, sat down behind the scarred little desk in there, and immersed myself in the *Form*. Jefferson came in and out a couple of times and we chatted, and then, a little before ten, Quinlan stuck his head in the door. "Want some coffee?" he asked.

We walked to the kitchen, had a quick cup together, and came back in about twenty minutes. The trainer was no longer angry, but he was nervous, chain-smoking, and even more taciturn than usual. I knew that this was because he had entered Dragoon in the second race on the card and had begun to think he had made a mistake. He confided as much to me on our way back to the barn. "You told me he'd run well fresh," I pointed out.

"Yeah, I know," he said, "but he may be a little short. I shoulda put one more work into him."

"Why didn't you?"

"Because there ain't nothin' in the book for him next week," he explained. "I got to run him today or wait some more. He ain't too sound and Welch is tired of waitin'."

I had a feeling that Quinlan would never run his horses, if he could get away with it. That's the trouble with horsemen who really care about their animals; they keep their charges healthy, but they don't win the money. I didn't say this to Red, of course, because basically I admired him and sympathized with his concern. The world of big-time racing may belong to the titans of the sport we read about in the newspapers and to the con men like Gerald Monkton, but its true heroes are the Red Quinlans.

We got back to the barn just as a man named Fats Brown turned the corner of the tack room and came up to us. "Hiya, Andy," he said. "Van's around the other side. You all set?"

Quinlan nodded and Jefferson went to the stall to get Dragoon. The three of us then walked around the barn as Fats Brown told us about the state of his health. "You see how I am?" he said. "Look at that blue mark there, you see that? That's from the penicillin they shot into me last week, when I had that bad cold. I can't take that penicillin, you know. The doc says I got to get me a tag to wear around my neck in case I'm ever in an accident or something. I could die from that penicillin."

The van, huge and vaguely menacing, was parked beside the barn. It was large enough to accommodate six horses and there were four animals already inside, being comforted by their grooms. One of them was Basingstoke, Fulvio's five-year-old plodder, who was entered in Dragoon's race. But I knew he had no chance and had already told Anna the night before to inform Fulvio that we were not betting on him. Jefferson appeared and led Dragoon up a ramp and into one of the empty stalls. The old pro's coat gleamed, his ears were pricked, and he looked very ready to run. "Keep a good hold on him, Jeff," Quinlan said. "He knows where he's goin'." He turned to Fats, who was still jawing away at me about his medical problems. "Take it easy, Fats. Don't make any sudden stops."

The driver looked at him in surprise. "Sure thing, Andy," he said. "Never had an accident yet, you know that."

We stood in the road by the stable and watched the van drive away, taking Jefferson and Dragoon to the receiving barn at Aqueduct. When the truck had disappeared from view, Quinlan dropped the butt of his cigarette into the dirt at his feet and reached into his pocket for a fresh one. "Don't you know those things can kill you?" I said.

"I'm still here, ain't I?"

"Listen, Red, what are you so worried about? The horse looks great, he'll run great."

"A mile and an eighth is a long way off a layoff, Shifty."

"He's done it before."

"And then I got Saint Ivy up," the trainer said, referring to a French rider name Jacques St. Yves. "He's screwed up before."

"He's also won with him, right?"

"Yeah, but a mile and one-eighth on the turf, that's a long way for that frog to go without makin' a mistake."

"I'm betting two hundred dollars on him," I said. "I figure the money's in the bank."

"Yeah, you would," the trainer answered. "You ain't gonna die rich, Shifty."

I went off to have breakfast and study some more, but I caught up to Quinlan again in the Aqueduct paddock, about fifteen minutes before post time. He was in the process of saddling Dragoon, after which Jefferson led the horse out into the walking ring; he was trying to keep him relaxed and moving. Dragoon looked terrific and I had a strong feeling he'd run very well, but Quinlan seemed inconsolable. He eyed his animal dourly, like a banker weighing his chances of recouping a loan to Paraguay. When the jockeys appeared from under the stands and moved rapidly toward their mounts, the trainer didn't even bother to greet his rider.

Jacques St. Yves had a small, round face with rosy cheeks and a bulbous nose. He seemed tall and rather thin for a jockey, but he exuded an air of quiet professionalism. "Andy, how do you wish me to ride him?" he asked, just as Quinlan gave him a leg up into the saddle.

"Like you always do," the trainer told him, "only try not to fuck up this time. He may be a little short."

"He always runs good, Andy."

"He'll give you whatever he's got," the trainer said glumly.

We watched the horses move out onto the track, then ducked back under the stands and headed for the elevators. I decided to up the ante on Dragoon, who was four to one on the board, and I left Quinlan to go and bet four hundred dollars to win on him. When I rejoined the trainer in the Turf and Field Club, Nora had arrived. She was dressed in a blue suit and looked beautiful, but a little pale. "My goodness, what happened to you?" she asked.

I told her. "I was lucky, really."

"Yes, I'm sure you were."

"Where's Welch?" Quinlan asked.

"He went to bet more money on Dragoon," she said. "It seems there's a tip on him."

"I figured," the trainer said. "I told him the horse might be short."

"You know Jack, Andrew."

Her husband didn't answer but picked up his binoculars and watched Dragoon jog toward the starting gate. "He's movin' good," he murmured, as if to reassure himself. "Yeah, he's movin' all right."

I looked at the board. Dragoon had dropped to three to one, while Basingstoke was being ignored by the bettors; he was twenty-two to one in the nine-horse field, the second-longest shot on the board and rising. I glanced around the room, but I couldn't spot Monkton. I wondered if he had even bothered to show up.

Jack Welch came back to the table and sat down with a deep sigh. "Glad I got that one in," he said, folding up his *Form* and picking up his binoculars. "I hear all over he's a cinch."

"You didn't hear it from me," Quinlan said.

I glanced again at the odds. Dragoon had dropped to five to two and was now the clear second choice in the race. Basingstoke was twenty-five to one. "It is now post time," the loudspeaker announced.

We focused on the starting gate as the tote board winked its last-minute calculations. It was that long second now before the start, but no, not yet, not yet! Some horse had broken through the gate and had to be brought back and eased into position again. A minute passed and then another one. "That's not good," Quinlan murmured, still glued to his glasses. "He could fall asleep in there. He's standing in there like an old lead pony." Another interminable moment as the horses shifted in the gate, seemed to strain against the barrier, poised for flight. Quinlan moved to the edge of his seat. "Don't look at me, Junior," he commanded softly. "Get that head turned front." Finally, the gate opened and the horses burst into the clear, heading for the turn. Quinlan jumped, then sank back into his seat. Dragoon had broken next to last.

He couldn't overcome that bad a start, even though St. Yves rode him correctly the rest of the way. The jockey tucked his mount in along the rail to save ground around the first turn, then moved him out at the half to make his run. Dragoon passed half-a-dozen horses, but had to go four wide around the stretch turn to get within three lengths of the lead. It took too much out of him and he finished fifth, beaten five or six lengths, but still well ahead of Basingstoke, who floundered in seventh.

"I'll be goddamned," Welch said, taking a wad of parimutuel tickets out of his pocket and dropping them on the table. "Some tip."

Quinlan got up without a word and headed for the paddock. Nora smiled wanly at Welch. "I'm so sorry, Jack," she said, "but after that start . . ."

"Yeah, what are you gonna do?" the owner replied. "But I told Red not to put that Frenchman up again."

"Well, he knows the horse, Jack," Nora said, still smiling. "Dragoon has never been quick in the gate and he's such a long-striding horse that he does a lot of things wrong. He just didn't have any luck today. Next time, Jack."

"Yeah," Welch agreed, but without enthusiasm, "I guess. But that was a bad race he ran, a real stinker."

"I hope he came out of it all right, that's all," Nora said, "because in this business, Jack, any day you can get by without an accident is a good one."

"Yeah," the owner said, reaching for his *Form* again. "I gotta try and get out now."

I said goodbye to Nora and spent the rest of the day in the grandstand. I really didn't want to put in any more time around Jack Welch and I knew that both Red and Nora would not linger beyond the next race or two. I had no other bets to make that afternoon, but I thought I'd hang around for a few races and take notes, then maybe do a little advance work on the Thursday entries, since I was certain Fulvio would be raring to go. On my way to a seat in front of a television monitor, I bumped into Art Mendola again. He was steaming over St. Yves's failure to get Dragoon out of the gate. "That little prick cost me a grand," he informed me. "What the fuck happened to you?"

"I was mugged," I told him.

He blew his nose spectacularly into a wad of used Kleenex. "I don't even know what the fuck I'm doing out here," he mumbled. "I got pneumofuckingmonia and I'm running a fever and I got to put up with all this aggravation."

"Maybe you should go inside, Art," I said. "Don't you belong to the Turf and Field Club?"

"What are you, kidding me?" he said. "The only club I ever joined was the Aqua Velva Aftershave Club."

"What did you think of the way Monkton's horse ran?"

"It takes a bum to train a bum. But I seen you with him. I figured you liked him."

"Monkton's an acquired distaste."

Mendola sneezed and coughed up something monstrous into his Kleenex. "Between guys like him and fuckups like that frog jock, you could wind up cutting your throat out here. Excuse me." He shuffled morosely away toward the men's room, probably in quest of more tissues. I smiled at him. I don't know why, but Mendola made me feel better about life in general. Thunderclouds always seemed to be bunched around his brow, but he was clearly in touch with the forces of light.

As soon as I left the track that afternoon, I called Fulvio's apartment to bring him up-to-date and found Jeanine Lagrange on the premises. Anna answered the phone, but almost at once the manager interrupted her, as if she had snatched the receiver out of her hand. "Do you have any idea what you've done?" she asked, in a voice as balmy as an arctic zephyr. "Do you even understand what you're doing?"

"Would you mind being a little more specific?" I replied. "What's wrong?"

"Fulvio has a cold."

"Well, there's a lot of it going around," I said. "This town has a rotten climate."

"I don't suppose I'm making myself clear to you," she continued. "Fulvio may be unable to sing tonight."

"That's too bad. Does he have an understudy?"

"That is not the point, Anderson. The point is that the public is paying its money to hear Fulvio Gasparini, not Lloyd Keegan, as Otello," she said. "Fulvio insists on singing tonight and the opera management is prepared to allow him to. In fact, they want him to."

"That doesn't seem very sensible to me, but I'm sure you'll think of something. Have you tried chicken soup and aspirin?"

"I'm holding you personally responsible."

"Really? For what?"

"Anna informs me that you had a cold," she explained. "Even

166 • WILLIAM MURRAY

so, you allowed yourself to puff germs into Fulvio's face and took him to the races for three days in a row, which is very tiring."

"I couldn't have kept him from going to the track if I had surrounded the place with tanks," I said. "You don't know about horseplayers, Jeanine. They'd walk barefoot on hot coals to get down."

"You are sickening."

"Listen, I didn't make your client into a gambler," I argued. "All I've done is win money for him. And I didn't put him into the horse business with a crook either."

"What are you talking about?"

"Your man Monkton is a thief."

"That's outrageous."

"I thought so, too," I said. "And if you don't tell Fulvio about it, I'm going to."

"Anderson, I think you're a very bad influence on my client," she announced. "I'm going to do my best to keep him from ever seeing you again."

"You might lose him," I said. "Gamblers will give up everything but their habit, don't you know that? Anyway, let me talk to Fulvio now."

"That's out of the question," she snapped. "There's a throat specialist here with him and he can't talk. Please don't call again." And she hung up on me.

I did call back, of course, almost immediately, and this time Anna hung up on me, but not before I managed to inform her that we had lost four hundred dollars on the day and that Basingstoke had run poorly, as expected. "He's going to ask you, so you'd better tell him," I concluded rapidly. "Also, I'd stop seeing Gerald Monkton, if I were you." That was when she hung up on me.

I toyed with the idea of dropping by the Met that evening, but I soon decided against it. I'd had enough drama for one day and I didn't want to witness my favorite tenor in serious vocal difficulty. I was hoping he wouldn't sing at all, and then, as I was nosing through midtown traffic, I suddenly wondered if anybody had bothered to contact Achille Pipistrello, who knew Fulvio's voice better than anyone. The minute I got back to my room, I tried to call the old man. He wasn't home, but I was told by some clarion-voiced mezzo-soprano at the Castagno Opera Workshop that he might be attending the *Lucia* performance, which was being held that night at a public-school auditorium only a few blocks from the workshop. "He sometimes goes there, if he likes the singers," she trumpeted into my ear.

It took me about an hour and a half to sponge myself clean from the track, grab a bite to eat, and get uptown. I arrived there just as the performance was about to start and I sat down in the back of the hall. I knew there was nothing Pipistrello could do immediately about Fulvio, but I wanted to inform him of what was happening. And by that time I also had more questions of my own to ask him.

The high-school auditorium in which the Castagno Opera Workshop put on its public performances was a barren-looking hall with a high ceiling, light-yellow walls, and rows of plain wooden seats facing the stage and an open space directly below it, where the orchestra sat. I recognized Madam Castagno herself at the piano and then I also spotted Pipistrello. He was sitting at the end of an aisle five or six rows in front of me, his hands resting on the head of his cane. The room could accommodate about five hundred people, but its institutional barrenness made it seem vaster than it was. There were probably over three hundred in the audience, quite a few of them obviously friends and relatives of the singers, but the place looked more than half-empty. I was about to get up and join the maestro, when the lights dimmed and the conductor, a stocky, gray-haired man with glasses, appeared and the performance got under way.

It quickly proved to have a charm all its own. The orchestra, which seemed to be playing at a tempo somewhat at variance with the conductor's beat, hit some really interesting wrong notes and one of the violins played consistently just under the pitch. The lighting was so dark during the first act that it was hard to tell what was going on, but this served at least to disguise the set, which seemed to consist largely of a wrinkled blue backdrop, random pieces of secondhand furniture, and cardboard cutouts. The singers, however, were fine. They were all young and fresh-voiced and they sang with commendable ardor. When the curtain fell on act one, the audience applauded loudly and a few *"bravi"* rang out.

During the intermission, I went down and sat next to Pipistrello, who had not moved from his position. *"Dio mio,* what has happened?" he asked the minute he saw me.

"Somebody keeps hitting me over the head," I said. "You're a hard man to get on the phone, Achille."

"I am so seldom home. You called the workshop?"

"Yes, they said you might be here." I proceeded to tell him about Fulvio. "He may not be singing tonight."

The old man nodded gloomily. "That would be best, but I am not sure. They will not want to cancel."

"Somebody named Keegan is covering the part?"

"Yes, a dog with a voice like a goat," Pipistrello said. "They will not want him to sing. They will try to make Fulvio to sing."

"And will he?"

"Perhaps." He shrugged. "You see, in New York they do not listen to me. They do not even like me to be around Fulvio. The Metropolitan has its own people, and then the Lagrange woman . . ." He did not finish the sentence, but began, oddly, to hum tunelessly to himself, like a defective electrical device.

"Achille, what's going on here?" I asked. "I have this crazy feeling that somebody's following me around the country trying to hit me over the head. Am I paranoid or something? You mentioned a man they call the Hammer. Who is he?"

Instead of answering, he took out a handkerchief and blew his nose noisily into it. "Ah, I too have a cold," he said, and resumed his tuneless humming.

"Achille, you said there was a doctor. . . ."

Another minute or two passed and I didn't press him. The humming continued and then, quite suddenly and with no further preamble, he began to talk steadily in a soft, expressionless voice just above a whisper, so that I had to lean in very closely to hear him clearly. "The doctor's name is Renato De Caro," he said. "He was born in Ottaviano, near Naples, the village of Don Pippo. He was at first only a doctor, but then he was visited by a man who wish to avoid military service and ask for his help. De Caro refused, but he receive a visit by two other men, friends of Don Pippo, and he change his opinion. He help this person to avoid the army. That was the beginning."

"What period are we talking about?" I asked. "Recently?"

"No, no, many years ago," Pipistrello said. "It began during the war. De Caro was a very young doctor, just back from medical school."

The old man lapsed into silence again, but I prodded him. "Go on, Achille, please."

"Two or three days later, after the second visit, he is taken to see Don Pippo and they have a very nice chat. It is explained to the doctor that Don Pippo and his friends belong to a very important group of friends and friends of friends, all men of respect in the city. They wish him to join them. *Dottor* De Caro then also becomes a man of respect, with many friends, like Don Pippo."

"Mafia?"

"No, no. That is not a nice word, not *per bene*. In Naples it is called the Camorra. It is the honored society of Naples, you understand?" He did not wait for an answer, but proceeded with his tale. "For many years De Caro work for Don Pippo and he become very rich and powerful. He marry and he have children, and his family they become rich and powerful also."

"It sounds like one of those heartwarming fables of our time."

"This is a period of much activity in Naples," the old man continued. "After the war comes *il* boom and the men of respect profit very much from it. There is, first of all, the building, all done with permits from the city government, which is run by the friends of friends. This is the time of most respectability and honor. Then, in the sixties, all this ends. It ends with drugs and the industries depending on the drugs. There is also contraband—tobacco, liquor, guns, everything—but the drugs are the most important. There is so much money now that the whole of Naples is divided into zones of influence, but too many people have too big shares. There is fighting among the groups and there is betrayal and there is punishment. Don Pippo, he is against the drugs, because he says it is too dangerous and he don't wish to end his life dead or in jail. So he keep much control over what it is they are doing in his zone and he fight to keep the drugs out, away from his people. You understand?"

"I'm beginning to like him," I said.

"Oh, Don Pippo is a true man of respect, a man of honor," Pipistrello said. "He is of the old Camorra, which was once only men like him, men of much respect, men fighting together to protest against foreign oppression. It was the time of the Bourbons in Naples."

"A long time ago."

"Yes, a very long time ago."

He lapsed into silence and then resumed his tuneless humming. All around us people were beginning to come back to their seats for the start of act two. I waited impatiently for the old man to proceed, but he did not seem inclined to. "And then what, Achille?" I finally asked.

Pipstrello blew his nose again, then carefully folded up his handkerchief and tucked it back into his pocket. "By the end of five or six years ago, even Don Pippo is having trouble," he said. "There is the pressure of this money, you see? Some of his own people betray him, even some of the people very close to him. They become involved in the drugs. And so there is fighting and there is killing, much killing. Don Pippo remains a man of honor, but all around him now there is this killing. He is denounced, he is arrested."

"For drugs?"

"The people in the drugs have many friends in high places," the old man explained. "They wish to eliminate Don Pippo. They make a *denuncia*. But even from jail Don Pippo remains in charge. He has many friends who are loyal to him. It is not the friends of Don Pippo who shoot the judge. It is the friends of the others."

"What judge?"

"The *magistrato* who is investigating the drug traffic. They shoot at him in the street. 'Shooting at a judge,' Don Pippo says from the jail, 'that is a useless and damaging provocation.' Soon after, Don Pippo is released from jail. The judge who survive the shooting, he let him go. Don Pippo begins now to find out for serious who are his real enemies. There is a proverb in Italy, *mio caro:* 'From my enemies I can protect myself, but from my friends only God can save me.' "

"So what about this doctor?" I asked impatiently.

"He is a betrayer of Don Pippo. He is no longer to be trusted. His medical practice has put him among the sellers of the drugs. He has become even more rich than before. Don Pippo must eliminate him."

"He kills him?"

"They say it is an accident, but if so, it is a lucky one. *Dottor* De Caro drowns in his swimming pool on Capri."

"Okay, Achille, I follow you so far, but what does this have to do with me?"

"The doctor have a family and this family make a *vendetta*. Vengeance, you would say."

"Against a Camorra don?"

"The doctor, too, have friends, new and powerful friends. The war goes on."

"I'm still in the dark, Achille. How do I figure in this?"

"You are helping Fulvio, no?"

"Yes, but—"

Our conversation was interrupted by the reappearance of the conductor and the blinking of the house lights indicating the beginning of act two. I went back to my seat, where I had left my coat, intending to catch up to Pipistrello again either at the next intermission or after the opera. No sooner had the performance resumed, however, than I temporarily forgot Don Pippo and the Camorra and the whole bizarre story. I was whisked back into the more delightful unreality of Donizetti's rural Scotland, where everyone sings in Italian. Except for the famous sextet, during which the conductor simply stopped beating time and allowed his cast and orchestra to find their own way out, I had never heard *Lucia*. It wasn't Verdi, but it was wonderful just the same, full of good rollicking tunes. I especially enjoyed the tomb scene, during which the largest headstone, an unwieldy cardboard cutout, toppled over, revealing the legend SUNKIST ORANGES on the back, and the tenor, who had evidently forgotten his dagger, committed suicide by punching himself in the stomach. Obviously, this wasn't the Met, but it was opera and, as a new fan, I found I could be as tolerant and uncritical as even the hardiest buff. When the cast and the hapless conductor lined up to take their final bows, I applauded as lustily as the rest of the audience.

Pipistrello had left his seat during the second intermission and headed for backstage. He had not returned, so I had planned to catch up to him there later. When I finally began to look for him, however, he was nowhere to be found. I spotted what at first looked like a large blue tent, but turned out to be Madam Castagno, so I asked her if she had seen him. "Oh, yeah, he was here," she informed me. She had been standing off to one side, supervising the striking of the set, while the singers and their personal entourages of friends and relatives were hugging and kissing one another stage center. "He came back to tell the conductor to let the first violinist beat the time. But then I don't see him no more."

"Well, I'll probably talk to him tomorrow," I said. "By the way, congratulations. It was a terrific performance."

Madam Castagno smiled, a little wanly. "I got to have this dentist for a conductor," she said, "but he's the only one who can pay the musicians. So what happened to your head?"

"I tried to hit a high note and my skull cracked."

"Yeah, you're funny," she said. "You've got to be a little funny to stay in this business."

SEVENTEEN

◆

Carnal Pursuits

Fulvio and I did not go to Aqueduct the day after the second *Otello*. Anna called me about 9:00 A.M. from the apartment, as I was sipping coffee and idly perusing the *Times*, to inform me that the tenor was ill and in enforced seclusion. "Is it his cold?" I asked.

"He tried to sing last night," she said, "but he had to stop at the end of act one. Keegan finished up for him. You should have heard that bitch Pantaloni."

"What did she do?"

"When Fulvio had to release the A early at the end of the duet, she held on to her note so everyone would know he'd cracked," she explained, "and she came offstage laughing. Fulvio tried to kick her, but he missed and fell down."

"Is he okay?"

"He can't even talk. He's steaming."

"Still?"

"No, you don't understand. He's inhaling steam. It's the best thing you can do for a cold or a laryngitis. The doctor's coming over later."

"Tell him I don't much like the card today anyway," I said. "Does he know that one of his horses is running?"

"Which one?"

"Battle Flag."

"He'll want you to bet on him."

172

"No way. The horse has no chance. Monkton's got him in over his head and at the wrong distance."

"You could be wrong, of course."

"Not about this, no. But anyway, I don't want you to worry about Monkton."

"What do you mean by that?"

"I shouldn't have said anything," I told her. "Frankly, I don't care what you do on your own time. It's none of my business. But I am concerned about Fulvio."

"I don't know what you're talking about," she said icily and again hung up on me. It was getting to be a habit.

I spent the rest of the morning practicing in my room. With all the pressure on me to pick winners, I'd been neglecting my primary talent, so I put in a major session, especially on shuffling and dealing, techniques as basic to my profession as singing scales is to an opera star's. I needed another day off from the track and also I wanted to hang around, just in case Fulvio decided to contact me. I wasn't really on top of events, but I had a strong feeling that wheels were turning somewhere in the background of my life and that at some point I would find out something crucial to the situation. In any case, my room was probably the safest place to be, if there was indeed someone out there trying to ambush me.

At about noon I telephoned Pipistrello, but again I got no answer at home and this time no one at the Castagno Opera Workshop knew where he was either; he was not scheduled to coach that day. I shaved, showered, got dressed, and went out to lunch. When I came back, at about two-thirty, I found a message to call the Lagrange office. "Oh, I'm so glad we were able to get you," Gregory chirped into my ear. "Jeanine is so worried."

"Not about me, I'm sure."

"Wait, I'll put her on."

"Lou? I'm so happy you called," she began, in a tone so friendly I hardly recognized her voice.

"You are? What's going on?"

"Well, you know about Fulvio."

"Yes. How is he?"

"He's going to have to take it very easy for at least a week," she said, "which means he's going to miss the third *Otello* and maybe the last one as well. He should never have tried to sing last night. I did my best to stop him, but he's so stubborn."

"I guess I've noticed that."

"The doctor saw him this morning," she continued. "He has a

very slightly inflamed right vocal cord and they're both a little pink."

"I gather that's not good."

"It's a mild laryngitis, nothing terribly serious, but he can't sing or even talk for a few days at least. And, of course, he must stay in."

"Which means no racing either."

"No, definitely not," she said. "It's going to be very hard on him."

"Well, he can always send money out with me, if he wants the action, which I'm sure he does."

"I really would like to talk about this whole situation with you," she said. "I'm very concerned about it."

"I can understand that."

"I was up awfully late last night and I'm pretty tired," she said. "I'm going home in about half an hour. Can you drop by for a drink later?"

"Sure."

"Good. Gregory will give you my address. I'm on Sutton Place South."

"I think I know where that is."

"At about six?"

"Fine. Jeanine?"

"Yes, Lou."

"What have I done recently to endear myself to you?"

"I've been thinking quite a bit since our last unfortunate conversation," she explained. "I guess I owe you an apology."

"It's not necessary, Jeanine."

"I get so wrapped up in my clients' careers, especially Fulvio's, that I sometimes can't see the whole picture," she said. "You struck me as a threat, but I'm beginning to understand that I was wrong. I hope you'll forgive me."

"I'm a little surprised."

"I don't wonder. Anyway, come by and let's put our heads together."

I spent the rest of the afternoon in a movie, some heavy Japanese epic loosely based on *King Lear* that would have been a lot more entertaining if it had had a score by Verdi, and I arrived at her place a few minutes after six.

She lived in a large, red-brick apartment house with a green awning thrust out over the sidewalk and with a crew of doormen and elevator operators to whom I had to identify myself before I could be admitted to the premises. I thought I might even be frisked, but, in this era of terrorists, bombers, and proliferating street criminals, I really wouldn't have minded. The elevator man eventually deposited me on her landing, but lingered long enough to make certain I was recognized by her before he departed. Maybe it was my bandaged head that made them so suspicious.

Jeanine herself answered the door. "Come in, Lou," she said, with a smile. "I'm so glad you could make it."

"Well, it isn't as if I have a terrifically busy schedule."

"How's your injury coming along?"

"It feels okay. I should have the stitches out in a couple of days."

"What a world," she said, with a sigh. "You can't go anywhere anymore and feel safe."

I followed her inside, but I was so astonished by the change in her that at first I hardly noticed my surroundings. It was not only her attitude, but her looks. She had put on some makeup and her hair hung loosely in flowing curls down to her shoulders. She was wearing sandals and some sort of a black silk kimono that was slit up both sides practically to her waist, allowing for tantalizing glimpses of her long legs every time she moved. Furthermore, I was convinced that she was naked underneath this single outer garment. It had been some time now since I had last romped with Simone in Las Vegas and I had been living the life of a cloistered monk ever since. In my enfeebled state, I was badly shaken by Jeanine's appearance.

I tried to cope with my agitation by studiously concentrating first on the ice-cold vodka martini she insisted on serving me, even though I'd feebly indicated a preference for wine, then by trying to take stock of my surroundings. We were sitting in an intimate corner of her living room, at right angles to each other on a curved, white settee facing a fireplace in which a pile of burning logs crackled cheerily, providing most of the illumination. A single floor lamp burned dimly in one corner, emanating just enough light for me to notice that the walls were covered with very authentic-looking French Impressionist art, but otherwise I was too befuddled to notice much of anything else. Every time I glanced toward my hostess, I could see that I was within touching distance of her knee, a glorious-looking joint encased in the sort of satiny skin and firm flesh every libidinous male dreams of. Jeanine was clearly her own best work of art.

"How's your drink? Are you all right?" she asked, after several minutes of aimless chitchat about the traffic, the weather, and crime in the streets.

"It's fine, thanks."

"Now, what *are* we going to do about Fulvio?"

I set my drink down and turned again to look at her. She was leaning intently toward me, her elbows resting on her knees, and I could quite literally smell her. I still don't quite know how I dared, but without a word I simply leaned forward and kissed her. She did not actively respond, but she didn't pull away either. "I apologize," I said. "I don't know why I did that."

"It was very pleasant," she said softly. "Can we talk about Fulvio now?"

"Sure. Ask me anything you want."

"I suppose I really need to know how long you think this sort of thing can go on."

"What sort of thing? His gambling?"

"Yes."

"Forever. You're not going to get Fulvio to join Gamblers Anonymous, you know that as well as I do. He's hooked, but it can be controlled."

"How, Lou?"

"Well, he has his singing, that's more important to him than anything."

"Sometimes I wonder about that."

"Most gamblers substitute their habit for everything else in their lives," I continued. "Fulvio doesn't. He's a terrible gambler, but he's not the worst."

"What can we do about it?"

"Exactly what we are doing," I said. "Try to keep him away from casino games and bookies and in the one area where I can help him."

"For how long, Lou?"

"Well, that's a good point," I admitted. "I'm not going to be around forever. But I have a friend who's at least as good a handicapper as I am and he could take over for me. He'd love to travel. Perhaps we could split Fulvio between us, several months at a time."

"Who's your friend?"

"His name is Fox, Jay Fox. The one time of the year we'd both be unavailable is the summer, from the end of July to mid-September."

"What happens then?"

"That's the Del Mar meet, seven weeks of racing by the ocean in Southern California," I said, smiling. "We never miss Del Mar. We build our whole year around it."

"How odd," Jeanine said, "how very strange."

"It is, I admit, but then look at you, look at Fulvio," I pointed out. "What's more peculiar, wanting to see a horse race or paying money to sit for four hours in a theater to watch a bunch of overweight people dressed in ridiculous costumes screaming at each other in foreign languages?"

She laughed, the first time I had ever heard her do so, a throaty, contralto sound churning up from the bottom of a deep well. There wasn't much mirth in it, but it was interesting. "You have a point," she admitted.

"Of course that's not the way I feel about it," I said, "but most people do."

"Well, Fulvio often goes home in the summers," she said. "Perhaps I could book his dates so that he'd always be home then. Carmela keeps a pretty firm grip on him."

"Gambling is not his only problem at the moment."

"No? What else?"

"There's Gerald Monkton."

She stiffened visibly. "What about him?"

"Why are you so defensive about this guy? It's not your fault he's a crook."

"How can you say that, Lou? What proof do you have?"

"Look, I don't know how you got involved with him and I don't care," I said. "I'm sure he comes well recommended. He's a terrific con man, good-looking, talks a great game and all that. But he's a thief."

"You can't prove that."

"Actually, I could." I told her about the sale of Le Duc. "And if he'll steal at one end, he'll steal at the other. I'd bet you even-money he pockets some loot every time one of Fulvio's horses moves in or out of his stable. He's not unique in the horse business, Jeanine, but he's a pretty flagrant example of what used to be called a hotel trainer. Some years ago he must have figured out it was easier to stiff people than try to win races. How much has Fulvio lost so far? I'll bet it's a hell of a lot more than he's thrown away gambling."

She didn't answer right away, but got up to freshen our drinks. She moved with a silent, feline grace that suddenly reminded me of Simone and, in my weakened condition, set my blood to churning again. "What you say is very disturbing," she declared, as she dropped ice cubes into the shaker and stirred the contents. "I was introduced to Gerry through people in the business whose opinion I value highly. I was looking for an investment with a quick depreciation and I was told you can recover the cost of purchased horses over either a three- or a five-year period. Then there are operating expenses that can be deducted and a very good capital gains prospect. I estimated that we could turn a handsome profit from time to time and it seemed to fit in with what Fulvio likes to do."

"You'd need at least one top horse every few years, an animal whose value would multiply dramatically based on purses won, right?"

"Yes, something like that."

"But your man Monkton is buying stiffs," I said. "He's spending bunches of Fulvio's money on overpriced, mostly foreign horses with good pedigrees but no ability or who are already cripples. You don't make money that way, especially when you know that the buyer has a vested interest in making you pay too much. It's a very rich man's game, Jeanine. You may be a very smart lady in your field, but you don't know anything about horses. You've given this guy a license to steal."

"You haven't said anything to Fulvio about this, have you?" she asked, turning now to look at me.

"No, but I told you I would and I will, if you don't."

"He'd simply become very agitated and this is not the time," she said. "Fulvio's frantic about his voice right now and he has to take care of himself. That's all he should be concerned with. I hope you agree." She came back to the sofa, handed me my drink, and raised her glass to me. "Chin chin."

We drank and then she sat down again. The kimono parted and most of one leg came into dramatic view. She made no effort to cover it up and it remained there, glowing softly in the firelight and as irresistible to me as the sirens must have been to Ulysses and his merry crew. "I'll take care of Monkton," she said. "It's my fault. I should have paid much closer attention than I have."

"My guess is that you have well over a million dollars invested with him," I said, forcing myself to look away from her. "That's a lot of money on trust alone."

"I'll take care of it," she repeated. "But you mustn't alarm Fulvio, certainly not now. Lou?"

"Yes."

"Why don't you look at me?"

"Because you're a very disturbing sight."

She laughed that dark laugh of hers again, then turned my head with her hand. "So why don't you make love to me?" she asked.

How could I refuse such an offer? I almost shredded the kimono as I struggled to peel it off her, before we descended to the rug in front of the fireplace and I practically nailed her to the floor. In my frenzy I don't think I even bothered to remove all of my own clothes. Foreplay and concern for my partner were ideals I ignored totally, as I performed with the grace of Godzilla. When it was over, about a minute and a half later, and I toppled off her to lie, dazed with spent lust, by her side, she looked up at me and smiled. "Shifty?" she asked. "Are you sure it isn't Swifty?"

"I'm really sorry," I said. "Please give me a couple of minutes. I improve with practice."

"Come on." She stood up, took me by the hand, and led me into her bedroom, where we spent much of the next two hours in a more elaborate carnal romp, during which I managed to make some amends for my earlier boorishness. Jeanine proved to be a sexually skillful partner and made a good show of enjoying herself, but there was little tenderness in our lovemaking. And when it was over, she began briskly to reassemble herself for the rest of the evening, with the cool efficiency of a set designer erecting an elegant façade. She had clearly finished with me, if only temporarily, and I found myself wondering if she was expecting anyone else that night.

By the time I emerged from the bathroom and began to dress, she had already moved out to the living room, where I could hear her on the phone, once again dealing soothingly and professionally with some client who had obviously called her earlier, probably from abroad.

As I was buttoning up my shirt, I happened to glance idly at the top of her dresser, where she had mounted about a dozen small, framed photographs of friends, relations, and clients, some of them with herself in the picture. I recognized Fulvio, of course, and a couple of other major artists, and then my eye was caught by a color snapshot at the very rear of the group. It showed a full-grown lion up to his neck in the blue water of a swimming pool, flanked by a man and a woman. The lion was roaring with discomfort or dismay, but the couple was smiling broadly; they had their arms around the beast. I guessed that the photograph was probably three or four years old, but I knew that the lion was Wotan, because the people in the water with him were Tristan and Simone.

◆   ◆   ◆

I was ravenously hungry when I left Jeanine's place, about twenty minutes later. She was still on the phone, conversing with someone in French, when I reached the door and she ushered me out into the night with a casual, abstracted wave of the hand, as if we had spent the past two and a half hours together playing Trivial Pursuit. I walked west on Fifty-seventh Street for a while, mainly to clear my head, then I picked up a taxi at Lexington and went back to my little Italian restaurant on West Forty-eighth. I had no intention of walking home from there again, but the food was the best I had found, at a reasonable price, in the city. On the way, at a corner newsstand on Seventh Avenue, I picked up a copy of the *Post*, my favorite trashy newspaper, primarily to scan the next day's entries. It was still too early to buy the *Form*, which generally hit the streets at around eight-thirty. While waiting for my linguini with fresh clams to arrive, I browsed through the sports pages and looked over the names of the horses listed at Aqueduct. I marked a couple of races that looked promising, then set the paper aside to concentrate on my dinner.

The item about Achille Pipistrello did not hit me until after the salad course, when I turned to the front section of the *Post*, for the sort of luridly fascinating stories this publication had almost succeeded in elevating into an art form. A distraught mother in Queens had strangled her two tots and kept their little bodies in her freezer for two months. A Long Island handyman had been arrested for the torture murders of several young boys in his VW van. A swarm of poisonous African killer moths was invading Central America and massing for an assault on Mexico and later the U.S. Fifty thousand people were reported dead in a nuclear accident in Siberia that the Soviets had successfully covered up. Bloodsucking vampire bats were wiping out cattle herds in Argentina. A psychiatrist in California had been arrested for prescribing hallucinogenic mushrooms at weekend retreats for his patients. The minister of a Church of Satan congregation in Indiana had sacrificed his twelve-year-old niece on the altar during the course of a Black Mass attended mainly by members of a local motorcycle gang. After such startling revelations, I hardly even noticed the small headline in a lower righthand corner that said, MAN HAMMERED TO DEATH. I began reading it simply for want of anything else to glance at.

The body of a seventy-three-year-old vocal coach named Achille Pipistrello had been found at about 5:00 A.M. that morning in the alley beside his apartment house, on West Twenty-seventh Street.

A crew for the Department of Sanitation had discovered the corpse behind a trash bin. The old man's head had been bashed in by a number of severe blows from a small, blunt object. "Who knows and what difference does it make," an exasperated paramedic on the scene had been heard to say to a police officer, "but it sure looks like a hammer to me. It chopped him up pretty good." The killer must have been waiting for his victim either in the alley or in the street near the front entrance, and, judging from the state of the corpse, the attack had probably occurred sometime between midnight and 2:00 A.M. "This neighborhood is terrible," a nearby resident told the *Post* reporter. "We've had two other muggings and four robberies here just this last week. It's all these dope peddlers in the welfare hotels around here." The old man's money was missing, but his gold watch was on his wrist and his wallet had not been taken. "It is not known if the victim has any family," the story concluded.

I was sick. I sat there for five minutes until I felt sure I wouldn't heave my insides out all over the tablecloth, then I made it to the men's room and did throw up. When I came out five minutes later, I had to go to the bar for change, so I could make some telephone calls. "You look terrible," the bartender observed. "You okay?"

"I'm all right," I said. "I just got some bad news. I'm okay."

I went back to the public phone near the restrooms and called Fulvio's apartment, but I got his answering service instead. "We're not supposed to disturb him on any account," the operator informed me.

"It's an emergency. Is there anyone with him?"

"Miss Willows said she would call in."

"Then please ring through."

"I can't do that—"

"There's been a death," I explained. "Please put the call through."

"Fulvio's sleeping," Anna hissed into my ear. "You can't talk to him. I told the damn service—"

"Pipistrello's been murdered."

"What?"

I filled her in on some of the details. "Are you going to tell Fulvio or shall I?"

"I can't tell him now, for God's sake," she said. "I just got him to take a sleeping pill. He wanted you to call earlier."

"I couldn't. And there was nothing to talk about."

"What about tomorrow?"

"I'm going out of town for a day or two."

"You can't do that."

"Yes, I can. I have a family emergency."

"Fulvio won't like that."

"Tough. I'll be back by the weekend, I hope. You don't care about Achille, do you?"

"He was a boring little man."

"On second thought, don't tell Fulvio. Let him find out on his own."

"I'd rather, actually."

"You're really a cunt, Anna, you know that?" This time I hung up on her.

EIGHTEEN

◆

The Hammer

Vince Michaels picked me up at the airport in Las Vegas the next morning. He was waiting for me by the gate when I came off the plane and his face looked drawn. "What's the matter? What's happened?" he asked.

"I'm sorry I couldn't tell you very much last night," I said, "but I was pretty upset."

"You look terrible. What happened to your head?"

On the way into town I filled him in about what had been going on, but without explaining what my purpose was in coming to Vegas. "Don't worry about my head," I added, "it looks worse than it is. I should get the stitches out in a couple of days."

"Shifty, you're in too deep again," he said. "It seems to be a pattern with you. Why don't you just stick to magic?"

"I'm going to get back to it, Vince," I answered, "but I promised Fulvio six months. Also, we're making a lot of money. I'm handicapping like a god."

"If you live through it."

"And I've discovered opera, Vince. It's the greatest."

"Really? You think that?"

"Well, Verdi is the greatest," I elaborated. "Donizetti and Puccini are also fine. I'm keeping an open ear on the others."

"I hope you don't get into Wagner."

"I've only heard bits and pieces."

"Someone once took me in New York to hear *Parsifal*," Vince

183

reminisced. "It had some nice moments, but you had to wait about two hours for them."

"I'm reserving judgment, Vince."

He had moved since I'd last seen him, into a medium-sized apartment complex that looked like a miniature Versailles, two blocks off the Strip. It had a large interior courtyard, a sizable swimming pool, tennis courts, and a communal Jacuzzi. To get to his place, on a corner of the ground floor, we had to walk past the pool, around which several fine-looking bodies were basking in the desert sun. "This is nice, Vince," I said. "In New York they have winters. Good-looking neighbors, too."

"A lot of the kids in the MGM and Hilton shows live here," he explained. "It can get noisy when there are parties around the pool, but most of the time it's quiet."

"You like it better than your old digs?"

"Oh, yeah, I've got more room."

He was right, even though the premises looked very much like his old place, with magic posters and a couple of old oil paintings depicting medieval acts of legerdemain on the walls, piles of books on the profession spilling out from his shelves into heaps all over the floor, and odd bits and pieces of our craft lying about here and there, as if dropped at random from above. "Your housekeeping hasn't improved," I noted, with a smile. "You could clutter up the Grand Canyon."

"Look who's talking," he answered. "And I even made your bed. How long are you staying?"

"Just tonight, I hope." I asked him about Dawn.

"She's still at Circus Circus," he said. "You going to call her?"

I shook my head. "If you see her, tell her you talked to me and say hello."

"Sure."

"I miss her. I haven't been meeting any nice women recently, if you except the wife of a horse trainer I know."

"Be like me. Do without."

"I wish I could, but I don't seem to be able to. Can I use your phone?"

"Why not? That's what it's there for. You can call from your room, if you want privacy."

"I think I will, Vince," I said. "The less you know about any of this, the better."

"I agree. But when you finish I'm going to show you a couple of new moves I've been working on."

Detective Larry Sturm had not yet come to work, I was informed by the Las Vegas Police Department, but he was expected around three o'clock. I left my name and reminded the officer on duty I'd be dropping in. "I was a mugging victim here a few weeks ago," I declared. "I left word for Larry last night and told him I'd be coming by today."

"Look at this," Vince said, when I emerged from the bedroom. "Watch." He was standing behind the coffee table in his living room, rolling two fifty-cent pieces back and forth in his hands over a couple of coffee cups. I sat down. I knew better than to walk away from Vince when he had a new effect to try out and I wasn't disappointed. For the next half-hour I watched him move those coins under, into, and out of the cups, make them vanish, then change them into English pence, French francs, and Italian lire. The moves were hardly original, but Vince pulled them off with the panache of a master showman. For a finale, he clapped his hands and the coins simply vanished into air. "You like?" he asked, beaming.

"Great, Vince, really."

"And what have you got to show me?"

"Nothing, Vince. But I'm working on a few things."

"Like what?"

"I'm trying to materialize a murderer," I said. "It's not easy."

"Shifty, what's to become of you?"

"Good question, Vince. I don't have an answer right now."

I had an hour or so to kill, so Vince loaned me a pair of shorts I could barely squeeze into and I went out to bask in a little poolside sunshine. I commandeered an empty beach chair facing the diving board, lay down, and promptly dozed off. When I woke up about twenty minutes later, I found myself looking at the lean, bronzed body of a young man sitting on the end of the diving board. He had long black hair and a mustache and a jeweled crucifix dangled from a gold chain around his neck. He was talking to a couple of other willowy males sunbathing on rubber mats to one side of him. He laughed at something one of them said, then gracefully slid off the end of the board and swam four or five laps before reemerging, this time at my end of the pool. He reached for a towel and began briskly to rub himself dry. "Hello, Felix," I said. "Remember me?"

He looked up. "Oh, hi," he said, smiling. "Where have you been?"

"New York. I've been working. How's Tristan?"

"Fine, I guess."

"You aren't together anymore?"

"Oh, God, no," he said, with a little shiver. "I couldn't take that scene. I mean, I've done things in my life—well, you know, a little group stuff—but like, wow, I've never been into the real heavy numbers."

I immediately decided to pretend I knew exactly what he was talking about. "I know what you mean," I said. "That's why I broke up with Simone."

"They're too much, those two. I heard all about you, of course. Simone was furious."

"About Milù? Yeah, I know. That thing attacked me."

"Listen, you should have seen what they do with him at the parties," he said. "I mean, is it weird! Here's Tristan all tied up and stuff and everybody running around in their gear and she just turns that cat loose while it's all going on. I mean, what if he took a bite out of someone while they're just hanging there? It's dangerous!"

"Maybe that's part of getting their kicks."

"You got it, Shifty, believe me. Anyway, she's wilder than any cat. Did you ever see her all dressed up in that black rubber outfit she wears?"

"No. I guess she figured I wasn't quite ready for that."

"She just goes crazy. Boys, girls, animals—I mean, it's the whole scene. They wanted to tie me up one night in that harness they have in there, but I'm not into that stuff." He laughed. "I kind of wondered about you when I found out what they like and all, but then when you split I figured you didn't want any part of that scene either. One night she had some guy there who was really just a thug. I mean, he didn't get into costume or anything. He just kind of liked to beat people up, I think. She'd think up things to do and he'd do them. He was like a gangster."

"Who was he?"

"Oh, I don't know. Somebody I'd never even seen before. He just showed up the night of the last big party and he had these poppers."

"What's a popper?"

"Oh, God, sweetie, you don't know anything, do you?"

"Not much."

"A popper is what they call these little plastic capsules which have amyl nitrate in them," he explained. "You're supposed to like sniff them when you're getting off. It gives you a terrific high for like a few seconds, but it's dangerous. I mean, I have to stay in some kind of shape, you know? I'm a dancer and I just can't do drugs. Oh, it was all so sick. And you know what's sad?"

"What?"

"Tristan. I mean, he's so nice and sweet. I really thought we had something going there, the two of us. I had no idea he was so kinky. But I think it's really her fault. She kind of runs everything, you know? I mean, I think she got him into it."

"This guy with the poppers, did you get his name?"

"She called him Charlie. I don't know what his whole name is."

"What did he look like?"

"I told you, like a gangster. He was kind of short and dark, with a lot of disgusting hair all over him, like an ape. Oh, he was terrible. I can't imagine what Simone saw in him. He'd just go up to any girl he wanted and, you know, do her. I mean, he was so brutal. Anyway, that's not my scene at all. I got the hell out of there and fast. Tristan called me a couple of times, but I'm afraid to go over there now."

"Yes, I was glad to get out of there, too."

He finished drying himself and draped the towel around his shoulders. "Well, it's nice to see you," he said. "What happened to your head?"

"I was mugged."

"Goodness!"

"Anyway, it's just a cut," I said. "I'm fine, really."

"Well, I have to go to work now," he said. "We're rehearsing the new show. It was nice seeing you again."

"Same here, Felix. Be good."

"Up to a point, sweetie, but I'm not going to overdo it."

After he'd gone, I lay back to let the sun finish baking the New York cold out of my bones, while I tried to assimilate what Felix had revealed into the still vague picture now forming in my head. I was pretty sure of a couple of designs in it, but I couldn't imagine a logical reason for what was going on, certainly not one to justify clubbing a helpless old man to death in the street. That part of the picture agitated me too much to allow me to relax again, so I went back inside and began to dress. Vince was sitting at a card table, working on his moves; he didn't even look up when I said good-bye to him.

"Oh, yeah, I remember you," Larry Sturm said, as I sat down at his desk. "What happened? You got hit again?"

"Yes, but not here," I said. "In New York."

"That's where you called me from last night?"

"That's right. I need your help."

"My help? You need a bodyguard."

"Larry, I think the same guy hit me in New York." Then I told him about the attack on Hugo in L.A. and finally all about what had happened to Pipistrello. "Nobody's had a really good look at this guy," I concluded, "but the descriptions I do have are similar in every case. He's short and stocky and dark. He wears brown suits and sports a black fedora. He hits people on the head with a blunt object. It could be a pipe or a sap of some kind, but I think it's a hammer. He takes your money, but that's all. He leaves your jewelry, watch, wallet untouched. He may be a sadist, he's certainly some kind of pervert."

"A hammer?" the detective asked. "Why a hammer?"

"You tell me."

"It doesn't ring any kind of bell, Anderson. Sorry." He leaned back in his chair and put his hands behind his head, looking at me out of those pale, flat blue eyes with the mild contempt of the old pro for a pretentious rookie. "Did you tell this story to the police in New York?"

"No, of course not. It wouldn't make any sense to them."

"And you think it makes sense to me?"

"Frankly, Larry, I'm not interested in whether it makes sense to you at this point," I said. "But you may be able to help me."

"I doubt it, friend."

I plunged ahead anyway, sailing full tilt into the head wind of his professional disdain. "You know about Tristan and Simone?"

"The magic act? What about them?"

"They got any kind of record?"

"Record? Criminal record?" He sat up now, the blue eyes widened in amazement. "What the hell are you driving at, Anderson?"

"I don't mean I think they did it, Larry," I hastily explained. "What I really want to know is whether Simone was ever involved, or may still be involved, with a hood named either Charlie or Agostino."

"Charlie or Agostino? You—wait a minute, okay?" He got up, walked out of his cubicle for a minute or two, long enough to ask some subordinate to look up a charge sheet for him, then stepped back to his desk. "How'd you get to this guy?"

I told him everything I'd heard about Simone and her possible involvement with a hood of some kind, including what I'd gleaned just an hour or so earlier from my chance encounter with Felix. Sturm heard me out, but far more attentively than earlier in our meeting and with no trace of his apparently habitual cynicism. I was just finishing up my account when a young officer stuck his head around a corner of the partition. "Here it is, Lieutenant," he said, handing Sturm a fairly bulky manila folder.

Sturm thanked him and took it, then browsed through the contents for several minutes, while I sat there and waited. Finally, he looked up. "Carlo Agostino Martello," he said. "That's his real name. He's also known as Charlie August. Ever seen him before?" He thrust a mug shot across the desk at me.

The man in the photograph could have been typed for the role of a small-time thug by Central Casting. He was a stocky, bull-necked man in his mid-forties, unshaven, going bald, with a tight, unsmiling mouth and small, black eyes set close together over a broad, flat nose. "This could be the guy, but I couldn't swear to it in court," I had to admit. "Who is he?"

"We know him," Sturm said. "He's got a record, all right, but nothing sensational. He was an enforcer or collector for a bookie in Chicago. He came out here five or six years ago and opened a jewelry store out in Nugget. We suspected it was a front of some kind, maybe hookers, money laundering, we don't know. Anyway, it failed, or he closed it up after a year. After that, he's just been around. He had a private limousine service for a while. We know he's had a small string of working girls from time to time. He beat a couple of them up. He's supplied girls for parties, conventions, stuff like that. He did time back in Illinois for assault and battery and he worked as a bartender-bouncer out in some B-girl joint in Cicero. He likes to beat up on people, I guess."

"He probably met Simone by running girls to her parties."

"I wouldn't know. That's your guess."

"Yeah. Is he Mafia connected?"

"If he is, he's way down the pecking order, because we haven't heard of him. He may be a soldier for some family or other, but I doubt it. My guess is he's just a punk for hire. For five hundred bucks, you can get anybody maimed in this town."

"Plus he gets to keep your money."

"Sure, you can't trace the bills. That's why he doesn't take your watch or your credit cards. The money is like a little bonus for a job well done." The detective smiled. "There are perks in every business."

"Was he born in Chicago?"

Sturm glanced at his sheet. "Rome. He came over here right after World War Two, when he was three or four. His father had a brother in Chicago and he was raised there. Apparently the family

is straight, so he must be the black sheep. This isn't a hell of a lot to
go on, is it?"

"It helps, Larry."

"It doesn't give you a motive and you can't identify the guy. I
sure couldn't pick him up on what you told me."

"I know that. By the way, Martello—I wonder if that name
means anything in Italian," I said, pushing my chair back and
getting ready to leave.

Sturm preceded me to the door. "Hey, Tom," he called out
across the room, where I could hear a dozen or so officers moving
about or talking on the telephone, "what's *martello* mean in Italian?
Anything?"

"Sure," a male voice shot back. "It means 'hammer.' "

"Well, what do you think of that?" Sturm asked me, with a
broad smile.

"We couldn't make that stick in court either, could we?" I asked.

"Not a chance, Anderson. These guys all have lawyers. Watch
yourself, hear? And call if you find out anything. Don't be a hero."

"I'm a child at heart and my needs are simple," I assured him. "I
just like to deal cards and play horses."

"That's a hell of a way to live."

"I think it is."

The act was still terrific, even more dazzling than I'd remembered it. They had added an African elephant to replace Wotan,
and Tristan made his entrance on the beast, while Simone floated
toward him from the wings to alight on the very tip of the beast's
upraised trunk. Encased in shimmering black, she seemed to hover
there like a sinister humming bird, her face isolated by a spot. At
Tristan's command, the pachyderm lowered Simone slowly to the
floor, then, at a clap of the magician's hands, she rose again into
the air on her own and vanished in a puff of orange smoke. The
rest of the routine was pretty much as I remembered it, with Milù
once again an intrinsic and intimidating participant. At the very
end, as Simone, dangling by her heels from her trapeze, swung out
over the audience, I stood up, smiled, and waved at her. By
greasing the headwaiter, I had secured a table in the center of the
room, so she couldn't miss seeing me. For an instant she seemed to
freeze in space, her face an icy mask, then she quickly recovered
her composure, but did not drag out her farewell. With a final
wave and a smile, she and Tristan disappeared into the final blackout.

On the pretext of knowing one of the chorus girls, I managed to get backstage and encountered Tristan on his way below to take care of his animals. "Ah, Shifty, *mein freund*," he said, with a worried half-smile, "Simone is very upset. She knows you are here. What is wrong with your head?"

"An accident, nothing serious," I told him. "I didn't mean to upset her. I just want to see her for a couple of minutes."

"I don't think she wish to see you, Shifty," he countered. "She is still so angry from the thing with Milù. I have talk to her, but it is no good. You must give her more time."

"There is no more time, Tristan," I said. "I'm only here one night and I do really need to see her. Where is she? In her dressing room?"

"*Ya*," he answered, nodding unhappily. "You be careful. She is so violent sometimes."

"Yes, I know."

"You must excuse now, I must go to the animals." He turned and headed for the stairs.

"Tristan," I called after him, "it wasn't an accident." But in the crush and noise of chattering bodies passing around us, he didn't hear me, and I didn't pursue him. He obviously had his own problems, some of them bordering on the pathological, and who was I to exacerbate them? I liked Tristan and felt sorry for him.

I waited until the traffic in the corridor had thinned out perceptibly and then I knocked on Simone's door. No answer. I knocked again and then, doing my best to disguise my voice, I called out, "Signorina De Caro, please!"

A moment passed, then the door swung open and I was confronted by Simone. She was dressed in a short terrycloth robe that came halfway down her thighs and her face was partly covered with cold cream. Even so she looked as sexually desirable as ever, but her eyes were alive with anger. I also sensed alarm in her demeanor, which pleased me. Behind her, from his cage against the wall, I heard Milù's familiar hiss. "What do you want?" she asked in a whisper. "Haven't you done enough already?"

"Your maiden name *is* De Caro, isn't it?"

"What difference does it make?"

"Quite a lot of difference, to me." I touched my bandaged ear. "Your pal Charlie August, better known as the Hammer, is running around everywhere hitting people over the head. He tried to kill me and he succeeded in killing poor old Achille Pipistrello."

"I have no idea what you are talking about." She tried to close the door on me, but I stuck my foot in it and leaned against it.

"I want to know why, Simone," I said. "I think I know quite a bit now or maybe I can guess, but I want you to tell me. Then maybe we can reach some sort of understanding."

"You are being ridiculous."

"You don't even know somebody named Charlie August?"

"Of course not. Take your foot out of my door or I will call someone."

"Go ahead," I urged her. "We can talk about this in public, if you like."

"Damn you, what is it you want?"

"I want to stay alive, Simone. By the way, I've discussed this whole matter with some people in the Las Vegas Police Department. They know who Charlie August is. Or do you call him Carlo? Or Agostino? What *do* you call him when he runs in the girls for your kinky soirees? Is what he does there also part of his commission? And how come you never asked me to one of your little orgies? What was I, sacred love? Were the profane events reserved for others? Or were you acting on instructions, Simone? Combining business and pleasure, were you? Did you imagine—"

She gave a sort of little cry that sounded like something you'd hear in one of those nature programs on TV, a call in the depths of the jungle from a small, enraged animal in distress. Then she took the edge of the door with both hands and with all her considerable strength slammed it shut against me. I hadn't been ready for her and the violence of the act succeeded; I staggered back a few paces. By the time I recovered, the door had been locked shut in my face. I hesitated, one hand raised to knock for readmittance, but the incident had not passed unnoticed. A stagehand at the far end of the hall, near the stage door, had heard and seen enough to stop and look. "Hey," he called out, "you looking for something, mister?"

I smiled, shrugged helplessly, and walked toward him. "Not anymore," I said. "I think I found it."

NINETEEN

♦

Requiems

The funeral Mass for Achille Pipi-
strello took place the day after I got back from Las Vegas. Anna
told me about it when I called the apartment to inform Fulvio of
my return. "He's been asking about you," she said. "Weren't you
supposed to be here yesterday?"

"I had to stay over an extra day to take care of some personal
business," I explained. "How's he doing?"

"Much better," she said. "He may be able to sing by the middle
of next week, which means he'll be here for the last *Otello*. But
he's very upset about the old man. He heard about it from Gregory."

"I knew you wouldn't tell him."

"Fuck you, Anderson," she suggested pleasantly. "Fulvio still
can't talk, but he wants to hear from you. He wants to know about
this coming weekend."

"I have to look at the entries. He won't be going, will he?"

"No. He's not supposed to go out for another three or four days.
But he insists on attending the funeral."

"When is it?"

"Tomorrow morning, at ten o'clock." She gave me the address.
"What a bore."

"You have true compassion, Anna. You're one of nature's great
noblewomen."

She hung up on me. Of course.

It began to snow that night. By morning several inches had fallen
and the city had begun to grind to a standstill. I was happy about it,

because I realized that the track would be closed for a few days; I didn't exactly have horses on my mind at the moment. I walked from my motel to the church, a modest-looking gray-stone edifice on Lexington Avenue, in the East Seventies, and arrived there after the ceremony had started. To my surprise, the place was more than half full, mostly, I quickly realized, with members of the Castagno Opera Workshop. I slid into a pew toward the rear and immediately spotted Fulvio. Flanked by Anna and Gregory, he was sitting in one of the front rows. He was wearing a blue beret and a heavy fur coat with the collar pulled up around his ears, and his nose and throat were guarded by a thick woolen scarf wound tightly around the lower half of his face. He looked like a terrorist. I didn't see Jeanine anywhere.

The service itself was moving. I didn't understand much of the formal part of it, but several members of the Castagno sang, the young tenor I had heard at the *Bohème* rehearsal brought us all to tears with a very sweet, lyrical interpretation of a piece from the Verdi *Requiem*. What a composer! Fulvio was weeping visibly, his huge shoulders jerking spasmodically with grief. Anna did not touch him, but Gregory, I was glad to see, had his arm around him, or as far around him as he could reach, which must have been at least of some comfort to him.

I left before the end, as the mourners bowed their heads in final prayer, and went outside. The storm showed no sign of slackening and snow had already settled solidly on buildings and sidewalks, imparting an eerily beautiful look to even the ugliest structures. The buses were still running and a few taxis were in evidence, but most private cars had disappeared and the greatly reduced traffic moved slowly, purring softly over the accumulating carpet of white as if afraid to disturb a highly theatrical effect. The silent downfall had stilled the clamor of the city and bathed the scene in muted glory, transforming it into a dreamlike evocation of childhood memories, when I had lived in the East and romped often in the winter snow. I was standing there, on the church steps, bemused by this unexpected recollection, when someone came quietly up beside me and said softly into my unbandaged ear, "Come on, Anderson, we're going to see Paulie."

I started to turn around, but felt an iron hand on my upper arm propelling me toward the sidewalk. "Hey, wait a minute—" I started to protest.

"You want your arm broken?" the voice beside me asked quietly. "Don't say nothin'. Just move."

As we hit the sidewalk, the rear door of a black Cadillac limousine swung open and I was swiftly hustled toward it. "Don't do nothin' stupid now," the voice said. "It's okay. Paulie only wants to talk to you."

I made a last attempt to get free. I turned, intending to break away, but found myself clasped face to face with my assailant. My first impression was of cold, impersonal fury, the eyes of a snake above high cheekbones and a thin, tight mouth. I could also now feel the muzzle of a large gun jammed into my stomach, just below my rib cage. "You could go right here," the man said. "Or you can talk to Paulie."

I really had no choice. I climbed into the sedan and was shoved into the backseat, next to another man sitting in the far corner. My kidnapper climbed in behind me and took one of the jump seats, sitting with his back to the driver and facing me, one hand still in his coat pocket, obviously holding the pistol. He smiled at me as the car pulled silently away from the curb. The whole maneuver, I realized later, couldn't have taken more than thirty or forty seconds and I was certain no one near us had noticed anything in the least unusual.

"This the guy?" my kidnapper asked.

The passenger in the corner reached out and patted his knee. "Yeah, you did good, Benny," he said. "Relax. Shifty here knows better than to behave foolishly, don't you? You aren't going to do anything stupid, are you?"

"Not if I can help it," I said. "But I don't know what you want."

"It isn't what we want, Shifty," the man said. "We're doing a friend a favor, that's all. We just want to talk to you."

"Who are you?"

The man smiled and waved one hand deprecatingly in the air. "I'm a friend of friends," he said. "We just want to ask you a few questions."

"And you answer them right, asshole," Benny chimed in, "or I'll break your fuckin' face open."

"Somebody's already tried to do that," I said.

"Benny, please," the man in the corner said. "There's no need yet. Calm down." He smiled affably at me. "Now then, Shifty, I'm sure you'll cooperate. This shouldn't take very long."

"I'll tell you what I can, sure," I said, doing my best to ignore the hostile Benny. "What do you want to know?"

"Who are you? What are you doing here?"

"That's easy." I told him the whole story, from my chance encounter with Fulvio at the tables in Las Vegas to my subsequent appearance and big winning day in New York. As I talked, my questioner gazed abstractedly out the window at the falling snow. He was a thin, very small man of about seventy, nattily dressed, with little pointed shoes that barely touched the floor. The top part of his head and eyes were obscured by a black homburg, but he had a small black mustache and several gold rings on his manicured fingers. He spoke articulately in a low, pleasant baritone, but as if he had studied hard to overcome an earlier deficiency, perhaps a street argot of some kind. He could have been a William Morris agent. And as we talked, the limousine continued to move slowly uptown, weaving gradually through narrow side streets toward the East River Drive. "Where are we going?" I asked, when I had concluded my account.

"Don't worry about it," Paulie said, turning back to me with a smile. "We'll get you home all right."

"Unless you fuck up," Benny added.

"What were you doing in Vegas?" Paulie asked.

"I was taking care of some private business."

"Asshole," Benny said, leaning in toward me. "I'll whack you right now."

"You went to the police," Paulie said. "Why?"

I told him why. "I think somebody sicced this guy August or Agostino onto me," I added. "I also think he beat the old man to death. I'm not sure why, but I do know he was involved with Simone Krueger. I had to go to Vegas to make sure. I only talked to Sturm and he pretty much confirmed my feeling."

"You talked to the broad, too?"

"I went to see her backstage," I said. "She slammed the door in my face. People have been doing that kind of thing a lot to me lately. I find it depressing."

"You was fuckin' the cunt," Benny said, with his customary *savoir dire.*

"Benny, shut the fuck up," Paulie said, in a new tone I hadn't heard before; it could have sliced through concrete. Benny grunted unhappily, but sat back on his seat, temporarily out of it. I was grateful for that, at least.

"Simone and I had an affair," I explained. "She takes a lot of satisfying, more than any one person can provide, I guess. I'm not into orgies and S and M. Anyway, she got tired of me and it ended."

"But it didn't end, did it?"

"No, I guess not. I went to Vegas to find out why."

"And did you find out?"

"No, only about Charlie August," I lied. I knew it was risky, but it could be riskier still, I decided, to admit to knowing too much. "I get a little antsy when some guy is running around the country bashing me and my friends over the head," I continued. "I want Simone or whoever to pull this guy off me. I have a vested interest in life."

For the first time Paulie smiled, revealing an even row of white, perfectly capped little teeth. He reminded me of a small, efficient killing animal of some kind, like a ferret or a polecat. "Okay, so now, Shifty, I want you to tell me what you think is going on," he said. "What do you make of all this?"

"What do I make of it?" I asked. "You mean about Fulvio?"

Benny grunted angrily and stirred on his jump seat, but Paulie flashed him a look that froze him in place. "Just tell me what you think this is all about. That's not so hard, is it?"

"No, I guess not," I said, as the limousine now turned onto the drive at Ninety-sixth Street and we began to move up along the river toward the Triboro Bridge. "Basically, I think everybody's exploiting Fulvio. He's a great singer and a fine artist, but he's a child. He's got a girlfriend who screws around on him. He's got a manager who uses him and who may be in cahoots with this horse trainer, Monkton. They're robbing him blind, or at least he is. And you know that Fulvio's a diseased gambler. He really needs a twenty-four-hour guard to keep him from temptation and he should have somebody with him to manage his money for him."

"You've been doing good for him, I hear."

"If he sticks to horses, I can make him some money, nothing like the one big day we had at Aqueduct," I said, "but we could win, with disciplined play. Fulvio's not big on discipline. I can't make him a winner in the casinos or with bookies, no one can. All I could do is cut his losses. We've been very, very lucky so far."

Paulie assimilated the information, but did not pursue the topic. He stared out the window as we drove across the bridge and into Queens. I couldn't imagine why I was being whisked out of Manhattan. At first I thought we were headed for the track, but then I realized there would almost certainly be no racing today and I began to sweat. I had a vision suddenly of being taken to some empty building or parking lot somewhere and being turned over to the kindly ministrations of Benny, who obviously enjoyed his work and would relish eliminating me from the scene. The moment we left the parkway and began to head for a factory area not far from the waterfront, I decided to make a run for it, no matter how desperate my chances. I planned to lunge for the door on my side, while jabbing fingers into Benny's eyes, and bolt. I didn't really think I'd get away with this crude maneuver, but I was not simply going to let Benny whack me, as he would so graciously put it. I am not one to go quietly into the fading of the light.

I was poised to make my move and waiting only for Benny's concentration to waver even for a second, when the car suddenly swooped in toward the curb and stopped in front of a large, rust-colored warehouse. Several dark-green and orange moving vans belonging to a company called Mercury Van and Storage were parked nearby, but otherwise the street was empty. "Okay, Shifty," Paulie said, "Benny and I get out here. Jimmy will take you home."

Benny looked disappointed, but said nothing. "This is the deal," Paulie continued. "You just go on doing what you're doing, only you don't ask any more questions of anyone and you don't talk to the police again anywhere, is that clear?"

"Yes, but—"

"No buts," Paulie said, holding up one delicate little hand to cut me off. "No buts and no whys, no nothing." He moved to get out of the car, but turned with his hand on the door handle for one last word. "And you ain't—you're *not* to worry about Charlie August anymore. It's being taken care of." He now spoke to the driver, a burly man who had not said a word or even glanced once at us the entire time. "Jimmy, you take Mr. Anderson here back to his hotel or wherever he wants to go." He got out of the car and walked swiftly across the snowy sidewalk toward the warehouse entrance, followed by Benny, who shot me one last, withering look as he went.

I smiled and waved cheerily at him, as we pulled away from the curb. A foolhardy gesture, I suppose, but my mother once told me it always pays to be nice to everyone.

Jeanine was sitting in the lobby of the motel, waiting for me. She stood up when she saw me, but lingered in place until I had picked up my room key. She was dressed simply, in black slacks and a dark green turtleneck sweater, and her hair was pulled back into a no-nonsense bun. She looked much the same as the day I met her, a very attractive woman who seemed to be indifferent to or playing down her sexuality, but there was a noticeable difference in her attitude. She was frightened. As I rang the elevator bell, she came up beside me and put a hand on my arm. "Lou, I must talk to you."

I let her follow me up to my room and then shut the door behind us. "Please lock it," she said.

I slid the bolt into place and added the chain for good measure, then turned back to her. She was staring out the corner window at the snow blowing in flurries across the adjacent rooftops and over the gray water of the Hudson, a slice of which was visible from there. "Want a drink?" I asked. "Or some coffee?"

"No," she said, pivoting to look at me and then leaning back on the sill, her hands braced against it as if to take off at a moment's notice. "You went to see Simonetta."

"Yes. So that is her real name. I figured she'd have told you I showed up."

"You threatened her."

"No, I didn't. I just asked her a few questions she didn't seem to want to answer."

"How much do you know about us?"

"Enough, Jeanine."

"Tell me. I want to hear for myself."

"Well, I could start by asking you a question or two."

"I may not answer."

"I think you will." I sat down on the bed, propped the pillows behind my back, and put my feet up. I wasn't at all relaxed, but I wanted her to think I was. From where she stood, with the light now behind her, I couldn't see her face too clearly, but it didn't matter to me. She had ceased to exist for me as a woman; I couldn't even remember now what it had been like to make love to her. "How old were you when your father died?" I asked.

"What?"

"You are Renato De Caro's daughter, aren't you?"

She did not move and the silence grew between us like an invisible wall. I waited; I knew she would have to come through the wall to me sooner or later, or she would not have sought me out at all. "What difference can that make?" she asked. "What possible difference?"

"It has something to do with the way I now feel about you and Simone," I explained. "If you were very young—"

"I was eight. Simone was four. So what?" she snapped. "But I remember. I found him."

"In his swimming pool?"

"Yes. He was lying on his back at the bottom of the pool," she said, in a voice as lifeless as the corpse itself. "I went out with my governess to have a swim. He was lying there on the bottom of the pool. His eyes and mouth were open and he was dressed in his white summer suit. They told me he had drowned."

"And he hadn't."

"He had been strangled. There were heavy stones in his pockets. I learned all that later from my mother."

"And they never found out who did it."

"Of course not. The police said it was an accident, that he had fallen into the pool and drowned."

"So then what happened?"

"There was a big funeral. Many people came to it. My father was a very well-known doctor in Naples, but I suppose you know that already."

"Did Don Pippo come to the funeral?"

"I told you, everyone came," she said harshly. "Everyone. Even his murderers."

"It must have been hard on you," I said. "Did you love your father?"

"I—I hardly ever saw him." She stood up suddenly, turned away, and began to stare out the window again at the falling snow.

"When did you come to America?" I asked.

"Very soon after the funeral," she answered, with her back still to me. "My mother and her brother, my uncle, they brought us. We had plenty of money. My family had—connections. We lived in Boston till I was twelve, then we moved to New York."

"You never went back to Naples?"

"No. Never."

"Where's your family now?"

"We have no family. My uncle disappeared a few weeks after we got here. We never saw him again. My mother raised us. She died two years ago. She had cancer."

"They only kill the men in that world," I observed. "I guess they didn't anticipate any trouble from a couple of little girls brought up in America."

Now she swung around to look at me again and I could make out her expression. She was angry, but wary, much too afraid to reveal the possible extent of her cold fury. "I didn't waste my whole life plotting revenge, if that's what you mean," she said, in a flat, even voice, as if reciting a catechism. "I made a career for myself. I never thought about what happened. I put it behind me."

"Did you really?"

"Well, I used to have nightmares. I'd always see his face there, staring up at me through the green water, and I'd wake up screaming," she continued. "But by the time I was in my teens, the dreams came less often. Eventually they stopped coming at all."

"Tell me about Simonetta," I said. "It's an odd profession for someone with her background."

"She always had this thing with animals. And she loved gymnastics."

"And the kinky stuff?"

"I don't know. I don't know where that comes from. Does anyone?" she answered. "She was always that way, from the age of thirteen or fourteen. She was thrown out of three boarding schools and she ran away to join a carnival. She went to Europe. I didn't see her for three years. Not till she showed up one spring with the circus, here in New York. We've been in touch ever since."

"I guess you have."

"How did you find out about us? Who told you?"

"No one," I said. "I sort of pieced it together, Jeanine. Simone calls her sister in New York. She refers to you as Gianna. So does Fulvio, once. You tell me you're from Naples. It doesn't take Sherlock Holmes. When did you Frenchify your name? When you married Jean Claude?"

"Who did you talk to in Las Vegas?"

"The police."

"Why?"

"I've been trying to find out who this guy is who's running around the country bashing people over the head."

"And did you?"

"Not so I could prove it in court, but I know who he is."

"Tell me."

"His name's Carlo Agostino Martello, but he's better known as Charlie August," I said. "He's also called the Hammer, because he likes to hit people on the head with that particular tool. It matches his last name, so it's probably a simpleminded manifestation of his macho male ego. Simone was involved with him at one time. We both know why. Now he runs hookers into their late-night parties. He's not a lot of fun to be around."

"How do you know all this?"

"That's my business, Jeanine. Why should I tell you? You might sic the guy onto someone else."

"I didn't sic him onto anybody. What are you talking about?"

"I suppose I should tell you at this point that I've shared my information with the police in Vegas," I lied.

"It's just your story," she said. "You can't prove it."

"No, but I want them to know where to look in case anything happens to me."

"Are you accusing me of having ordered this man to beat you up?" she said. "That's fantastic! That's incredible!" She began to move toward the door. "I'm leaving."

I stood up and confronted her. "What did you come here for, Jeanine?"

"To see how you were. Now get out of my way."

"Bullshit." She tried to push past me. I held her back at first, but then I let her go and she got her hand on the lock. "You came because you're scared out of your wits," I said. "You think Fulvio's people may be on to you. You came here to find out how much I know."

She didn't answer, but released the chain, unbolted the door, and opened it. Before she could walk out into the corridor, I said, "They do know about you, Jeanine."

She turned and stared at me. Her face was pale, her eyes wide and dark with fear. "Fulvio? What does he know?"

"Fulvio's a child," I said, "it doesn't matter what he knows. Outside of the opera house or the concert stage, he's helpless and you know it. You should have figured all along that Carmela would keep an eye on him and what happens to him wherever he goes. Or maybe you did figure it out, but you made a serious mistake. You put Charlie August onto the old man and got him killed."

"Simone—"

"Simone nothing. You're the one who called the shots."

She seemed to hover in the doorway, undecided whether to flee or to find out exactly how much I knew. She wanted desperately to leave, to make at least a symbolic escape, but she had to ascertain exactly where I stood and whether I could now be of use to her, so, as I had foreseen, she closed the door behind her. She did not come back into the room, but lingered there, arms folded, her shoulders leaning against the door. Her face was a mask of indifference, but her eyes gleamed like those of a prowling night animal caught in a sudden glare of unexpected light. She was frightened and she was dangerous.

I walked across the room away from her and sat down in a chair facing her. She had come without a purse and I didn't think she was armed, but I couldn't be certain. I kept an eye on her hands as I talked. "I guess I'm the one who screwed up your plans," I said, "which just goes to prove how unpredictable and chancy life is. Funny, isn't it?"

"I don't find anything you do or say amusing," she answered.

"Okay, then I'll just stick to the facts, as I interpret them. How's that?"

"Say what you have to say."

"For me it began, of course, when Fulvio picked me up at the dice table in the Xanadu," I said. "I suddenly became an unknown factor in the game. Anna told you about me. You probably have her on your payroll and my guess is you threw her at Fulvio, knowing that Carmela would not object to her, or she herself would be traveling with him. Latin women, I've been told, are fairly tolerant about what their men are up to on the road, especially when they have a house to run and children to raise. She didn't know who you were. Your name meant nothing to anyone in Naples. I don't know how you became Fulvio's manager, possibly in the normal run of events. You're good at what you do. You must be, because you have other prominent musical artists on your roster. My guess is you got into concert and opera management at about the time you met your husband."

"I did it on my own," she snapped. "I'm the best in the business."

"I can believe that. Anyway, you knew who Fulvio was and at some point you began to steal from him. His gambling made it easy for you. All you had to do was feed his habit. You found Gerald Monkton and a game you can steal millions in with very little chance of getting caught—the horse business. You probably don't need the money, but it gave you some satisfaction. Until then you hadn't thought much about getting even with the Cupiellos, who had your father killed, and probably your uncle, too. But you had your nightmares to remind you and your mother must have kept the flame of hatred alive as you were growing up and now here was your chance. You found yourself managing the finances of this simpleminded man who was married to the only daughter of your father's murderer. Not only that, but Fulvio had obviously become a surrogate son to Don Pippo, who had no male heirs of his own. You couldn't have Fulvio killed, your vendetta couldn't carry you that far, as it would have risked exposing your real identity. Also, why bother? You could ruin him financially while continuing to make money off him. Remember how angry you got when I pointed out that your cut of the pie comes off the top? How sweet it is to get some measure of revenge and get rich at the same time. How am I doing so far?"

"You certainly have a fervid imagination."

"I was a small insect in the soup," I continued. "I turned Fulvio into a winner. I wasn't a real threat yet, just an inconvenience. But when I proved difficult to deal with directly and Anna informed you that Fulvio proposed to add me as a semipermanent member of his touring entourage, you sicced Simone onto me. First she got the Hammer to level me in the parking lot and that delayed me, all right, but only briefly. Then she indulged herself in an affair with me, which was a lark for her and did almost sidetrack me, but not quite. I was running out of money, always a problem with me. So she tried having me ambushed by her pet cat and then she sent Charlie August to L.A. to do a second and more definitive job on me, but he bopped my prospective tenant over the head instead of me. He might have killed him, except that he realized at some point that he'd hammered the wrong man. Charlie is undoubtedly not heavy on brains, but he's not totally dumb. He took Hugo's money, but he let him keep his jewelry and live."

She stepped away from the door and sat down on the edge of the bed facing me. "What do you want, Anderson?"

"Want? What exactly did you have in mind?"

"You said you always need money."

"Let me get the price up a little bit first," I said. "I haven't quite finished."

"I've heard enough."

"Really? How about this?" I leaned into her now, anxious, even eager to nail her with the rest of it. After all, this woman had tried to kill me. "When I made it to New York, you decided I had become a real threat. Not only had I turned Fulvio, at least temporarily, into a winner, but I had figured out that Monkton was robbing him blind on the horse deals and that you were in on it. So you had your sister's private thug come to New York to do a final job on me and he almost succeeded. Then you threw your own body into the fray and that worked, up to a point. It's a very beautiful body and I'm a tremendous admirer of your sex. But you kept on making little mistakes and they damaged your credibility."

"Such as?"

"I'll mention just a couple of the more recent ones. When I showed up at your apartment the other night, you obviously already knew all about my injury."

"I heard about it from Gregory."

"How did he know? But never mind. You also left a snapshot of your sister and brother-in-law on your dresser for me to admire. I mean, all the pieces added up, don't you see? I began to make out a complete picture; I had enough bits and pieces here and there so I could imagine the blank spaces and fill them in. It's not a pretty scene, Jeanine. It's a composite of revenge and greed and something even worse—ruthlessness."

"Fifty thousand dollars," she said. "Cash. And that's it. You disappear."

"I'm a magician, Jeanine, and a good one," I said, "but not quite that good. I could make myself vanish, I suppose, but what about Achille Pipistrello?"

"What about him? He was mugged. I had nothing to do with that."

I sighed. "Oh, Jeanine, I'm really disappointed in you. That poor old man was your only really disastrous mistake. You see, at first he didn't know about you either. He sensed something, and he definitely distrusted you, but it took him a while, too, to figure out your motives and who you were. He was smart, but not criminal smart. He just reported what he saw, heard, and felt. You must have known he was Don Pippo's eyes and ears in regard to Fulvio. You were afraid of him for that reason, but you felt secure enough in your chosen identity. You didn't really begin to worry about him until I also began sniffing bad odors in the wind. You decided he had become too much of a threat as well and so you sent Charlie August to silence him. But you were too late."

"Fifty thousand dollars now, in cash," she said, in an absolutely dead voice. "And fifty thousand more in six months. And that's it."

"A generous offer, but it's too late, Jeanine," I told her. "Even if I agreed, I'd have to worry forever about the Hammer or some other playmate of yours and Simone's coming after me again at some point, probably sooner than later. But even so, I couldn't say yes, not if I were as corrupt and greedy as your pal Monkton. You see, Don Pippo knows all about you now."

Her face was so empty of color it almost became transparent. I imagined I could see her skull through it. She sat there for another few seconds in the cold, gray light of my motel room, with the snow beating softly against the windowpanes, and then she stood up and turned slowly toward the door. I sat in place and watched her until, moving as deliberately as if in a trance, she opened it. "Somebody named Paulie asked me all about you after the funeral this morning," I said. "I couldn't very well not tell him anything.

He had an employee or a friend named Benny with him who struck me as a far more efficient version of your man Martello. I have this strange distaste for violence and I'm really afraid of dying."

She stepped out into the hall and hesitated there for a moment, as if weighing her chances or perhaps considering one last offer. I stood up, anxious now to usher her out of my life forever. "You know what poor old Pipistrello told me?" I said. " 'Don Pippo has very long arms,' he said. 'They can reach around the world.' " And I shut the door on her retreating back.

TWENTY

◆

Finales

Fulvio recovered his voice in time to sing the fourth *Otello*, which I enjoyed from an eighth-row-center seat in the orchestra that the tenor had thoughtfully managed to procure for me. He and Caterina sang magnificently and the death scene moved me to tears. The next afternoon we went back to Aqueduct, but this time had no luck at all. We lost three photos, finished one–three in two Exactas, got set down on a foul claim, and departed the premises four thousand dollars poorer. We'd have lost a lot more than that, if I hadn't fought ferociously to keep Fulvio from tossing great chunks of capital at losers in an effort to get even. "Fulvio, you don't understand the basic principle," I told him in the limousine, on our way back into the city. "In gambling, when your luck turns bad, you wrap up and you ride it out. You press only when you are winning. What would you do without me out here?"

"You are so right, my wizard, I know that you are so right," he said, with a great heave of his massive shoulders. "What I do without you, *mago*? Is necessary you stay always with me."

"No, Fulvio, I really can't do that," I said. "In fact, I'm not going to Naples with you either."

"What?" He turned in his seat to look at me, his broad, bearded face alive with astonishment and concern. "But we have tickets for tomorrow. Why you not come? I have tell Carmela you are coming."

"I know, I'm sorry," I said, "but in Naples I can't help you, Fulvio. And I'm through gambling in clubs or casinos with you.

207

We'll lose eventually and I'll get the blame. I've been thinking very hard about it."

"Who will blame you, my wizard?"

"Carmela. Don Pippo. I don't know who else. But you have a lot of strange friends, Fulvio. I've met a couple of them."

"Who?"

So I told him about my conversation on the way to Queens in Paulie's limousine a few days earlier. "Who is he, Fulvio? Do you know?"

He remained silent for a few minutes, staring out the window of the car at the dismal passing scene along Woodhaven Boulevard. Grubby two-family houses, small stores, cracked sidewalks—Archie Bunker country. "Farruccio," he finally answered. "It must be Paolo Farruccio. Is old family friend."

"Of Don Pippo's, right?"

He nodded. "Sì. He make the import-export business with Don Pippo here. Is nice man, Sheefty."

"Very nice," I agreed, "very congenial. He'll kill you with kindness. I don't care much for his pal Benny either."

"Who?"

"Some young punk," I explained. "He's the one who sort of invited me to take the ride with them. I don't think he's so nice, Fulvio."

The tenor didn't answer. The car passed an old cemetery, looking bleak and sad, with headstones poking up through the gray snow under the black, naked branches of tall trees. "Isn't there an old saying about Naples?" I asked. "Something about dying?"

"See Naples and die," Fulvio said. "Is because it's so beautiful."

"I don't want to see Naples and die. I want to see L.A. and live."

"No, *mago*, you don't understand. Is not you—" He interrupted himself and I could almost hear the wheels churning in his head. "You promise me, *mago*," he finally added. "You promise."

"I promised you I'd give it a try," I said. "You'll be back in three weeks, right? Maybe I'll be here and we'll go racing again."

"What I tell Carmela?"

"Explain how I feel to her, she'll understand. And be sure you also explain to Don Pippo."

"Carmela tell him everything. He know everything."

"I rather imagined he did."

The tenor shifted in his seat to look at me more closely. He seemed a bit petulant, like a small boy suddenly being denied a promised treat. "You don't trust me, my wizard?"

"I trust you, Fulvio, but you have to trust me, too," I said. "The way you gamble, I can't help you. I don't want to take the blame for it. At the track, all I can do is my best for you and maybe we can keep winning. We might do this again in March, when you get back. How long will you be here then?"

"Two months," he replied. "I have two more *Otellos* and then comes *Ballo in Maschera*, which I am also doing in Naples. Is great opera. I sing very good in *Ballo*. Is much lighter than *Otello*."

"It's got to be great," I said, "it's Verdi. I'm looking forward to it."

"I am singing it in Naples. You come, Sheefty."

I shook my head. "No, Fulvio, I really need some time to myself now. If I'm here when you get back, I'll be ready. You want to keep winning, don't you? I've got to stay on top of these animals here for us. Don't you see?"

I should have thought of that argument earlier. I could see it take hold of him, as the memory of our big winning day and the prospects of repeating it suddenly flooded into his head, like sunshine pouring into a room through open shutters. By the time we reached the bridge and began to inch tortuously across it through the sludge of homeward-bound traffic, he had not only accepted my decision but had become positively ebullient about it. "Is good, my wizard, is excellent," he said, exuding bonhomie. "Then in the summer is Covent Garden in London and Verona and then Napoli again. You come with me then."

"Maybe. We'll see, Fulvio. But only if you promise not to gamble there. I can only help you here. And in California, of course."

"Ah, California," he said. "Next fall I have a *Tosca* in San Francisco."

"Good. Maybe I'll send my old pal Jay Fox up to counsel you."

"And you? Where you go?"

"Back to magic, Fulvio. Back to my own life."

"I wish so much for you to meet Carmela."

"I'll meet her, Fulvio," I assured him. "If not this trip, maybe in July." I didn't mean it, of course. I didn't remind him that my summers were built around Del Mar and that nothing, not even a personal summons from Don Pippo himself, could budge me from there during the seven weeks of the summer race meet. There was a time and a place for everything. My one thought now was to get

Fulvio out of town and get back, however temporarily, to my own concerns.

When the limousine dropped us off in front of his apartment building, Fulvio threw his arms around me, crushed me to his chest, and kissed me resoundingly on both cheeks. *"Addio, mago,"* he said. "Stay well. I give your regards to Carmela."

"And to Don Pippo," I reminded him. "Don't, whatever you do, forget to convey my respects to Don Pippo."

"I don't forget," he said. "I tell him everything about you."

That could be fatal, I thought glumly, as I watched him waddle away into the lobby. All I had to worry about now was to hope that I had had a good recommendation from our friend Paulie.

A week after Fulvio's departure, the body of a small-time hood named Carlo Agostino Martello was found weighted with bricks at the bottom of a motel swimming pool on the outskirts of Las Vegas. He had been beaten up and apparently drowned alive. The following night, Simone Krueger fell from her trapeze during the finale of her act at the Stardust and toppled into a large screaming wedding party, breaking her back. She was expected to recover, but would probably remain partly paralyzed for the rest of her life. It was discovered that somebody had sawed through the crossbar, causing the trapeze to break when she was in mid-flight, hanging by her heels forty feet above the audience. During her second day in the ICU, her black panther, Milù, died of eating poisoned meat. Tristan refused to talk to the press about these events and then was arrested on suspicion of having tried to murder his wife. Vince called two days later to tell me about it and to fill me in on the details, but added that Tristan had also now been released and was no longer a suspect. "Word's out about the parties, however," Vince informed me, "and the police are questioning everyone and anyone they can find who used to attend those things. You know anything about this, Shifty?"

"No, Vince, I don't," I lied. "And you don't either, okay?"

"The cops also picked up one of Tristan's boyfriends here, a dancer named Felix Bolton, and they're asking him about it," Vince continued. "Apparently he's spilling the beans on all the kinky stuff."

"The *Post* here will love it," I said. "I'm sorry for Tristan. He's not responsible for hurting anyone."

"Whatever happens, he's through in this town."

"He needs help, Vince," I said. "He's really not a bad guy."

"What are you going to do now, Shifty?"

"I'm going home, Vince," I said. "I'm getting out of this."

"It's about time," Vince said. "Listen, Shifty, we're just little mice running around in a big arena full of fat cats. You understand what I mean?"

"Yeah, Vince, I do. I'll be talking to you. And thanks for calling."

I probably would have left New York that night, but in Fulvio's absence I had been doing so well at Aqueduct that I decided to linger on for one more racing day. Red Quinlan's reliable old gelding Dragoon was entered in the fifth the next afternoon and I didn't want to miss a chance to make one more big score before leaving; after his last race, I estimated he'd be at least five or six to one. I had also been going to the Met every night, sitting wherever I could pick up a ticket, and I was becoming an opera fanatic. I had a seat that evening for my first Wagner opus, *Lohengrin,* and I wasn't going to give that up either. Tomorrow night would be time enough to go home.

At about six, when I got back from the track, I called Happy Hal Mancuso, who was not surprised to hear from me. "I knew it wouldn't work," he said, when I told him I was coming back to L.A. "You tapped out, right?"

"Wrong, Hal," I said, "I'm doing just fine. But I don't like New York. I miss all that smog and sunshine back there."

"It's been raining. Anyway, I didn't cancel your cruises in March," he said. "I knew you'd be back."

"That's what makes you a great agent, Hal," I said. "By the way, I'm really into opera now."

"You never cease to amaze me, Shifty," Hal said. "You go from one rotten, no-future endeavor to another. You going to become a singer now?"

"No, but I want you to book me into San Francisco next fall," I said. "They have a great season there."

"There's nothing in San Francisco but queers," he said. "You want to be a bottomless waiter in a gay joint?"

"Good-bye, Hal. How's Hugo?"

"He's telling Mexican and Polish jokes. Want to hear one?"

"No. I'll see you in a couple of days."

"I'm agog with excitement, Shifty. Until I heard from you, I was wondering how I was going to make a living this year."

The *Lohengrin* was my first disappointment in the opera house. There seemed to be very few really good tunes, apart from the famous wedding march, and here were all these plump types standing around interminably in their bathrobes, while holding spears and swords and shields and acting mildly concerned about the doings of somebody who travels around in a swan boat. The soprano, who looked a lot like Madam Castagno, sang a decent aria in the first act that sounded like, "I'm here, Morgenthau, bring the muffins," and in the last scene the tenor announced fairly melodiously that he was going home because he was tired of people asking him his name (a not unreasonable request if you expect them to go to bed with you) and because "in furnace land, the iron's stricken," which I guess is some sort of Teutonic problem. Anyway, the experience cured me of Wagner for a while.

In the lobby, on my way out, Gregory came running up to me. He had apparently also suffered through the performance, because he seemed genuinely distressed. I was wrong about the reason. "Have you heard about Jeanine?" he asked.

"No, what about her?"

"She's very sick."

"What's wrong with her?"

"She ate some very bad mushrooms the other night. She's in the hospital."

"She was poisoned?"

"Yes. They call it amanitoxin poisoning," he said. "They must have been in the salad. We went with a whole group of people to this restaurant downtown the other night, but she's the only one who got sick. Isn't that ghastly?"

"It certainly is. How is she doing?"

"Badly. She has very serious liver damage. She started throwing up the next morning and I got her to the hospital. She was all pale and sort of yellow. She's really very sick. I'm going there now. Do you want to come?"

"No, Gregory, I don't think she wants to see me. I'm sorry."

"It was such a nice dinner party, too, with several of our old clients. We'd only been there once before, with Fulvio. Somebody had told him about it."

"An Italian place?"

"Yes, Il Miracolo, in the Village. Have you ever been there?"

"No."

"She's the only one in the whole party who got sick. Isn't that incredible?"

"Yes, Gregory, it certainly is."

Don Pippo was obviously not your leisurely, run-of-the-mill man of respect. I made certain, when I got back to my room, that my plane reservations were in order for the following evening. I planned to go directly from the track to the airport. I took a pill to get to sleep, but I tossed and turned most of the night and at five I was fully awake. I packed and then spent the rest of the morning on the *Form*.

At the last minute I almost didn't go, as I was more than a little anxious by then to get out of town, but I couldn't pass up Dragoon, so I stuck to my original plan. I had lunch in the clubhouse and let the first couple of races go by, while I isolated my action for the day, then I went up to the Turf and Field Club, where I found Red and Nora at their usual table on race days. "Where's Welch?" I asked, as I joined them.

"Betting, where'd you think he'd be?" the trainer answered.

"Shifty, you look better since they took the wraps off," Nora observed.

"He looks lopsided," Quinlan said.

I explained that they had had to shave off some of my hair above the injured ear to clean up the wound and put the stitches in. "It'll grow out eventually. Maybe I should wear a hat for a while."

"You look just fine," Nora said. "Doesn't he, Andrew?"

"You haven't been around in the mornings," the trainer observed.

"Only in the afternoons," I said. "I've been going to the opera a lot and it keeps me up late. I need my sleep, if I'm going to survive out here."

"Dragon'll win today. Only he won't pay much."

"Five to one, I figure."

The trainer shook his head. "He'll be favored."

"How come?"

"The dumb exercise boy blew him out in thirty-five and two the other morning," he said. "It got in the *Form* and they've made him five to two in the morning line."

"He'll be seven to two, no lower," I told him. "Bettors are dumber than you think they are."

"Welch has got a big mouth on him," the trainer said. "He's tellin' the world Dragon'll breeze."

"Swell."

I saw Gerald Monkton, elegantly dressed in a cashmere sports jacket and wearing his dark glasses, come in and join a large party of people on the level below us. He had a maiden named Quick Fix entered in the sixth that had been working well and was one of the favorites. I had thrown her out, mainly because I had made a firm decision never to bet on any animal trained by Gerald Monkton, a commitment to honesty that I knew would save me money in the long run.

Red Quinlan was right; the word was out on Dragoon and he was bet down to two to one by the time I headed for the windows. There was a long line to get down in the Turf and Field Club, so I went out into the grandstand area to bet. As I was standing there, with four hundred dollars in my hand to wager on Dragoon, I was suddenly approached by Benny. He was dressed in a slick, pinstriped sharkskin suit and looked positively lethal. "Well, if it ain't the magician," he said, smiling coldly. "Who do you like here, magician?"

"Nothing," I said. "I'm betting the next race early."

"Yeah? So who is it?"

"Quick Fix."

"The first-time starter? You think he'll win?"

"He's a dead crab," I said.

"A what?"

"A mortal lock. Can't lose."

"So you know something?"

"Will not blow. Tap-out city."

"Okay, asshole. On your say-so." He gave me another of those barracuda smiles again and turned his back on me.

Quick Fix, I found out the next morning, got left in the gate and ran eighth in a nine-horse field as the eight-to-five favorite. The loss cheered me up somewhat, but didn't really compensate for the four hundred dollars I had blown on Dragoon. Quinlan's horse again got another faulty ride from St. Yves, going four wide around both turns, and finished second, beaten a head by a thirty-to-one shot that should have finished up the track. "Oh, dear, I hope he doesn't say anything to Andrew," Nora commented, after a livid Jack Welch had risen from the table in fury and rushed out of the premises. "He'll be even more upset than Jack."

"It's a tough racket you're in," I said, kissing her cheek as I got up to leave. "I've got a plane to catch. Say good-bye to Red for me, will you?"

"Will we ever see you again, Shifty?"

"Oh, sure, Nora. Unless they shut all the tracks down. Then I'd have to move to Europe."

On the way out I skirted a bunch of people gathered around a middle-aged man lying on the ground. He was on a stretcher and a paramedic was administering oxygen, but the victim had his eyes shut and wasn't moving. Art Mendola was standing at the edge of the group, looking sorrowfully down on the scene. "You know the guy, Art?" I asked.

"Oh, yeah," the tout replied, "I've known Tony for years. He's got a bum ticker."

"Is he alive?"

"Only to the three horse," Art said.

Jeanine Lagrange died three days after I got back to Los Angeles. Gregory sent me clippings of the obits in the *Times* and the *Post*, which both included cabled expressions of regret from her most famous client, Fulvio Gasparini, then singing *Un Ballo in Maschera* at the San Carlo in Naples. Two weeks later, I came across a story in the *Los Angeles Times* about an investigation into mob activities at the nation's major airports, especially Kennedy, in New York, and O'Hare, in Chicago. Many tons of merchandise were being stolen, whole trucks were being hijacked. There was a picture of a man named Paul (the Dandy) Farruccio, who was suspected of masterminding the robberies in New York. He had been arrested after a raid on a warehouse in Queens belonging to Mercury Van and Storage had turned up mountains of contraband, imported mainly from Italy. Paul was unsmiling as he was being led away in handcuffs, but by the time I read the piece he had already been released on bail.

I received a large envelope from Fulvio in late February. *"Caro mago,* I am singing like a god," the note inside began and went on to inform me that he would be returning to New York in a couple of weeks, as scheduled. Carmela would be coming back with him. "I am to selling the horses," he wrote, "and it is necessary to finding a new manager. Carmela will help. You must come to New York, *mio caro,* and we go racing again. Here is greetings from everyone." He had included an eight-by-ten glossy of a huge *festa* for at least thirty people that had presumably been held at his house near Pozzuoli. Fulvio was standing at the end of a long table, which was all but invisible under the weight of food and drink. He had a glass of wine in one hand, raised in a toast, presumably to me. On his right was a small, dumpy-looking woman with a barely discernible mustache, obviously Carmela. She was dressed in black, with a double strand of pearls around her thick neck, and she did not look excessively benign. Next to her was a rather sad-looking, corpulent old man wearing a vest and a black beret. He was the only guest in the picture not looking at the camera. His eyes were half-closed and he seemed to be dozing. He was either Padre Rambi or Don Pippo, I guessed, but I never found out for sure.

I did not go back to New York that winter or spring and I never contacted Fulvio, nor did he ever try to get in touch with me. Perhaps Carmela had taken full charge of him by the time he got back. I wondered if he would be allowed to gamble anymore. I rather doubted it. One thing was certain: he was singing better than ever. I heard him one Saturday on the Met broadcast, doing *Un Ballo in Maschera*. I picked it up on the car radio on the way out to Santa Anita and I sat in the parking lot, with the radio on, until the opera was over. I missed the double and passed up a ten-to-one shot Jay Fox had told me about in the third. Even horses have to take a backseat to art, especially when the fat man sings.